"YOU REALLY EXPECT ME TO WEAR THIS?"

"I do. I should have outfitted you with one of these a long time ago. Keeping a pistol in your purse hasn't worked too well."

"The only reason I lost my gun was because Ruth swerved to keep from hitting that pig."

"Pig notwithstanding, this will at least keep you from having to dig in your purse to find the gun. Here, let me show you how to put it on."

"That's a great line, Dixon. I think I can figure it out. It looks like yours."

"It's a little different. It's made for a woman. I ordered it from the department."

I slipped my arm through the opening, wrapped the belt around my chest, and fastened the buckle.

"It's a little loose. I'll tighten it." Dixon took his time adjusting the strap in back. "How does that feel?"

"Awkward. And heavy."

"You'll get used to it. Wear a sweater or jacket and you'll be well covered." Dixon slid my new .22 into the holster and adjusted the straps again. "It should be snug, but not too tight."

"I feel like Annie Oakley."

"You look like a million bucks. If I weren't so hungry, I'd suggest we play a game of cops and robbers. But I've been in town for two days and I have yet to pass one shrimp down my throat. Any ideas where to go?"

"I do. Only one place. Gaidos. It's been around for more than forty years. It's got a reputation for fantastic shrimp. Trust me."

"Oh, I do."

Welcome to
Kathleen Kaska's

MURDER at the GALVEZ

"Fast paced and great fun, Kathleen Kaska's Murder at the Galvez takes readers on a breathless jaunt into the past. Sydney Lockhart is a strong, spirited protagonist, good company in this suspenseful and entertaining thriller."

—*Kathryn Casey, mystery and true crime author*

MURDER AT
THE GALVEZ

Miriam,

Life's a mystery

Kathleen Kaska

Also by Kathleen Kaska

The Sydney Lockhart Mystery Series
Murder at the Arlington
Murder at the Luther
Murder at the Galvez
Murder at the Driskill
Murder at the Menger (coming soon)

The Man Who Saved the Whooping Crane:
The Robert Porter Allen Story

The Kate Caraway Mystery Series
Run Dog Run
A Two Horse Town

The Classic Mystery TriviographyTM Series
The Sherlock Holmes Quiz Book
The Agatha Christie Triviography and Quiz Book
The Alfred Hitchcock Triviography and Quiz Book

Do You Have a Catharsis Handy? Five-Minute Writing Tips

MURDER AT

THE GALVEZ

Kathleen Kaska

Anamcara Press LLC

Published in 2021 by Anamcara Press LLC
Author © 2021 by Kathleen Kaska
Cover and Book design by Maureen Carroll
Arial, Tomarik, Lato, Parkway Motel
Printed in the United States of America.

Book description: Something fishy is going on in Galveston, Texas, and reporter Sydney Lockhart finds herself smack dab in the middle of it when she checks into the historic Galvez Hotel, a place which, for her, holds disturbing memories. Eighteen years earlier, she discovered her grandfather, the hotel's doorman, murdered in the foyer. Sydney's there to get a story. Instead, she's handed another hotel murder and a load of nightmares. If this wasn't bad enough, the you-know-what hits the fan at her parent's house a few blocks from the hotel. Bullets spray and sparks fly, and the crisis going on in Galveston just might rival the Great Storm of 1900.

ANAMCARA PRESS LLC
P.O. Box 442072, Lawrence, KS 66044
https://anamcara-press.com

Ordering Information:
Quantity sales. Special discounts are available on quantity purchases by corporations, associations, and others. For details, contact the publisher at the address above. Orders by U.S. trade bookstores and wholesalers. Please contact Ingram Distribution.

ISBN-13: Murder at the Galvez, 978-1-941237-82-3 (Paperback)
ISBN-13: Murder at the Galvez, 978-1-941237-84-7 (EBook)
ISBN-13: Murder at the Galvez, 978-1-941237-83-0 (Hardcover)
FIC022040   FICTION / Mystery & Detective / Women Sleuths
FIC022070   FICTION / Mystery & Detective / Cozy / General
FIC027250   FICTION / Romance / Romantic Comedy
Library of Congress Control Number: 2021945020

For Lloyd
my Galveston Guy

CHAPTER ONE

WHILE MY GRANDFATHER POPO WAS ALIVE, he worked as a doorman at the Hotel Galvez on the seawall in Galveston. He wore a dark maroon coat trimmed in black cording, which hung down past his knees, and he proudly donned a cap with "HG" stitched on the brim with golden thread. Whenever my family came to the island for a visit, I'd make a beeline to the hotel and stand with him while he greeted guests. People who saw us together knew in an instant that I was his granddaughter. We were cut from the same mold: tall, thin, and redheaded. I was proud of that fact, for James Robert Lockhart was the most handsome man I'd ever seen. When I found him crumpled on the floor in the hotel foyer, his body riddled with bullet holes, I knew my life would never be the same. Now, as I stepped into the lobby eighteen years later, the memory of that day hit me square in the gut.

My name is Sydney Jean Lockhart. I'm thirty, single, and I recently tossed aside a perfectly fine, secure career as a science teacher to try to make a go of it in a man's world. The year is 1953, and I'm the first female reporter hired by The Austin American Statesman. After my last assignment—covering a political powwow in Palacios, Texas—turned into an exposé on murder, scandal, and deception of which I was a surviving victim, my opportunities as a journalist have escalated. My editor, Ernest Turney, learned of my connections with the island and asked me to write a piece on another political situation, this one brewing in Galveston. At first, I hesitated: the event was to be held at the Hotel Galvez. My reluctance was not only because my grandfather had been murdered at the hotel, but because Galveston was where my parents had chosen to live after my father retired.

Returning to the scene of my grandfather's murder was going to be difficult. Figuring out how to avoid my parents while in town was the real challenge. But this assignment was too hot to pass up; it would add another feather to my fedora, which I often wore to hide my gender while on assignment. By the time I'd finished packing, several lies to keep my mother, Mary Lou Lockhart, at bay had formed in my devious brain.

I'd just finished cleaning my Smith Corona and replacing the ribbon when the doorbell rang and Jeremiah waltzed in, wearing white linen slacks and a lavender sweater.

"You need to lock your doors, dear. You never know who might walk in."

Monroe jumped from the sofa, slid across my hardwood floor, regained traction, and hopped up to plant her front paws on her uncle-in-law's shoulders.

"This dog's gotten fat." Jeremiah hugged my seventy-pound poodle.

"What do you expect after a ten-day stay with my father?" I walked over and gave my brother's roommate a well-deserved hug. "Scott won't mind being away from you for a few days?"

"Are you kidding? Do you think he'd notice? Do you think he appreciates the nice things I do for him? Do you think he ever says thank you for making sure the house is clean and comfy? Leaving him on his own for a few day will be good for the boy." He headed down the hall, running his finger along my bookcase to check for dust.

Jeremiah lives with my brother, Scott, in a stylish neighborhood in his too-expensive home overlooking Barton Springs. Except for taking care of Scott, Jeremiah doesn't work for a living. He doesn't have to. We don't know where he gets his money. He just has it, a lot of it.

"How's my brother doing anyway? He never calls."

"Working two jobs keeps him busy, and having to take off a few days to help sort through your family's latest crisis has put him in the hole." Jeremiah called from the kitchen. "I offered to cover this month's mortgage, but he, being a proud, stubborn Lockhart, wouldn't hear of it. So, I keep my nose out of his business. I cook, clean, and do whatever. How old is this chicken?" he said, pulling his head out of my icebox.

"I baked it last night. The pantry is full and the icebox is stocked. You should be set for a few days. Scott didn't have to take off work." I stood in the kitchen doorway and watched Jeremiah make himself at home in my tiny kitchen.

"You're looking at the top student in home-ec class—four years in a row." He shook the crumbs from my toaster, squeezed the bread, and then sniffed the potato salad. "Besides, when does Scott not jump when your mother calls? By the way, how's the new cousin? When do I get to meet her?"

A couple of weeks ago, we found out that my mother's deceased brother had fathered a child with his mistress. Not only did Uncle Martin support the woman, but he put their daughter through law school. Marcella Wheatly showed up in my life during my last assignment to help defend me against a murder charge. Her half-sister, my dear cousin Ruth, has not quite warmed up to Marcella, although Ruth donated blood when Marcella needed it.

"She's out of the hospital. But don't expect to see her at the next family reunion. Do me a favor—run interference for me if my parents call."

"This potato salad needs more mayo and ... something else." He picked up the pepper shaker. "You're going to have to use your male disguise if you plan to gallivant around Galveston right under their noses. I could lend you some of my clothes. We're about the same size."

"Your clothes are too flashy for me, and a bit too feminine, if you don't mind me saying so."

"Which should tell you something about your wardrobe."

"How about this?" I said. "I could tell my parents that I got the assignment at the last minute and was about to pick up the phone and call."

"Weak."

"Okay. This one's better. Since you two just reconciled, I wanted to give you some time to yourselves."

"Better." He was now dicing the chicken into tiny bits. "Let's hear another."

"I'm a grown woman, and I don't have to tell you a damn thing about my plans."

"Too honest. Your mother will have a hissy and she'll know you're up to something. Go with the reconciliation story." He placed the chicken on a saucer. "Where's the kitty?"

"Hiding under the bed. You know how she gets when someone comes over."

"Yes, but I'm her favorite person. This should lure her out."

A split second after the sound of the dish clinked on my tile floor, an orange, football-sized mass of fur dashed into the kitchen. "Don't worry about a thing. Go do your job. The girls and I will have a fine old time." He cradled Mealworm in his arms and showered her with kisses, causing a purr to reverberate through the room—not an easy task for a cat with a mouth full of baked chicken.

"I should have this assignment wrapped up in a few days." I sat my luggage by the front door. Monroe began whimpering. I reached down and nuzzled her soft ears, and began whimpering myself.

"Don't worry about it. I'll be here. Quick, before you leave, tell me about the new boyfriend. Ruth said—"

"He's not my boyfriend."

"—that you two were hitting it off pretty well and that he was ready to prop—"

"Since when do you listen to what Ruth says?" I gave Monroe a reassuring kiss on her curly head, looked around for the cat, who'd disappeared, picked up my luggage, and left before Jeremiah could ask any more questions.

JUST AFTER ONE O'CLOCK I PULLED UP under the back portico of the Galvez. I left my car and luggage to the valet, grabbed my clutch, and stood looking up at the seven-story structure, then took a deep breath and went inside. When I was little, I used to run up the hotel's front steps and PoPo would say, "Let me get the door for you, ma'am." He'd bow and open the door with a flourish. As I passed, he'd say, "Welcome to the Galvez, Miss Lockhart. Enjoy your stay." I would lift my chin like a queen. Then I'd reach into his coat pocket and pull out a pack of Teaberry chewing gum.

Standing in the lobby, I swear I could still taste that sweet flavor of the gum.

Now, as I marched to the front desk, I questioned my sanity for taking this assignment. I don't know what it is with me and desk clerks, but we get along as well as two wet cats in a small cage. "I have a reservation," I said to a man who looked more like a referee at a cockfight than a desk clerk.

"Name, please." He looked down at his registration book.

"Sydney Lockhart."

He peeked at me under his brow and then glanced toward the front door, then toward the back door, then around the lobby. I turned to see what he was looking for when he said, "Is your husband here? Are you Mrs. Lockhart?"

"There is no husband, and it's Miss Sydney Lockhart."

"I see," he said. "Please fill out the card." He paused. "I'm sorry. Whoever took the reservation didn't write down a check-out date."

I pulled the registration card over and picked up the fountain pen. "I didn't give one."

"I see," he said again. "What day should I put down?"

"I'm not sure when I'll check out. Is that a problem, because if it is, I'm sure Mr. Cahill will settle things?"

Upon hearing his boss's name, he said, "That won't be necessary, Miss Lockhart. Check-in time isn't until three o'clock, but since your room is ready, I'll do you a favor. Here's your key. Room 559. Turn left when you get off the elevator. Is there anything else I can do for you?"

"Yes, I'd like an extra pillow. Can you arrange that?"

"I'll see what I can do. Anything else?"

I thought of the bottle of champagne that had been waiting for me when I checked into my room at the Arlington Hotel in Hot Springs, Arkansas last November, but what had also been waiting for me was a dead body in the bathtub. Ellison James, throat slashed and naked as a jaybird, had been murdered only moments before I walked in. I decided not to push my luck. "If I think of anything, I'll let you know."

Once I had my room key, I headed for the foyer. I was never one to leave the dirty work until last. I'd much rather face my demons head-on and be done with them. Another doorman stood where PoPo used to stand. The uniform was the same, but the look on the man's face spoke of boredom. Nevertheless, he smiled and opened the door for me.

"Thank you," I said, "but I'm not leaving right now."

He turned to assist an elderly woman with her luggage.

At first, I'd thought PoPo was playing a joke on me, lying there on the floor with his hat tossed to the side, but the slackness of his jaw had told me he was dead. It wasn't until I knelt down beside him that I saw the blood. I was eleven years old.

My family would come to Galveston to visit my grandparents, and as soon as I said my hellos to my grandmother, I'd run out of the back door, jump on a bicycle my grandfather kept for me in the garage, and peddle to the hotel a few blocks away. It had been a quiet Tuesday in the summer. I remember hearing what I thought were firecrackers as I approached the entrance. Tires squealed, and I darted onto the grass as a car spun away, almost taking out the oleander bushes. The case had never been solved. Random violence was the theory. Galveston in the mid-1930s had a reputation as a rough town. It wasn't much better today.

My throat closed, and I had to remind myself to breathe. Suddenly, I felt a hand on my arm.

"Miss Lockhart?"

I jumped as a voice behind me brought me back to the present.

"Sorry, I didn't mean to frighten you. I'm Leonard Cahill. Mr. Cameron told me you were here." My face must have shown the foreboding I still felt. Leonard Cahill paused and studied me closely before he continued. "We're very happy to have you staying with us. After you're settled in, I'll go over the events we have scheduled over the next few days and give you a tour of the hotel."

Fresh air finally reached my brain, and I was able to speak.

"Thank you, Mr. Cahill. I'll unpack and then we can visit."

"Wonderful. I'll walk you to your room."

"That won't be necessary. I'll see you in about an hour."

"Just come to the front desk, and Mr. Cameron will find me." He hesitated. "Miss Lockhart? I just wanted to let you know that I...well, I'm aware of what happened to your grandfather years ago." He paused again, and his cheeriness turned to concern. "I worked in catering back then. It must be difficult for you. If there's anything I can do, let me know."

I smiled. "Thank you, but I'll be fine."

I shook away the vision of my grandfather lying on the floor and followed Mr. Cahill back into the lobby. Several groups of businessmen were milling around the front desk, waiting to check in. Suddenly I felt the electricity in the air, and my melancholy feelings disappeared.

The purpose of the convention was to announce the development of Pelican Island, a place that was known as the dump when I was growing up. Until now, no one had shown much interest in the island. The Texas Legislature had given it to Galveston in 1856 to use as a Confederate bluff of strength, complete with fake guns to ward off the enemy. When the Houston and Galveston Ship Channels were dredged, the muck was deposited on Pelican Island. Except for shorebirds, snakes, and a few burrowing animals, the island wasn't of much interest to anyone. But that was all about to change, and not everyone was happy about it.

The controversy surrounding the island's development is what drew me to the assignment. This story had potential— many angles for my devious mind to explore. A few months ago, the City of Galveston had formed a navigation district, and the voters, excited by the economic prospects for their island, voted to allot $6 million to build a bridge and move ahead with the development of the island. It turned out the city had been favoring a syndicate of investors from New York despite numerous bids from developers in the Lone Star State. Then, a couple of weeks ago, the New York company lost out to one from Houston located just fifty miles up the road. Seemed that the squeaky wheel had gotten the grease. There was also a growing grassroots group that opposed the development for environmental reasons. Just seeing the convocation of energized, opinionated, influential men (and a few women) ready to spew their information and debate their causes aroused my inquisitive nature. I couldn't wait to pick their brains and maybe even ferret out some juicy tidbits.

The elevator seemed to inch its way up. I'm not usually claustrophobic, but the box was crowded. I focused on the floor numbers and watched them light up, one after another, until I heard the final ding. The elevator attendant slid the door open and nodded. I stepped off onto the fifth floor.

Room 559 had a water view, and I stood at the window for several minutes watching the waves crash onto the beach. It was one of those beautiful late-January days when spring comes around to check things out for a possible early arrival. For once, the Galveston surf didn't look like murky chocolate milk. The water was as blue as the sky and the waves gentle. A few fishermen, standing knee-deep, were casting their luck about fifty yards out. I looked closely to make sure my father wasn't one of them. A knock at the door made me jump.

"Who is it?" I asked. I'd learned the hard way not to open my hotel-room door until I knew who was knocking.

"Bellboy, ma'am. I have your luggage and the extra pillow you asked for."

I dug around in my clutch for some change and handed him his tip. As he was leaving, he turned back and said, "Oh, I almost forgot. A message came for you." He reached into his breast pocket and pulled out a slip of paper.

Hotel messages made me as nervous as knocks on my room door. They often brought news that my family was experiencing some sort of crisis, like my mother was running away from home—again—or my brother had gotten his feelings hurt because Jeremiah had vetoed Scott's request for his favorite dessert, or my cousin Ruth's hangnail had ruined her new pair of stockings. The unexpected note made me wonder if Ruth was on my trail. Her meddling nature and my adventurous affairs went together like suction cups and starfish. I hadn't told her where I was, but her bloodhound instincts could track me down before I had a chance to unpack my PJs. Or, heaven forbid, it could be my mother, who might have already spotted my convertible in the parking lot.

The note was short and sweet: Don't get too comfortable. Your stay will be short. No signature. Great. Who had I offended this time? I called the front desk. Mr. Chambers answered.

"This is Miss Lockhart in 559. The bellboy just brought me a phone message. Do you know who took the call?"

"I took the call, Miss Lockhart."

"Did the caller say anything else?"

"No, ma'am."

"Don't you think the message is kind of strange, in a threatening sort of way?"

"After working in the hotel business, nothing seems strange to me."

"Was the caller a man or woman?"

"A woman, at least that's the way it sounded."

"Why didn't you transfer the call to my room?"

"Because you weren't in your room yet. The call came in just as you got on the elevator."

"If I get any more such calls when I'm not in my room, could you ask who the caller is, please?"

"I don't run a messenger service down here, ma'am."

"Your hospitality overwhelms me. I have one more question. Did the caller ask for me by name?"

"No ma'am. The woman just said she had a message for the person staying in 559."

"Then the message could have been for the previous guest, don't you think?"

"Quite possibly, ma'am."

"Right." I hung up a little too hard and hoped I'd made my point with the mordant Mr. Chambers.

The message couldn't possibly be for me. I hadn't had a chance to get into any trouble yet. Whoever had stayed in this room before me was probably a cheating husband whose wife had gotten wind of his exploits.

CHAPTER TWO

I had one more unpleasant task to take care of before I unpacked. Although visiting the foyer where PoPo was murdered was far more serious, checking out my room, as I had also learned from experience, was paramount to my safety. I pulled back my shoulders, headed for the bathroom, and jerked back the shower curtain. The tub was empty—whistle clean. I turned to the closet, picked up a vase from the credenza, and snapped open the door. The only thing inside was a neat row of wooden hangers. No one lurked under the bed; there were no bloody clothes in any of the dresser drawers. I was beginning to like this place. I looked at my watch. I had twenty minutes to wash off the road dust, change into fresh clothes, and meet Mr. Cahill for our appointment.

My progress was stalled when I noticed that my dreamy bathroom was without towels. I didn't want to speak to the desk clerk so soon after rupturing his eardrum. When I'd gotten off the elevator, I'd noticed a maid's cart, so I scurried down the hall in my stocking feet and grabbed a few towels. As I passed room 553, I heard sobbing coming from the open door. I peeked in. The room looked like the aftermath of an atomic bomb. The floor was littered with garbage: a nice collection of takeout food boxes, some with remnants of what looked like meatloaf and mashed potatoes, a few empty beer bottles, and a brown banana peel. The ice bucket had become a giant ashtray, full of butts. The sheets were a tangled mess, and woven into that mess were the leftovers of a wild night—a tie, one black sock, a lacy slip, an empty bottle of champagne, and a pair of panties.

I figured the crying was coming from the owner of the panties until I saw a housemaid picking through the rubble. I'd cry too if it were my job to clean up this room.

"Are you okay?" I asked.

She screamed and tripped over a throw pillow hidden under a pile of towels.

"Don't sneak up on people!"

"Sorry. Are you okay?" I repeated. "Maybe you can get someone to help you. I can't believe how people leave their rooms."

"This is nothing," she said. She blew her nose in one of the towels. "None of the furniture is broken and I haven't found any cigarette burns in the upholstery. At least they were courteous and used the bucket."

"Then why are you crying?"

"Oh, you know."

"I do?"

"No, I guess you wouldn't." She glanced at my left hand. "Not yet anyway."

I regretted coming to her rescue. Seeing no blood or broken bones, I edged toward the door.

"You will, though," she called. And when I responded with a grunt, she followed me. "It happens to us. All of us. Our kids grow up, our husbands get fat and lazy, and just like that," she snapped her fingers, "it's all over. No one needs me but this hotel. So I come to work and clean up after"—she picked up the toilet brush and used it to hoist the panties—"heathens."

I really felt sorry for the old gal, but I didn't have the time or desire to hear about her pathetic life. "I helped myself to some towels. There were none in my room. I hope you don't mind."

"What room are you in?" she gasped.

"559. But it's okay. Just an oversight."

"That new girl is as dumb as a mule."

"Actually, mules are pretty smart. Stubborn is what they are."

"Who cares? When I get hold of Marlene, I'm gonna give her a piece of my mind. I'm in charge of the rooms on this floor. My name is Blanche. You just call down to housekeeping and ask for me, and I'll get you whatever you need."

"Thanks, Blanche." I turned to leave.

"And believe you me, when you reach my age, the same thing will happen to you. You can't stop it. You better start training your future husband now before it's too late."

"I'm thinking about not getting married."

"Good for you. Now run along. My advice-giving time is over. I got work to do." The slip now dangled on the end of her toilet brush. "I need a hobby," she mumbled to herself. "Something that would keep my mind off work."

My plan to luxuriate in the huge Victorian bathtub was squelched thanks to Blanche. I dressed, checked my seams in the mirror, grabbed my writing pad, and opted for the stairs.

Mr. Chambers was chasing some swim-suited children from the lobby, as if the nearest beach were thousands of miles from here rather than right across the street. One little boy, not dressed for the beach except for the swimming goggles that covered his eyes, wore a pair of red cowboy boots, a fringed vest with an aluminum star pinned above the heart, and toy six-shooters strapped around his hips. Mr. Chambers grabbed the little guy by his arm. "Outside, young man," he said. "You cannot jump all over the lobby furniture." The little boy broke from Mr. Chamber's grasp and pulled out his gun.

"Pow! You're dead!"

"You missed," Chambers said. "Outside!"

He walked back behind the front desk, but I didn't wait for the color to return to his face. "I have an appointment with Mr. Cahill. Please tell him I'm here."

"Yes, ma'am." He switched on the intercom. "Miss Lockhart is here to see you. Yes, sir." He disconnected and handed me a slip of paper. "Here. I called your room, but you didn't answer. I asked, like you instructed, but she refused to leave her name. And this time there was no mistake." He cocked his head and smiled. "She asked for you by name."

I wanted to take my pencil and erase that wicked grin from his face. Instead, I returned his smile with one just as wicked.

The note was simple: "I'm not joking, Miss Lockhart." Heat rose from my ears, and I knew my face had become as red as my hair—an angry red, as my father loved to say.

"Miss Lockhart, let's start by me showing you around the hotel."

I heard Mr. Cahill's voice, but it sounded as far away as yesterday's serenity.

"Are you okay, Miss Lockhart?"

"No, I'm not, Mr. Cahill." I showed him the note. "There's another one upstairs in my room." I told him what it said. He looked over at Mr. Chambers, whose evil smile had turned to one of innocence.

"If Miss Lockhart receives any more of these inappropriate calls, direct them to me. Understand?"

"Yes, sir."

"Shall we start with the pool and verandah?"

We walked outside to a glorious day.

"I wouldn't worry about the prank calls. I'm embarrassed to say, but that happens on occasion, especially when we have such a controversial event as this, and you being a reporter... well, it's probably some old crank trying to make a statement."

I liked hearing myself referred to as a reporter. It had a nice ring—Sydney Lockhart, reporter. When I resigned from teaching after having had a few travel articles published, I imagined my writing continuing in that vein. However, I managed to publish a few opinionated pieces, and those have landed me some challenging jobs. Who knows where this will take me, but after lesson plans, whiny adolescents, and early-morning faculty meetings, I was ready for anything.

The verandah looked like a Hawaiian paradise. Palm trees grew tall around the perimeter of the pool. Oleanders, blooming in every color imaginable, filled huge stone planters. White-and-green striped lounge chairs lay side by side, and next to each one was a small drink table. Several guests were already imbibing early-afternoon cocktails, and the children Mr. Chambers had chased out of the lobby were now in inner tubes bobbing in the pool. The scent of rum, suntan location, and chlorine hung in the air, reminding me that Galveston was a hotspot on the Texas tourist map. I looked across the seawall at the gentle incoming waves.

Mr. Cahill caught my gaze and laughed. "I know what you're thinking. Why the pool when the beach is across the street?"

"I can answer that. The beach doesn't have a waiter, and the kids won't arrive back in the hotel room with sand in their bathing suits. I spent a lot of time here as a child. After a day at the beach, my grandmother used to hose down my brother and me in the backyard before she'd let us in the house."

"It's a constant battle—removing sand and salt from the lobby floors, mattresses and rugs in the rooms, and believe it or not, out of the plumbing. Sometimes I think our janitors work harder than anyone here." He shrugged. "But it's all part of running a beach resort hotel."

We walked through the garden and followed the path around to the front of the building. The fresh, unencumbered breeze was welcome.

"Let's go inside." Mr. Cahill patted down his wind-blown hair. "I'll show you the conference rooms where the gathering will take place. We'll stop by my office, and I'll let you take a peek at the agenda. The mayor is kicking off the event with a press conference at three o'clock today. Most of the other reporters aren't arriving until then, so you have a head start."

I wondered why I was receiving this special treatment, not that I was complaining. It could have been because of my family roots here on the island, although I wasn't BOI (born on the island)—but more likely it was the tragedy of my grandfather's murder.

More than two hundred people were scheduled to attend the conference—influential and powerful people who planned to shape the future of Galveston, transforming the town from a rough-and-tumble gambling venue to a viable port city where commerce would become the key to the area's prosperity. In the late 1800s, Galveston was vying with Houston to control the shipping industry and become the port city of the South. Houston sprinted ahead in the race when a hurricane almost destroyed the island in what has become known as the Great Storm of 1900. Galveston has been in slow recovery mode ever since. If the city fathers could pull off the Pelican Island Development Project and get rid of the riffraff, Galveston's economy might experience a much-needed growth spurt. I smiled inwardly. Where would my father go if the Balinese Room shut down, especially now that my mother had moved back home? His need for an occasional escape would be even stronger.

Mr. Cahill's office was a buzz of activity. Secretaries clacked away on their typewriters, phones rang, and everyone talked at once. From a pile of papers and files on his desk, Mr. Cahill unearthed a folder and lifted out a slip of paper. He pulled out his chair and cleared a space on his desk. "Have a seat. Here's the agenda. You can copy it in your notebook if you'd like."

"Mr. Cahill, excuse me, but Joyce has double-booked the Island Room." A young woman walked up and shoved a calendar under his nose. She looked as if she'd been on the project for days. "We'll have to move one of the parties, but we have no place to put them."

"Oh, Lord, let me take a look at the schedule book." He turned back to me. "Make yourself comfortable. I'll be back in a second."

I opened my notebook and began copying the agenda for the next two days. The morning's keynote speaker, Maurice Roland, with the Houston development firm of Briscoe, Roland, and Cooper, was to speak first. His credentials ran on for half a page. His claim to fame was the successful beach resort he'd built outside of Mobile, Alabama. His speech was to last an hour, followed by comments from Dal Quinn, Galveston's newly elected mayor, then a few words from the president of the Chamber of Commerce, the city planning commissioner, and finally, the governor of our great state, Allan Shivers. Shivers is no stranger to the Gulf Coast—he'd grown up in Port Arthur. Soon after he took office, the federal government had tried to secure the rights to the state's oil-rich tidelands, and Shivers had slapped their hand so hard that the feds had been afraid of a second Civil War. They backed off, and Texas got to keep its underground sludge.

There was a short break in the schedule, and then the true business of planning began, with several meetings scheduled throughout the hotel. I copied the entire list and placed check marks where I thought I'd find the most valuable information.

I'd promised Ernest I'd keep him informed of my progress. This was my third major story for the paper, and although my first two had been well received, I still had to prove myself.

I finished just as Mr. Cahill returned. "If I survive this week, it will be a miracle," he laughed, mopping his forehead with his handkerchief.

"Looks like you've got quite a crew here."

"Everyone's working overtime, and it's starting to show. Even though the conference doesn't start until tomorrow, we've been planning this for months. No matter how much we prepare, last-minute problems always crop up once folks start arriving. Someone doesn't like a conference room—it's too cold or too hot—another group doesn't like the menu we've planned even though someone at their office had already approved it, then someone else complains that the guests staying next door are loud and obnoxious. It's one big juggling act."

Joyce ran up again, looking even more harassed than before. "Sorry, Mr. Cahill..."

"I'd better let you get back to work," I said. I picked up my notes. "This was helpful. Thank you again."

"Good luck, Miss Lockhart. Call if I can be of more help." He paused as if he'd just thought of one more bit of information, but before he could say another word, Joyce took him by the elbow and pulled him into a fray of anxious employees.

My growling stomach chastised me for skipping lunch so I headed for the dining room. Waiting for tables was a line of people that snaked out into the lobby. I did a quick U-turn and decided to find another place to eat. Reilly's Coffee Shop, a local greasy spoon, served the best gumbo on the island, and it was only two blocks away. I was hesitant about showing my face on the street, but my mother never rose before noon, and then it took her most of the afternoon to decide what to wear. Dad usually spent his days fishing or puttering in the yard. Feeling safe that I'd go undetected by the Lockhart faction, I strolled over to Reilly's and found a booth by the window. I spread out my notes and ordered a bowl of seafood gumbo and a salad.

The proposed development of the small island was much more extensive than I had imagined. The land was to be divided into three areas: industrial, residential, and commercial/recreational, requiring an estimated expenditure of $17 million spread out over ten years. My meal arrived, and minutes later, my plate was empty. I considered ordering a slice of the pineapple upside-down cake that sat on a cake stand on the counter, but when I saw Lattie the Lush, my parents' neighbor who has had her inebriated eye on my dad, pull up into the parking lot, I threw some money on the table and exited fast.

When I reached the hotel, I ran up the stairs, dashed to my room, and changed into a sweater, slacks, and my saddle shoes. After the press conference I'd planned to pay a visit to Pelican Island. Just as I grabbed my jacket and camera, the phone rang. Anticipating another threatening message, I said in a firm, what-the-hell-is-this-about voice, "Hello!"

"Syd, dear, you sound out of breath. I don't want to spoil your fun, but your mother's been calling."

"When?"

"All morning."

"Jeremiah, you haven't told her where I am, have you?"

"Nope."

"What does she want?"

"I don't know. I haven't exactly talked to her."

"Then how do you know it was her calling?"

"A new pattern. She hangs up on the ninth ring. Then, to make sure she had the right number, she calls right back. Scott figured it out. If he wants to talk, he picks up the second time and makes some excuse for not picking up the first time."

"How many times has she called?"

"Five double-calls in two hours. You'd better call, or she'll go on a tear."

"Thanks, I'll do that now. How are the girls?"

"Wonderful! I spent the morning at that new poodle boutique. Monroe looks fabulous in yellow."

"I don't want to hear it. Keep on screening Mom's calls. Talk to you soon."

I liked the call-screening idea. I'd have to think of a ring code for Dixon. When we parted in Palacios, we agreed, amazingly so, to talk over the phone every Friday morning. But then I'd have no excuse for not picking up the phone, even though I promised him I'd stop doing that. Well, I'd better get this over with, I thought. I made sure my door was locked and called home.

"Hey, Mom, what's up?"

"Where on earth have you been?"

"Working."

"You don't have a job."

"I'm a reporter, Mom. They pay me money for writing. That, in my book, is a job."

"Don't get sassy with me. Now, listen. I need you to come home right now and help me."

"Help you what?"

"This crazy celebration your insane father insists we have."

"The anniversary party?"

"He wants to have it on Stewart Beach and roast hot dogs."

"That sounds like a good plan."

"Don't be ridiculous! The new West Side Country Club would work better."

"I'm sure you'll have no trouble convincing him of that. You don't need my help."

"Of course I need your help. There are decorations, invitations, a band to book, a menu to plan."

Neither of my parents worked. My dad is retired, and my mother dabbles in community theater, but otherwise their days are free. The only reason she wanted me around was to ruin my peaceful life. I knew if I flat out refused to help, she'd never let up. A compromise was in order. "Listen, I can't drop what I'm doing. I'm right in the middle of researching a story. Send me your guest list and invitations and I'll address them.

"I don't have time to do that. You have to come to Galveston today. The party's this Saturday. If you leave now, you can get here before it gets dark. See you then."

Click.

"Mom!"

I picked up the phone and called Scott's office. I rarely called him at work, but this was an emergency.

"Hey, Sis, what's up?"

"Don't 'hey, Sis' me. Did you know about this anniversary party?"

"Sure, Mom's been planning it for months, except for that time she left Dad and moved out to the beach hut."

"No, I mean, her latest plan. She's having it this Saturday!"

"Good. Get it over with is what I say."

"She insists I leave right now to help her."

"You're already in Galveston—that will be easy."

"Listen, Scott, you know good and well she doesn't know I'm here. I'm on assignment and I don't plan—"

Click.

Like mother like son.

I picked up the phone again. Desperate circumstances call for desperate measures.

"Hello."

"Ruth, how's my cousin?" I asked.

"I haven't spoken to her. Just because I saved her life doesn't mean I want to have anything to do with that woman. Just the thought of that horrible experience is causing me some residual dizziness. I need to sit down."

"I'm talking about you, Ruth. How are you doing?"

"Oh, I still feel a bit weak, but I'll recover."

"Weak? You donated blood for Marcella three weeks ago. It doesn't take that long to recover—a couple of cookies and a glass of orange juice, that's it."

"Maybe for most people, but I have a delicate constitution."

"You do not. You recovered from that gunshot wound in Hot Springs and from Wilson drugging you in Palacios in a matter of hours. You're one tough gal."

"All of which wouldn't have happened if it weren't for you. What do you want?"

"I need your help."

"Oh, no, not again."

"Okay, bye." I had the receiver halfway to the cradle when I heard her say, "Wait. At least,"

I put the receiver back to my ear. "—I can listen."

"This is right up your alley. Mom has this harebrained idea to have the anniversary party this Saturday at that new country club. She needs someone to help with the planning and I'm working. I thought maybe you and your mom could pitch in."

"No way. I'm got several meetings scheduled this week with the board of directors. We're finalizing things for the St. Mary's Home for Unwed Mothers."

"The what?"

"You heard me."

"How does Mary figure into this?"

"She became pregnant before she got married."

"That's a bit different, Ruth. She was conceived by the Holy Spirit and then, to make things legit, Joseph married her. I wouldn't call her an unwed mother. Besides, St. Mary's Home sounds like a convent of sorts."

"Maybe you have a point. Don't bother me. I've got work to do."

When Ruth's father died from a heart attack in the bed of his mistress, Ruth and her mother were not only surprised by Uncle Martin's philandering, they were flabbergasted by how much he was really worth. Ruth, despite her self-indulgence, wanted to donate some of her wealth to a worthy cause. After considering several ridiculous charitable ideas, she settled on a home for unwed mothers.

"You need to delegate, assign a committee to do the work. Hop on a plane at Love Field. You can be at the Hobby Airport in Houston, rent a car, and be on the island in less than three hours."

"I'm the brains behind this operation. I can't leave!"

Ruth's brains were behind something, but it wasn't any operation. "Fine, maybe Marcella can help."

Click. This time I was the one who hung up. I had no intention of calling my newfound cousin. Besides, I knew she'd be busy with her law practice, which, I was afraid, was working her to an early grave. I checked my watch. If my calculations were right, Ruth should arrive at my parents' house before dinner. At least I bought myself some time. With a little luck, I should be able to wrap this story up and be at George and Mary Lou Lockhart's doorstep to offer assistance on Friday afternoon. By that time, my mother would be in such a frenzy she wouldn't have time to rag on me.

CHAPTER THREE

When I walked into the conference room, I scanned the crowd to see if I recognized anyone. I hadn't expected to, since most of my previous time on the island had been spent on the beach in a bathing suit, toting a sand bucket. Once I was sure there were no familiar faces in the room, I grabbed a seat in front and took out my notepad.

Five minutes later, Mayor Dal Quinn stepped up to the podium. He looked to be in his mid-forties. His thick, wavy, auburn hair was tamed with a respectable amount of Brylcreem. A burly but neatly trimmed mustache covered his top lip. His swarthy complexion made his otherwise plain features appear attractive. He hooked a pair of rimless glasses over his ears and cleared his throat. "Thank you for coming today, gentlemen." He noticed me, winked, and quickly added, "and lady."

I looked around, and sure enough, I was the only female reporter in the room. Mayor Quinn said all the right things: How the development of Pelican Island would boost Galveston's sagging economy; how Galveston was growing and needed the expansion if it planned to attract more businesses; how Galveston was destined to become the vacation Mecca of the Gulf Coast. When he asked for questions, hands shot in the air, including mine. He handled the questions concerning the enormous expenditures and environmental issues like a pro. Although most of my questions had been answered, he did not call on me.

Twenty-five minutes later, the mayor thanked everyone for coming and turned to leave even though my arm was still in the air. I assumed he hadn't seen me—the tall redheaded woman in the front row—so I went ahead with my question: "Mr. Quinn, what made you decide at the last minute to go with the development company from Houston?"

Mayor Quinn turned and looked directly at me. He smiled as if he were about to address a naughty kitten, "Just good business sense, little lady."

Since my question was essentially ignored with that rude comment, I tried again. "Is it true, Mayor, that you've received death threats over the development of the island?" It pays to do a little research beforehand.

"No more than I received when I announced that I was running for mayor, honey."

His response sent a chuckle through the crowd. He waved and ducked away. I was trying to keep the steam from escaping my ears and curling my hair even more, when the guy sitting next to me spoke up: "Good questions." He held out his hand. "Chuck Conrad with The Galveston Tribune. Our good mayor is famous for both his charisma and his evasiveness. Don't take it personally."

Chuck Conrad looked ready for retirement. Pale blue eyes sank under heavy brows. His wrinkles etched deep. Ink stained the tips of the fingers on his left hand.

"Sydney Lockhart." I shook his hand. "With The Austin American Statesman. Evasiveness I can handle. Being called 'little lady' and 'honey' irks me."

"I don't doubt it. Neither did the mayor. I saw that look he gave you."

"Patronizing, to say the least."

"Maybe. What I saw was a tiny bit of fear. He works a crowd well. Gives pertinent information, presents both sides, asks for questions, and darts away just as things heat up." Mr. Conrad stood up. "Maybe we can compare notes sometimes."

I gathered my things. "Sounds good. I'm staying at the hotel."

"You can find me at the paper. I seem to live there. Keep asking those direct questions. But I don't have to tell you that, right?" He cocked his head and gave me a curious look.

"What?" I said.

"Read your story about the murders in Palacios. Your investigative skills are something to be reckoned with. If you don't make it as a journalist, you can always hang out a PI shingle." He tipped his hat and left.

I was beginning to learn how small the community of newspaper writers really is. Joining that community felt empowering. I thought of the heroic efforts of journalist Ruth Gruber and then began to picture myself covering some covert operation overseas, parachuting behind enemy lines to cover a story no one else had the guts to take on. Then, suddenly, I thought of Ralph Dixon—something I did a lot lately. The thoughts were a mixture of excitement and fear. Was that part of the attraction between us? Two people who had the desire and tenacity to snoop into other people's business. Friday morning was ninety hours away. I guess I could wait.

THE BRIDGE OVER TO PELICAN ISLAND WAS ONLY A VISION, a mere architect's sketch on a display board. I parked my car where 51st Street dead-ended. About a mile across the Galveston Ship Channel, Pelican Island sat in all its forgotten glory. Marsh grass had staked its claim along the water's edge, and sea oats and cordgrass stabilized the dunes. A few tired, old shrubs battered into submission by one too many hurricanes managed to hang on by the skin of their roots.

Several construction barges were in place in the channel; drilling had begun. I noticed some activity on the island. Vehicles that had been ferried over appeared to be moving debris from one area to another. I noticed a guy decked out in work clothes and a hard hat giving orders to a group of men about to board a boat. I walked over and introduced myself.

"This ain't no beach, lady. You're on the wrong side of the island if you're looking to get a suntan."

"Actually, I'd like to hitch a ride over to Pelican Island."

"What do I look like, a tour guide? This is a construction site, and we ain't in the business of entertaining tourists."

"I won't be any trouble. I'm a reporter covering the island's development. I just want a look around."

He pointed to the boat landing where a boat was ready to take off. "That launch's coming back over in an hour. Be on it or swim back."

"Right. Thank you."

Five minutes later, I hopped off the boat and onto a muddy shore. As I approached the dunes, the mud turned to hard-packed sand and walking along the beach became much easier. A gray curtain swished and swirled overhead, creating an enormous shadow—a flock of sanderlings landed and began feeding on swarms of sand flies. Squawking gulls, mixed with a few raucous terns that had migrated in for the winter, were diving for fish in the surf. A few yards farther down, a crow picked at the remains of someone's recent campfire. The bird grabbed its prize and flew off with a large, dark chunk in its beak. I poked at what looked like huge, charred, baked potatoes among the coals. Another crow flew in and landed nearby, squawking at my intrusion into what was clearly his campfire. The beach sounds were momentarily drowned out by the engine noise of a dump truck rumbling down the road. The driver waved and disappeared in a cloud of dust.

About a quarter mile down to where the truck was heading, I noticed the beginning of the new resort. The dunes had been leveled, and the landscape took the shape of a giant football field. The city was not wasting time. The bridge was at least a year away from completion, and the construction on the island was already under way. I looked back at the birds. "You can't stop progress," I told them. "It's necessary for the economy." I wondered if they felt the same sense of intrusion that I did. A hefty herring gull squawked and deposited a slimy white blob a few feet in front of me. Evidently so.

I decided to walk over to the site and see if anyone could give me a scoop on the development, maybe a contractor or engineer who didn't mind talking. I misjudged the distance, and by the time I got there, I realized that the return boat was scheduled to leave in fifteen minutes. I saw the friendly truck driver returning and I waved him down.

"Mind if I catch a ride?"

"Hop in. I was wondering what you were doing here."

I ran around to the passenger's side and climbed in. "Scoping things out," I said. "Are you driving onto the ferry?"

"Don't plan on paddling this baby across the water."

"Right. I came across on that boat, but I guess I can get back with you. Is that the location of the resort back there?"

"So I've been told."

"Kind of early to start with the bridge not built yet, isn't it?"

"I don't ask. I just move dirt and collect my check."

We drove up to a temporary boat ramp. My chauffeur got out of the truck and helped the pilot secure the ferry for loading. Moments later, we were aboard, and soon I was back on Galveston Island. I thanked the driver and waved to Mr. Hard Hat. He rolled his eyes and walked away. I love it when I make a good impression on people.

I trekked back to my car and instantly saw that something was wrong. My little convertible leaned slightly to the right. "Damn!" I cried. That's all I needed, getting stuck in the sand. I should know better. Then I saw that the right front tire was flat. Digging out of sand could be a pain, but I could fix a flat with my eyes closed, thanks to my dad, who insisted I learn the basics of car repair and maintenance before getting my driver's license. I walked around to the trunk to retrieve the spare and quickly realized that one spare wouldn't help much. The left rear was flat, too.

The rumble of a dump truck told me I was to have company.

"Having trouble, ma'am?" The guy who had given me a ride leaned out the window and cut the engine.

"Slightly. Someone has slashed my tires."

"Maybe you ran over something. Been bringing a lot of construction supplies over the last few days." He got out of his truck to come over for a closer look.

"I didn't run over anything. The gashes are on the side, near the whitewalls."

"Yep, I think you're right. Someone made several jabs before cutting into the tire. You made any enemies?"

"Not in the last fifteen minutes," I wanted to say, but answered with a shrug instead.

"I can give you a ride over to Bob's Station," he said.

"No! I mean, isn't there someplace closer?"

He scratched his head and looked at me as if I was the biggest moron this side of the Mason-Dixon Line. Actually, that's exactly how I felt. Bob's Station was where my father did business. Before Bob could lift the second tire from the axle, my dad would find out I was in town and rush over.

"Looks to me like you can't be too choosy."

"Bob's is all the way over on 61st Street."

He scratched his head again. "Got a point. I need to be back here as soon as possible. There's the Red Top Garage on 25th Street just a couple of miles from here. He sells new tires, and, believe me, you're going to need some. Bob probably don't have these fancy whitewalls anyway."

"Red Top sounds fine," I said. "And thanks so much for your help."

WALLY BRIGHTON AT THE RED TOP GARAGE was dressed in a jumpsuit covered with so much grime and grease that it glistened in the sun. He puffed on a stogie and listened to my problem. "Kids," he said. "Up to no good. What kind of car did you say you have?"

"It's a red 1953 Chevy Bel Air Deluxe with whitewalls."

He whistled. "Some car. Sounds like I better tow it in. If the tires are slashed like you said, I doubt I can fix 'em. You'll probably have to buy two new ones. Expensive, you know."

"I don't have a choice. How long?"

"I'll send one of my boys to get it. Should be ready in a couple of hours. Police station is around the block. You might want to report this—not that it will do much good."

I thanked Wally and dropped a dime into the soft-drink machine. I sipped on a Royal Crown Cola and pondered what to do. Wally was right. Finding out who slashed my tires would not be high on the priority list of Galveston's finest. But if someone was out to frighten me away, their threats and intimidations could escalate. It could be smart to get this incident on record. I finished my cola and told Wally I'd be back soon. Instead of going to the police, I walked down 25th Street to The Galveston Tribune building. The receptionist directed me to the second floor, where I found Chuck Conrad banging away on a typewriter that looked as old as he did. A cigarette dangled from his lips and his tie hung loose. He glanced up, plucked the cigarette from his mouth, and pointed for me to sit down.

"How's it going?"

"Not so good. Have a minute?"

"For you? Sure. What's up?"

"Who would slash my tires out on 51st Street?"

He leaned back in his chair. "In Galveston? Are you kidding?"

"No. I'm bugged, Mr. Conrad."

He laughed. "Call me Chuck. Probably some teenagers who had nothing better to do."

"I don't think so. I also received two threatening messages right after I checked into the hotel."

"You got my attention. What did they say?"

"The first one came while I was on the way up to my room. The caller, a woman, left a message with the desk clerk for me not to get too comfortable, that my stay would be short. Since I'd checked in early, I figured the call was for the previous guest. Then the second one came a few minutes later. This time the woman asked for me by name, saying she was serious about her first message."

"A woman, uh?"

"Right. And then the tires."

"You think they're connected?"

I gave Chuck a what-do-you-think look.

"I see what you mean. No coincidences."

"No coincidences. Do you think it's related to the reason I'm here?"

"To report on the conference? If that were the case, we'd all have gotten threats. Unless you know something the rest of us reporters don't."

"I just got here. I don't know any more than you. I haven't begun to snoop."

Chuck took a hard pull on his cigarette. He stared at his stained fingers. He loosened his tie another inch. "Sounds to me like someone anticipated you'd be trouble. You got that first message right after you arrived."

"What trouble could I possibly be?"

"Are you kidding? You sleuthed out that killer in Palacios a few weeks ago and even exposed a plot to swindle an oil company. You're good, Miss Lockhart, really good."

"Thanks, but I don't know what the hell I'm supposed to know."

"Haven't a clue. Call me if you have any more trouble. For now, I wouldn't go cruising around desolate areas alone."

"Because I'm a woman?"

"Because you're a smart, nosy woman. That's a compliment."

CHAPTER FOUR

I left Chuck to his work and decided to keep this crime from the police until I'd given the situation some more thought. The Red Top Garage closed at 6:30. That gave me—a smart, nosy woman—an hour to snoop.

Mayor Quinn's secretary graciously told me her boss was in a meeting, but if I didn't mind waiting, he might be able to see me before he left for the day. I took a seat, prepared to wait that long if necessary. If the mayor had received death threats over the issue of developing Pelican Island, then I wanted to know the person or group that was so opposed. I only had to wait five minutes before Mayor Quinn came out. After a slight hesitation, he smiled and introduced himself.

"Sydney Lockhart," I said. "I'm with The Austin American Statesman. Thanks for taking time to see me. I know you must be extremely busy."

"Ah, the lady reporter," he said. "Please come into my office. Lockhart? Are you related to the Lockharts who live on the island?"

"My grandparents lived here." I left out the part about my parents retiring to Galveston. If he'd heard about my mother, he would certainly not take me seriously.

"I knew your grandmother. Fine lady. Sorry about your grandfather. I was away at college, but I heard about the incident. Never found out what happened, did they?"

"No, the case was never solved. Mayor Quinn, I wanted to—"

"Yes, yes, please sit down. You heard the rumor about the death threats."

"Is it a rumor?"

"Miss Lockhart, don't be naïve. The development of Pelican Island has been a controversial issue, but that's nothing new. If you lived here, you'd be used to opinionated people."

"Most opinionated people aren't that strong about their convictions."

"They are here. Oh, they're all bluff. I wouldn't waste my time chasing after that story. There's no validity to it, Miss Lockhart."

"Who made the threats? You must have some idea."

"I don't, and I don't really care."

"Did they come by phone or mail?"

"By phone. Just some crackpot with nothing better to do. I don't expect you to understand, a young, novice reporter. I know you're after a story, but there's not one here."

"So I shouldn't worry my little head over the threats I've received today and the slashing of my tires, right?"

"Let me offer my sincere apologies. We like our visitors to feel safe in our fair city. Where did this happen?"

"Out on 51st Street across from Pelican Island."

"Well, there you go. Not the best part of town."

"That sort of things happens often in that area?"

"We had a few incidents soon after we broke ground, but nothing serious; a bunch of trash dumped on the site, a few tacky protest signs. Then the police began patrolling the area more frequently, and things have cooled down. It's predictable now that we're under way that the vandalism would start again. May I ask what you were doing out there?"

"I wanted to see the area. Things seem to be moving rapidly."

"Yes, they are."

The mayor's intercom buzzed. "Excuse me. Yes, Miss Howard. Tell her I'm on my way." He stood up. "That was my wife reminding me we're due at a dinner party in ten minutes. My advice to you, Miss Lockhart, is stick to the facts. Don't look for news where there isn't any. That's something seasoned journalists know. I admire your enthusiasm, though."

At that moment, Miss Howard walked in, and the mayor headed for his back door. "Miss Howard will show you out."

Once outside the reception area, I thanked Miss Howard

and told her I'd let myself out. I paused outside the door long enough to hear Miss Howard pick up the phone and tell her boss, "She's gone, Mr. Quinn."

So Mr. Quinn didn't get elected on his good looks alone. The man was sharp and slick, and a damn good liar.

WALLY HAD MY CAR READY WHEN I RETURNED, along with a bill for two new tires, a bill that punched a devastating hole in my wimpy savings account. He must have noticed the look of shock on my face.

"Threw in a free car wash. Gotta keep the salt spray off. Rust a car to dust living here on the coast."

"Thanks, Mr. Brighton. I'm just here for a few days. Could you tell what cut into my tires? Was it a knife?"

"I'd say it was something with a thicker blade. The rear rim had a small notch cut into it as if someone struck the tire hard. Maybe with a hatchet."

"A hatchet!"

"I'd say so, ma'am."

I DROVE AROUND THE HOTEL AND SCOPED out the surrounding neighborhood, avoiding my parents' street, of course. I didn't want my car sitting in the hotel parking lot waiting for the next vandal to have his way with her. A block away from the hotel sat one of the three Catholic churches on the island. The parking lot of St. Anthony's was shaped like an enormous L. Near the rectory, along the base of the L, ancient magnolia trees with drooping limbs provided a secluded place to park. It would be impossible to see my car from the street. In fact, it wasn't possible to see it from the rectory windows either, so hopefully the priests wouldn't notice the hot little sports car on their property.

I was on my way to the elevator when Mr. Chambers called my name. "Miss Lockhart, a message for you." He waved the paper in the air like a matador waving a cape at an angry bull. The man must live to see me seething with annoyance. "This time it's a telegram, and the sender left a name."

I thanked him and snatched the telegram from his hand. I

took it to the verandah, found a table, and ordered a martini. I waited for its arrival before reading the message.

HEY, HON–STOP–WORRIED ABOUT YOU–STOP–BUT I'M SURE BY NOW, YOU'VE TACKLED ALL THE GHOSTS OF THE PAST–STOP–

I swirled the olive, giving my first swallow of gin time to slow my pulse. During our conversation last Friday, I'd told Dixon the story about finding my grandfather. He had listened, and I'd felt the empathy, even through the phone lines. The weekly conversations were a good idea. Talking to him had become easy. We could get through a ten-minute conversation with only one disagreement. I picked up the telegram and read the rest.

I'LL CALL ON FRIDAY, SAME TIME, DIRECTLY TO YOUR ROOM 559–STOP–TOP FLOOR, CORNER ROOM WITH A WATER VIEW–STOP–I CHECKED–STOP–SOUNDS ROMANTIC–STOP–DIXON

I'm surprised he didn't know the color of the rug and the print on the wallpaper. Damn! Dating a detective makes it difficult to be mysterious or evasive. Sometimes I'm grateful he lives four hundred miles away. But when I least expect it, I feel an emptiness somewhere in the middle of my chest and a strong urging to have it filled. The rest of this martini should take care of that nonsense.

"Hey, lady, wanna ride my horse?"

I looked over, and standing by the pool was a short version of Hopalong Cassidy, the same little boy I'd seen earlier. This time, along with his vest and six-shooters, he was decked out in chaps and a red cowboy hat and boots.

"I don't see your horse," I said.

"Old Ned is tied up outside. He's a palomino. My name's Big Bad Jones. I'm a gunslinger, but you can call me Frankie."

"Well, Big Bad Frankie Jones, I'm going to have to take a rain check on the horse ride. Maybe some other time."

"Jones is my professional name. My other name is Franklin P. Leaky."

"What does the P. stand for?"

"My father says it stands for Pest, but it really stands for Pearce. What's your name?"

"Sydney."

"That's a boy's name."

"Not if it's spelled with a Y instead of an I."

"Girls are stupid."

I ignored the dig and handed Franklin Pearce Leaky, a.k.a. Big Bad Jones, my martini olive. "One day soon you'll change your mind about girls. Here. I don't have a carrot for Old Ned, but maybe he'd like an olive."

"Thanks, lady, but my horse don't eat olives." He spun around and ran back to his fantasy world.

I turned Dixon's telegram over and wrote my response.

IT IS ROMANTIC–STOP–IN A LONELY SORT OF WAY– STOP–SYD

I finished my drink and headed for the lobby. The phone booth was unoccupied. It was only Monday evening. What the hell? I placed the long-distance call. He answered on the first ring.

"Dixon."

"Collect call from a Miss Lockhart. Will you accept the charges?"

"Put her on."

"Go ahead, Miss Lockhart," the operator said.

"What's the color scheme?"

"Don't know, but I'll bet the bathroom soap is in the shape of a seashell."

"A conch. I hope you don't mind the early call."

"After the day I had, a call from you is a welcome."

"Did you just say something nice to me?"

He laughed—a sound I'd heard only a few times, and on each occasion, it sent flutters all the way to my toes.

"Hey," he said, "you're not in jail, are you?"

"Nope, I'm in the hotel lobby, gazing out on the gulf."

"That's a relief. Tell me about your first day on this assignment."

"You mean you haven't sent someone down here to keep tabs on me?"

"Would I do that?"

"You would and you have. Speaking of spies, how's my friend Billy doing?"

"He's working the beat with your other friend, Officer O'Riley. It's only temporary, though. I have big plans for Billy. Now tell me, what's going on there?"

"I got here around one, went directly to the foyer, where I experienced flashbacks. Before I made it up to my room, a nasty call came via the front desk, telling me, in so many words, to get out of town. Less than an hour later, a second call came in, just in case I didn't get the first one. Then Jeremiah called with a plea for me to phone my mother, who's planning the infamous anniversary party for this Saturday. Mom wants me to drop everything and help. Let's see. All that happened within the first couple of hours. Then I pissed off the mayor at the press conference. Got two of my tires slashed while I was conversing with the sea gulls on Pelican Island. Then I paid a personal visit to the mayor, and he ever so delicately threw me out. How am I doing?"

"I expected worse. You're not injured and you're not in jail. I'm relieved. What do you think those threats were about?"

"I have no idea. I thought they were linked to this assignment, but why would anyone not want me reporting on this? There are dozens of newspaper reporters here getting the same scoop."

"Yes, but you're different."

"How's that?"

"Bright, beautiful, and..."

"That's pretty much what Chuck Conrad told me."

"Chuck who?"

"A reporter for The Galveston Tribune. He knew all about the incident in Palacios. I should have taken Jeremiah's advice and come incognito."

"Too late now. Just be careful."

"I will. Thanks for listening. I'll call you on Friday."

"Maybe I should come down and tuck you in."

"I'm working."

"Sure. Hey, who's Conrad again?"

Yes, our conversations were definitely getting easier. And sometimes that scared me.

I stepped out of the elevator onto the fifth floor and knew immediately something was wrong. Even from where I stood,

I could see that my door was open a crack. I grabbed the vase from the hallway table and tiptoed to the door. I heard voices. These people, whoever they were, didn't waste time. I decided it was in my best interest not to barge in and demand an explanation. After all, I'd promised Dixon I'd be careful. I was backing away when the door flew open.

"Just bring it in. I've made room by the window."

"Ruth!"

"Oh, hi. I thought you were the bellboy. It's about time you got here. You can help me rearrange things."

I walked in and saw my bed covered with suitcases.

"Now don't give me that look," Ruth said. "There's a convention in town, as you very well know. I have no choice but to stay with you. Blanche is bringing more towels. The bellboy is bringing the cot for you to sleep on."

Ruth often left me speechless, but this time my brain lost all contact with my vocal cords.

"Well, you insisted I come to Galveston. And I'm certainly not staying with your parents since Mom's staying in the other bedroom. And I'm certainly not sleeping on a cot." She lifted her nose. "Have you had a martini already?" She stomped her size-2 foot. "No fair. Hey, let's go down to the bar. I have your mother's guest list and invitations right here." She picked up a shoebox. "We can address them while we drink. I have stamps and everything. This party is going to be such great fun." Then she noticed the telegram in my hand and grabbed and read it while I stood stock-still. "Well, well, seems like things are progressing rather nicely, hon."

The two bellboys came up behind me carrying the cot, and behind them was Blanche with an armload of towels and linens.

"Go ahead and set everything up," Ruth ordered. "Sydney and I will be in the bar."

"Good for you," Blanche said. "Live it up while you can."

We were in the elevator, creeping down toward the lobby, when I finally found my voice.

"A cot?"

"You know, after you called, I was so mad." She looped her arm around mine in a cuddly sort of way. "Then I thought about it for a minute and realized you were right. I have been working too hard. Anyway, I've arranged for my new secretary to take over and...well, here I am."

"The cot's for me?"

"Thank me later. Blanche and I will take care of you."

CHAPTER FIVE

The elevator bounced to a stop. Ruth nearly dropped the box of invitations. The attendant apologized for the hard landing. The sudden jar must have shaken something loose in my brain because peacefulness washed over me; the anxiety that, only moments ago, had stunned me into paralysis, was replaced by a dreamy calm.

Ruth and I found a table by a window, made ourselves comfortable, and placed our cocktail order.

"I'm glad you're here, Ruth. That outfit you're wearing looks nice on you."

"You're glad I'm here?" Her puzzled look lasted only a second. She smiled and winked. "You seem different, Sydney Jean Lockhart. I mean, hon. Do you really like this dress?"

"Coco Chanel?"

"Absolutely. That's the reason I'm a wee bit late. I had to stop by Neiman's on the way to the airport. What does one wear to a thirtieth-anniversary celebration?"

"Pray tell, what does one wear?"

"It's a surprise. It'll knock your socks off."

"So, since the time I spoke to you a few hours ago, you hired and trained a new secretary and bought a new wardrobe."

"I'm amazing, aren't I? While you were here in vacationland exchanging love notes with the lieutenant, I've been busy, which includes dealing with your crazy mother. You owe me big-time, Cousin."

"You didn't tell her I'm here?"

"Relax. I told her that you're in Africa writing about wildebeests."

"You did what?"

"Just kidding. You must relax, Dear Cousin. Your mother thinks you're in Austin working on some story. I told her that since you were low woman on the totem pole at the newspaper, you were given the assignment of reporting on the Junior League. She was impressed."

"You're such a good liar."

"Thank you. I obviously get that nasty trait from my father's side of the family. Frances is so honest, she couldn't fib if her life depended on it."

Our martinis arrived. I took a sip before my pleasant mood had a chance to evaporate. Ruth grabbed the waiter's arm. "We're starving. What's your special tonight?"

"Tonight it is Crab Louie."

"Perfect. We'll each have one. And the soup?"

"Tomato bisque."

"Two of those as well."

"You're on a roll. I thought you were feeling weak after your ordeal with Marcella."

"Helping those young unwed mothers lifts my spirits. Let's not talk about that woman. Just because I saved her life doesn't mean I like her. Now, tell me what trouble you've gotten yourself into." She rubbed her hands together as if she were about to dive onto a sale table at Neiman's. Then her perkiness vanished. She sat her martini down and grasped my hand. "Oh, dear. I forgot. How are you doing with...the—"

"With dealing with the memory of my grandfather? Not bad. I try to stay out of the foyer by taking the side or back entrance to the hotel."

"You poor thing."

"Speaking of talking about other things, let's change the subject. How's the home coming along?"

"Wonderfully! I've purchased an old hospital that's been closed for about five years. It was a small private hospital owned by a guy who helped people. He died, and the family didn't want to continue the business so it closed. I got the building really cheap. There's not a lot of remodeling to do. The rooms were made for two patients. We're changing them to single rooms, painting them, adding cozy rugs, homey furniture, and some comfy knickknacks. The kitchen is in perfect shape, but the dining room needs a major redo. The lights are too bright, and the metal tables and chairs are cold. I'm adding sofas and lounge chairs."

"So you're really making this happen."

"You doubted me?"

"Well, actually, yes."

"I forgive you."

"Are you actually going to run the place?"

"Oh, please! When would I have time to work? I've hired a director."

"That was fast. Who is she?"

"My friend Lucy Freeman's cousin, Lauren Patterson—she used to be a nurse. I think she will work out fine."

"What are her credentials? Does she have a business background?"

"I told you, she used to be a nurse. How hard is it to run a home?"

"Why isn't she still a nurse?"

"Who the hell knows! Don't be difficult. All I need now is a name for the place. You convinced me St. Mary's Home doesn't sound right, but I can't keep calling it the Echland Home for Unwed Mothers. It implies that I might have been in that situation myself."

"True. How about simply The Echland Home?"

"Not bad, but not quite right either."

"You'll think of something."

"Now that the important stuff is out of the way, tell me what trouble you've gotten into."

"There's someone who wants me to leave town."

"That's not unusual."

"I've had two threatening phone calls."

"Boring so far."

"Two of my tires were slashed while I was on Pelican Island."

Her eyebrows rose. "Now we're talking. Whom do you suspect? Tell me all about it."

"There's not much to tell," I had finished the entire story just as the waiter placed our first course in front of us.

"A woman, you said?" Ruth tasted her soup and added salt. "Maybe it has nothing to do with this Pelican Island thing. Maybe it's someone you knew in Houston. Some girl from high school whose boyfriend you stole who now lives here. She's been planning to get even all these years, just waiting for the right moment. And then, bingo! She's walking her dog on the seawall and notices you drive by in your fancy car and she snaps." Ruth looked around. "Maybe she works at this hotel."

"Only you would come up with a lame-brain story like that. I never stole anyone's boyfriend. Got any other ideas?"

"Give me time. But I wouldn't worry if I were you. Now that I'm here, we can handle whatever problems you attract."

"You'll be at my parents' house helping Mom with the party, remember? And another thing—I'm not sure about us staying in the same room."

"I thought about that, and I have an idea. Whoa, here come our Crab Louies. Let's eat, and while we're having dessert, we'll talk about that tiny room you had the gall to check into."

While we wolfed down our entrees, Ruth filled me in on George and Mary Lou's anniversary party. The band and caterer were booked. Mom was still trying to locate a photographer, but things were moving along rapidly. That was no surprise since the initial planning had been completed last November when the celebration was supposed to take place. Then, a few days before the event, my mother canceled everything and left my father when she began to suspect that their wedding had never taken place.

My parents had eloped to Hot Springs, Arkansas, and were married at the historic Arlington Resort and Spa, a ceremony of which my mother has no recollection due to the celebration beginning as soon as they hit the highway. When my mother began planning their thirtieth-anniversary party, she couldn't find their marriage certificate. She wanted it for a centerpiece on the cake table. My father had to confess that he'd left the certificate in a suitcase at the hotel. Mom, being somewhat suspicious, assumed they'd skipped the ceremony and gone straight to the honeymoon. Dad tried to get a copy of the certificate, but a fire in the Garland County Courthouse had destroyed the records. My stubborn mother would still be living in the beach house if I hadn't found the original marriage certificate while investigating murders at the Arlington Hotel. I'd discovered the certificate taped to the back of their wedding picture, which had been hanging on the wall along with those of several other newlyweds who'd tied the knot at the Arlington.

With all the party preparations running smoothly, I didn't understand why my mother was in such a panic to have me put my life on hold and help. My thoughts were interrupted when I heard Ruth say, "two hundred people."

"What?"

"We need to get these in the mail tomorrow."

"They've invited two hundred people! On the spur of the moment, they expect two hundred people to attend their celebration? There's no time for anyone to respond to the RSVPs. My mother has really lost her mind this time. What's the hurry anyway?"

"People are talking."

"What people? Talking about what?"

"Their separation. Your mother wants to dispel all the lies."

"Lies!"

"Lower your voice. People are beginning to stare."

"But they were separated. Mom flees whenever she gets a wild hair."

"Yes, but her new friends don't know that. Your mother has joined the West Side Country Club."

"Stop!" I pushed my half-eaten Louie away. "I don't want to hear it. My head hurts."

"You should have invited Ralph Dixon to the party."

"I thought you liked him. If he meets my mother, he'll probably never want to see me again."

"You know, Sydney, you tend to overreact where your mother is concerned." She placed the box of invitations on the table. "Let's address half of these now. Over dessert and coffee, I'll tell you my plan for Room 559; then we can finish the other half."

Surprisingly enough, I regained my composure by the time I'd reached the G's. I'd never heard of Jim and Sarah Gordon, who lived two doors down from my parents, probably some of my mother's many new friends.

"I'm going to write the return address on these envelopes. I've been to your parents' house many times, but I don't know the street name. All I know is the white house with green shutters on the corner across from the little park."

"P and a Half."

Ruth was busy scribbling away. "Pee in a hat? I've never heard that expression before. It's rather crass. If you have to go so bad, use the lobby restroom."

"No, that's the name of the street. It's 504 P and a Half. The city planners probably skipped that street when passing out names and had to add the 'half' to keep from renaming everything. Let's stop. The room. Your plans."

"I checked at the front desk. That nice Mr. Chambers was very helpful. There is a large room available now on the west side of the hotel, but he said that music from the bar across the street often continues into the wee hours of the morning. There's also a larger room across the hall, which should be available tomorrow if the people don't decide to stay over. We can have that one. Two beds, more space. So, you see, you only have to spend one night on the cot."

When Ruth made a surprise appearance in Palacios a few weeks ago, I was so angry I made her stay at the Baptist Encampment. I refused to share my room at The Luther Hotel. Was I feeling guilty over that incident? Was I so grateful to her for running interference with my mother, or was I, after all these years, growing accustomed to her annoying habits? No, it was something else, but I didn't know what. I feared my peaceful bubble would burst at any moment, but for now I'd hang on and float with it. Over a warm brandy, we finished the infernal invitations.

CHAPTER SIX

I persuaded Ruth not to unpack all six suitcases. We stacked them in the only uncluttered corner of the room and were asleep by midnight. Early the next morning while Ruth bathed, I licked two hundred stamps. I called for room service, and we had a nice breakfast of waffles, bacon, and scrambled eggs. Ruth dashed off to the post office and then to my parents' house, and after I stretched the kinks out of my muscles (sleeping on the cot was worse than I had imagined), I went to work.

I called Ernest to update him on what was happening and then began typing my notes from yesterday's interview with the mayor. I picked up the phone to order more coffee when Mr. Chambers called with the bad news. The people in the large room across the hall had decided to stay one more night. He sounded joyous, delivering that little bit of disappointment. I was not going to brood over having to spend another night on the cot. The first planning meeting was scheduled for ten o'clock, and I decided a brisk walk was in order. I'd check on my car, stroll the seawall while keeping an eye out for people whose cage I might have rattled in the past, and have my coffee on the verandah. I donned my gray slacks and red sweater, slipped my notebook into my satchel, and left my room feeling on top of the world.

Not two steps from my door, I was almost startled out of my shoes when the door next to mine swung open and a pistol poked out, followed by a loud "Pow!" Big Bad Jones pushed open the door and gave me the evil eye.

Great, just great, I thought. Having a six-year-old cowboy next door was all I needed.

"Is your horse in there?" I asked.

"Yep."

"Wonderful! I'll bring him a carrot when I come back."

"He likes apples better. And remember, no olives."

"Yeah, right."

Frankie followed me into the hall, firing his pistol.

"Find someone else to shoot, honey. I'm busy."

"Franklin Pearce!" came a voice from within the room. "Get your butt in here before I take that stupid pistol and fling it out the window!"

Frankie retreated, and I went on my way.

EXCEPT FOR A FEW SPLATTERS OF SEAGULL WASTE, my car was fine, but I didn't want to press my luck. I wanted to let the pastor know I'd parked my car in the parish lot, and I was thinking up a reasonable excuse for having done so when I saw my mother leaving the rectory. I ducked behind the parish hall and waited. I couldn't imagine what she was up to now. When we lived in Houston, we were members of St. John's Parish. I attended Catholic school, but my mother wasn't a regular churchgoer. Was this part of the new Mary Lou Lockhart? It wasn't yet nine o'clock and she was up and out and looking full of energy. Her ocean-blue suit caused her bleached-blond hair to shine like a globe on a light pole. My mother wasn't tall, but her heels added a few inches to her height. The party—of course, that was probably it. My mother was known to rise to the occasion, but only when that occasion benefited her.

Mom stood on the porch chatting and laughing with a young priest. I decided my car was safe where it was for a while longer, and I went in the opposite direction. With Mom in the neighborhood, strolling along the seawall was not a good idea. I went back inside the hotel and found a cozy spot on the verandah, made myself comfortable, and ordered coffee.

I read through the commercial/recreational development portion of the proposal the committee had prepared for the press.

The development of Pelican Island was outlined in a two-year plan. Once completed, it would consist of a 10,000-square-foot convention center, a posh hotel housing two hundred rooms, all with an ocean view, and a beach park complete with picnic tables, a pavilion, and a boardwalk. There were also plans for a midway sort of area where local businesses could set up their own concerns such as food stands, souvenir shops, and beach-supply rentals. How nice—tourists could lounge on the island made from channel dredge and watch oil tankers slide by on their way to Houston.

"Morning."

I looked up to see Chuck Conrad walking over.

"Hello," I said. "Grab a seat. Coffee?"

"Thanks. Police find out who slashed your tires?"

"No, haven't reported it. What's the use? Random violence." As soon as I said those words, I saw PoPo's body lying in the foyer and my breath caught.

"Are you okay?"

"Sure," I rubbed my eyes, trying to erase the image from my mind.

Chuck sat down and pulled out a pack of Salem's, tapped the box on the table, and offered me one. We lit up. A diligent waiter whisked by with a cup for Chuck.

"What do you think of the proposal?" he asked.

"The justification sounds reasonable. Construction jobs for islanders, a great boost in tourism..."

"But?"

"But why did they suddenly decide against giving the project to the company from New York and give it to Roland's company? Are Galveston's manual laborers acceptable, but the brains behind the operation not?"

"Good question."

"And what's behind the mayor's death threats?" I asked. "And who's making them? Quinn claims he doesn't know and doesn't care."

"Rumor has it they're coming from an organization called People for Pelican Island, an ecology-minded group."

"Just a rumor?"

"Although the group is outspoken and against the development, they deny the mayor's accusations."

Chuck looked at his watch. "Almost time to go. I'm sure you want a seat up front again."

I laughed. "So I can be noticed." I reached for my purse.

"Let me," he said, and threw four bits on the table.

Getting there early landed us our two seats in front. Chuck introduced me to some reporters he knew, one from The Houston Chronicle and the other from The San Antonio Express. Like Chuck, the two men were in their fifties or older and had probably been pounding the news beat for longer than I'd been alive. I scanned the room again, hoping to see some women and was happy to spot one. She was older than me, but it was good to see the mold of the traditional reporter starting to crack. Then the reporter from The Houston Chronicle said, "Not a great start. Our keynote speaker is late. The mayor looks nervous."

"Quinn?" Chuck said, "Mister Cool-as-a-Cucumber?"

"Not today," Chronicle said.

We all turned to the head table and podium, and sure enough, Mayor Quinn looked distressed. It was only ten minutes after ten, but the mayor was having words with some guy who stammered, unable to get out a complete sentence. At twenty after, the mayor finally stepped to the podium.

"Good morning. Thank you for coming. Mr. Roland has been detained but will arrive any moment. What did I tell you? With so many people flocking to our beautiful island, the line of traffic crossing the bridge is backed up all the way to Houston." The crowd chuckled as the mayor held up his hand to continue. "While we wait, let's hear from Mr. Billings."

Forty-five minutes later, Mr. Billings from the city planning commission was finishing up his presentation and was clearly stalling. He asked for questions and that stalled a bit longer. Finally, Mayor Quinn thanked him and announced that due to an unforeseen emergency, our keynote speaker had had to cancel. Nothing serious, he added. The agenda would be rearranged, and further information would be available later this afternoon. The mayor's secretary took the podium and gave an altered summary of the day's events.

"Well, that's it," I said.

"Oya will never allow it!" A shout from the back of the room had some reporters up out of their seats and others snickering. "This is her warning! You did not listen before!"

I turned to see a flash of lavender, a gauzy curtain flit through the air and disappear out the door.

"What the hell was that?"

"Our resident mystic, Asherah Astor," Chuck said. "I was wondering when she'd show up. She's been predicting the Second Coming for years now."

"Oya?"

"The Lady of Storms. She communicates through Asherah."

"She's warning us about Judgment Day?"

"More like the second hurricane. It seems that Asherah mollifies Oya, who, according to Asherah, was responsible for the Great Storm in 1900."

"And Oya is not happy with the development of Pelican Island?"

"Would you be happy if your home was turned into a resort? Ash claims Pelican Island is one of those cosmic places on the planet that emits strange sounds or lights or whatever. If the island is disturbed, Oya will unleash the fury of her wrath again."

"Would Asherah do something to stall the project?"

"Ash is harmless. She lives in a ratty houseboat somewhere on the bay. She has a small following of goddesses who assemble on the beach every now and then or on her boat, probably during some astrological occurrence like the solstice or an eclipse or when their moons are aligned with their planets. They dress in purple fairy outfits, burn incense, and chant. I'm heading back to the paper. By the way, I want to hear all about your adventure in Palacios. I read about it, but I want it straight from the mare's mouth."

"You got it."

I needed to take care of my car before the priests of St. Anthony's found it and had it towed. As I left the back door of the hotel, an ambulance flew by, followed by a cop car. Had they been traveling in the opposite direction, I would have worried that the party planning at the Lockharts had become too heated.

I walked around the corner, but couldn't get to the rectory; the emergency vehicles were blocking the way. Neighbors had gathered on the street, and I joined them. An elderly woman made the sign of the cross and began praying for a Father Albert. From her mutterings, I gathered that Father Albert was the elderly priest who had been on his deathbed after having a stroke last month. I watched, but no body was carted out; instead, three priests ran to the back parking lot, where a cluster of police officers stood around looking serious.

My car! Surely, my illegally parked convertible wouldn't cause all this commotion. I ran over to see, and sure enough, my car was the center of attention.

"Miss, step back. You need to leave the area," ordered a cop who looked like he could play linebacker for Green Bay.

"What's going on?" I tried to look over his shoulder.

He moved to block my view. "Please, Miss—"

I stepped aside and saw the trunk of my car wide open. Even from where I stood, I could see that something was inside, and it wasn't a spare tire.

"But that's my car," I said.

The cop changed his tone. "Come with me."

"Sergeant," the cop said to a guy who looked in charge. "This is the owner of that car."

All eyes turned from the body in my trunk to me.

CHAPTER SEVEN

W hat's your car doing parked back here, ma'am?" the
sergeant said.

The crowd that had begun to form leaned over as one giant
mass to hear what I had to say for myself.

"I'm staying at the Hotel Galvez." I thought about lying and
telling him that the parking lot was full, but there were plenty of
places on the street, so I came forth with the truth. "I was hiding
my car." Wrong words. If I hadn't had everyone's attention
before, I certainly had it now. "I mean, my car was vandalized
yesterday, and I didn't want that happening again."

The sergeant looked at a car in mint condition. "Two of my
tires were slashed," I added.

"Name, ma'am," the sergeant spoke.

"Sydney Lockhart. I'm a reporter covering the convention at
the hotel. I assume the man in my trunk is dead, Sergeant—"

"Bleaker. Who's your traveling companion?"

"You can't be serious. I've never seen the guy."

Bleaker turned to one of the police officers. "Finish up here.
Miss Lockhart and I are going to the station."

Not again. Why me? I peered into the trunk for one more
look. "I don't know that man or how he ended up in my car."

"We'll talk at the station. I need your statement." He directed
me to his car. No handcuffs—that was a good sign. Just then
Big Bad Jones wriggled his way through the crowd.

"If you rode a horse instead of driving a car, you wouldn't
have these kind of problems." He looked up at the sergeant.
"She's not very smart. She tried to feed my horse an olive."

"Maybe you should ride toward the sunset and keep going," I said.

ONCE AT THE STATION, I WAITED IN A SMELLY, windowless room for what seemed like forever. Claustrophobia crept up my back and curled itself around my neck. I was about to open the door for some fresh air when Sergeant Bleaker and another man came in. The new guy wore a rumpled suit and scruffy wing tips. His shifty eyes told me he was a detective. He could use some lessons from Dixon on how to dress.

"This is Miss Lockhart. Miss, right?" the sergeant said.

"That's right, Miss," I said.

"Detective Fidalgo," the guy said, and sat down across the table from me. He looked me straight in the eye and then squinted. "You look familiar."

I was about to deny having recognized him, but it was too late. "You're James Lockhart's granddaughter, aren't you?"

Detective Fidalgo was in uniform the last time I saw him. He was younger, and didn't quite know what to do with a hysterical eleven-year-old girl. The hardness around his eyes softened. "So, here you are again?"

"I can't believe you recognized me after all these years."

"A honed skill. Sorry about your grandfather."

"I hope you and your department manage to solve this murder."

"Right." His sympathy evaporated and his demeanor took on a harsher tone. He opened his notebook and got down to business. "How long was your car in that lot?"

"Since yesterday evening. I parked it there around 6:30."

"Did you move it any time after that?"

"No, I didn't."

"Anyone see you park it there? The priests?"

He knew the answer to that. I'm sure the priests at St. Anthony's had told him they didn't know whose car it was. "No, I suppose I should have told them, but being a weekday, I didn't think anyone would mind."

"Sergeant Bleaker tells me your car was vandalized."

"Yesterday when I was on Pelican Island. I went for a walk

along the beach, and when I returned I found two flat tires." I didn't mention the hatchet.

"You didn't report it?"

"No. I should have, but I didn't."

"Where were you last night?"

Alibi! I had one! Ruth. Was I having a premonition last night, seeing Ruth in my room and feeling okay with the fact that she'd barged in unannounced? Yes, that was it! "After I parked my car, I went back to the hotel for the evening."

"Can anyone substantiate that?"

"My cousin Ruth was there. I was with her the entire night. We shared a room together."

"Where is she now?"

Oh, boy. I didn't want to get into explaining that my parents lived here and why I wasn't staying with them. And why they didn't know I was even in town. "She's...visiting relatives, since I'm working today. She should be back at the hotel later this afternoon." My excuses weren't working. I saw the suspicion on Fidalgo's face, and I knew he didn't intend to wait for Ruth to show up. I envisioned police cars pulling up to my parents' home. I guess things could be worse—I could be behind bars again. I decided it was time for me to start asking the questions.

"Listen, am I in trouble?"

Fidalgo lit a cigarette and took his time answering. "The guy died between eight and midnight. Shot. As long as you can account for your whereabouts at that time, you are free to go... for now."

"I'll call my cousin. She can be here right away. Also, we were in the bar last night until after midnight. The waiter and bartender can vouch for us."

Fidalgo looked up at sergeant. "Check that out," he told Bleaker. He pointed to the phone. "Call your cousin."

I prayed Ruth would answer. She didn't, but Aunt Francie did. "Aunt Francie, this is Sydney. How's it going?" I smiled and listened to a rather lengthy explanation of how the band my mother had booked had canceled because the drummer was in the hospital with appendicitis. Aunt Francie rambled on about how the new country club wasn't yet set up to accommodate so many people, and how things were falling apart faster than sandcastles during a rising tide. I made sympathetic noises until Francie finally paused to catch her breath, and I jumped in. "Glad things are going well. Can you put Ruth on?"

"Sure, dear. Your mother wants to talk to you first."

"No!"

Detective Fidalgo jerked up from his notes.

"I'll talk to Mom later. Put Ruth on first."

It didn't work. "Sydney! Ruth has been working since early this morning making decorations while you're in Austin pretending to work." I smiled again at the detective, hoping he couldn't see the flush spreading across my face. I kept quiet and listened for another three minutes while Mom bitched. I mouthed the word "relatives," and rolled my eyes. Then I heard Ruth's voice in the background. "I'll handle her, Aunt Mary Lou. Just give me the phone. Sydney?"

"Ruth, I need to you come downtown to the police station, now. See you in a few minutes." I hung up and prayed she was smart enough to keep her mouth shut. "She's on her way."

While I waited for my cousin to arrive, I told Detective Fidalgo everything that had happened to me since I'd driven over the causeway yesterday, including the threatening calls. I asked him if he knew who the dead guy was. He said he didn't, or maybe he just didn't want to tell me. I asked how long they'd have my car.

"A while. These things take time."

I asked if there was blood in my trunk.

"Yes, most definitely."

"That means he was killed close by and dumped into my trunk right away. Did the priests or any of the neighbors hear gunshots?"

I heard the door behind me open as Detective Fidalgo said, "I'm the one in charge here. You ask too many questions."

"That's my fault. I taught her to be inquisitive."

I turned around to see my father standing there wearing his favorite fishing hat with little furry things dangling off hooks. Behind him was the backstabbing Ruth.

"Dad!"

"I had to tell him," Ruth said. "I can't handle everything. This party is a nightmare, and if you're going to get involved with murders again, I'll need help handling that as well."

Detective Fidalgo looked over at me and cocked his head. I put my head down on the table. "She's joking," I said. "My family is a riot." I raised my head. "How did you know this involved a murder?"

"Words spread fast," Dad said. "The neighborhood is buzzing."

"Well?" Fidalgo said, looking at Ruth. "Where were you last night?"

Ruth graciously confirmed my story that we were together at the hotel until around eight this morning and then added, "We even stayed in the same room—a tiny room, I might add. Although I am a heavy sleeper."

"Ruth!"

"Don't shout. I'm just trying to be helpful."

"Am I free to go?" I asked.

"We'll corroborate your story with the hotel employees. You can go, but stick around town."

Dad drove us back to the hotel, and the three of us went up to my tiny room. Unlike my mother, my father is the most tranquil person in the world. Finding me sitting in the police station's interrogation room didn't seem to surprise him. He assured me that my mother, although aware that a man had been found murdered a few blocks away, didn't know that his body was stuffed into my trunk, or even that I was in town. In fact, I didn't have to explain why I was keeping my presence a secret. He knew.

I noticed a looked of concern on his face, not the type of worried look I was used to seeing. Then I realized the cause of his consternation and felt like a real heel.

"It's the first time I've been in the hotel since that awful day."

"I know, Dad. This must not be easy. Have a seat. I'm ordering room service. If you've been out fishing all morning, you could probably use some lunch."

"It's okay. I don't know how long I'll be able to keep this from your mother. She's bound to find out, if she doesn't already know. Once Lattie hears that the car was a red Chevy Bel Air convertible owned by a tall, redheaded woman, she'll tell your mother and she'll figure it out. When did you get here?"

"Yesterday after lunch," I said. "I planned to stay until I wrapped up this story, and then I thought I'd present myself on Friday afternoon."

"I wish you'd told me you were coming."

"I'm working. You know how Mom gets when I'm around. And since she's planning this party..."

Dad looked around. "Party, damn. Maybe I should get a room here. Your mother is in a whirlwind. No, that's not true; she is the whirlwind. Then Frances arrived this morning, and now there are two whirlwinds. When those two women get together, it makes a hurricane seem like a mild breeze. I just recovered from the Marcella Wheatly saga, and now this."

"Poor Uncle George," Ruth put her arm around him.

"If I live through this, I can live through anything. You should have left our marriage certificate in Hot Springs. Your mother would still be in Los Angeles, and I'd have some peace of mind."

"I'm here," Ruth said to Dad. She gave me a dirty look, insinuating all this was my fault. I refrained from comment. Ruth's presence had saved my butt, so for the time being, I'd let her play the role of savior.

Someone knocked. We all turned and stared at the door. Then turned and stared at one another.

"Oh, good Lord," I said and went to answer it. It was Blanche.

"I saw a man come in here."

"Is that against the rules?" I said.

"No. I just wanted to know if I should bring extra towels." She tried to peer around the door. Not out of curiosity, I'm sure, but to see if a wild party was brewing so she'd have an idea of what kind of mess she'd have to clean up tomorrow.

"It's my dad. He was just leaving."

"Sure, honey." Blanche winked. "Whatever you say. Just remember what I told you." Then she lowered her voice. "Does he have money? If he has money, you can forget all that advice I gave you."

I slammed the door.

We had lunch, and Dad left to return to his own private storm. As soon as he walked out, the phone rang. It was Chuck Conrad. "Was that your car?"

"It was. I just gave my statement. What do you know?"

"The reason our keynote speaker didn't show."

"I was thinking that might be the case."

"Who is it?" Ruth said.

"A reporter with The Galveston Tribune," I said to her.

"I hope you had an alibi," Chuck said.

"I did—she's standing right here—my cousin Ruth."

Ruth waved.

"I'm beginning to wonder about this town," I said.

"Personal question?"

"Go ahead."

"James Lockhart, who was murdered at the hotel quite a few years back?"

"My grandfather."

"Damn."

"For a small town, Galveston seems to have its share of murders."

"Actually, things have rolled along fairly peacefully in the last decade or so. We have a few characters who take matters into their own hands every now and then. Hey, the mayor and police chief are about to have a press conference at the police station."

"I'm on my way," I said.

"See you there." Chuck hung up.

I grabbed my bag. "Let's go. We've got work to do, and it doesn't involve party planning. Our mothers can handle that. We're going to a press conference, and then I'm going to find out who's been mean to me. Slashed tires are one thing; blood in my trunk is another."

Ruth followed me out, skipping. "I'll get you another car."

"I don't want another car. I like that one."

"We'll trade it in for the newest model."

"That is the newest model."

"I can never ride in that car again," she said.

"What—a tough girl like you?—sure you can."

CHAPTER EIGHT

If my father thought there was a whirlwind at the Lockhart house, he should have seen the fiasco in front of city hall. Asherah Aster and several of her goddesses, all dressed in wispy, lavender-colored translucent robes, fluttered around chanting some nonsense and throwing what looked like fairy dust over anyone who walked by.

The press was swarming like an army of ants. Ruth and I walked in to find more people crammed into the lobby. A podium was being set up, and we were told the mayor would be out shortly to make an announcement. I saw Chuck and went over. "Never a dull moment," Chuck said. "How are you doing?"

"I'm fine," I said. "This is my cousin, Ruth Echland."

"I'm here to keep Sydney out of trouble."

Chuck looked at her.

"Sometimes the task is not easy," Ruth added.

"Why your car?" Chuck asked.

"Convenient," I said. "It was tucked away in the back of the church parking lot. I guess when the Red Top Garage replaced my spare, they forgot to lock the trunk."

"The killer could have just dragged the body into the bushes," Chuck said.

"Maybe they hoped I would drive it away."

Our speculations were interrupted as the mayor stepped forward. "I would like to express my sadness over the death of Mr. Maurice Roland. Our thoughts and prayers are with his family. Rest assured our police department will find out who is responsible. In the meantime, the Pelican Island Planning Conference has been temporarily canceled. However, the planning will continue"—the protesters booed—"in due time. I'll turn the microphone over to our police chief and his detective." He turned and walked down the hall.

The police chief gave the facts, some of which I already knew. Sometime between eight and midnight, Maurice Roland was shot in the chest at close range. They have no suspects but are following up several leads. As the chief turned to leave, one reporter shouted, "Does the murder have anything to do with the Pelican Island Development?" The chief ignored the question, and several reporters began shouting similar inquiries. The questions went unanswered. Reporters darted for the nearest phone booths, eager to get the latest news to their papers. I, on the other hand, was not so ready to accept these paltry bits of information.

"Not much info," Chuck said. "Not surprised."

"You mentioned some characters from way back when. Any names to go with them?"

"The main one that comes to mind is the Boedecker family. But from what I hear they are on the straight and narrow now." He scribbled in his notebook. "Gotta get back to the paper." As he turned to walk away, he called over his shoulder. "Be careful."

"What do we do now?" Ruth asked.

"After we talk to Asherah, we visit the detective and demand some answers."

"Fun." Ruth headed out the door, her Ferragamos clicking loudly across the hardwood floor.

Asherah and her fairy goddesses had gathered on the front steps where they were winding down their fluttery performance. We walked up and waited while Asherah finished giving instructions to the other women: "Let's meet again tomorrow night. This incident bought us some time, but don't think for one moment that the project has been canceled. We need to remain visible. Go home and meditate, envision Oya peaceful and happy. Then meet me on my boat tomorrow at midnight— and for Christ sake don't forget your fruit!"

The women nodded assuredly.

"Good, you know what to do." Asherah's entourage dispersed.

"Miss Aster?" I asked. She turned and when she noticed my notepad, she didn't need a proper introduction.

"Yes, I'm Asherah Aster, and you're a reporter." She stepped so close I could see the gray hairs growing on her chin. "Listen, you write this down. We plan to stop this project even if we have to plant ourselves in the sand on Pelican Island."

"Why the objection? Pelican Island isn't worth much to anyone." Asherah's round face turned scarlet, and she jabbed her finger in the middle of my notepad. "You just listen one minute, Miss. That little piece of land is a power center."

"Can you be more specific?"

"Oya is the goddess of wind and lightning. It is she who determines the fate of this island. If unhappy, she can transform a gentle gulf breeze into a wind powerful enough to destroy every structure on this island. She's the creator of hurricanes."

"And Oya was responsible for the Great Storm?"

Asherah stepped back and eyed me from top to bottom. "People forget. I was on the island when it happened. I can never forget. I was ten years old." A horrified look spread over her face.

"You're afraid that another hurricane will happen if Pelican Island is developed?"

"Oya's power comes from within. Disturb her island and she will retaliate." She pointed to my notebook. "You're not writing this down."

"I've got it up here." I pointed to my head.

"Get my name right. Asherah, A-S-H-E-R-A-H. It means "She Who Walks by the Sea.""

I scribbled it down, although this story would never make it across any news wire.

Ruth nudged me and cleared her throat. I got the message.

"Thanks for your time, Miss Aster."

Ash shot me the evil-eye, flared out her robe, and fluttered away.

"I read about something like that happening in Hawaii. It was in National Geographic. A volcano goddess got angry because tourists kept taking her rocks as souvenirs."

"And she erupted and destroyed an entire village? Ruth, sometimes I can't believe what comes out of your mouth."

"I amaze myself sometimes. I'm a walking encyclopedia."

"I thought you only looked at the pictures."

"Yeah, well, a picture's worth a thousand words."

"You're hopeless."

Ruth and I waited in the lobby of the police station only a few minutes before Fidalgo came out of his hole. "Anything to add to your statement, Miss Lockhart?"

"We want answers," Ruth said.

"What she means is—"

"I know what she means. I'm not ignorant about your crime-solving exploits. But we will have none of that here. You will not interfere with this investigation, understand? You—will—not!" He punctuated each word with a finger jab in my direction. "Now, if you don't have anything to add to your statement, I've got work to do."

"I figure it was someone Maurice Roland knew, since he was shot at close range."

"Muggers don't usually make an appointment with their victims. They can be quite furtive," he huffed.

"You're passing this off as another crime of random violence? Not good for the city's reputation, especially now."

"Good day, Miss Lockhart." He nodded a good-bye to Ruth and left.

"Furtive," Ruth said.

"It means secretive."

"I know what it means, smarty pants."

"You can contemplate Fidalgo's vocabulary later. Come on. Let's go."

"Where to?"

"The only place in town to get reliable information. I don't know why I hadn't thought of it before."

SITTING ON A LONG PIER JUTTING INTO THE WATER, the Balinese Room gave one the feeling of being on a cruise ship in dock. This is my father's frequent hangout. When I was little, he didn't know I was listening when he spoke of his visits to the infamous bar. There is something here for everyone. A gift store out front where vacationing families can purchase polished conch shells with GALVESTON ISLAND printed on the side, or those little ships stuffed inside little bottles. Next to the gift store is a restaurant famous for fried clams and coleslaw, and farther back, a lounge and ballroom famous for all sorts of tomfoolery. On the walls were autographed pictures of performers who had appeared here in the past. There was Old Blue Eyes himself, smiling sheepishly. Sophie Tucker, my father's heartthrob, relaxed on a divan with a cigarette in one hand and a highball in the other. Between photos of Bob Hope and the Marx Brothers, there's a sly and sexy Jayne Mansfield, whose nude body is slightly hidden behind a powder-blue fur. Below her autograph, she'd written, "I'll never tell." And, of course, if you had the moxie, gambling was at your disposal.

Even though it was midday, the Balinese Room was packed. Ruth and I made our way toward the lounge. Before you could say "martini shaker," a sleazy-looking guy with lustful eyes materialized from some dark corner, rushed over, and opened the door. We thanked him and hurried in before he could engage us in conversation. I looked at my watch. "Cocktail time doesn't start for another two hours."

Ruth looked around. "The bar is open."

"I know, but our cocktail time."

"You're joking."

"I'm not. I'm working. I need to keep a steady head."

"True," Ruth said pensively. "But what will it look like if we order two Dr Peppers? We can't get information if we don't fit in. I've an idea. We compromise."

We sat down and Ruth ordered two gin and tonics rather than our usual martinis. "Tonic and a lime squeeze, dilute the alcohol." Ruth pulled out her cigarettes and two ebony holders. Before she could flick her silver lighter, the sleazy guy waltzed over and flicked his.

"Can't let two beautiful dames light their own. Louis Maxwell." He slid his chrome Zippo back into his pocket and brushed back a strand of oily hair that had fallen over his left eye. "Mind if I join you?"

I wanted to tell the guy to take a hike, but we were here for information, and Louis looked like the type of guy who could supply it. Ruth raised her eyebrow and then blew a plume of smoke toward Louis.

"Sure," I said, "sit down. My name's Sydney and this is my cousin Ruth."

"Haven't seen you gals here before. On vacation?"

"We are, but we're thinking that maybe Galveston was a bad idea. We were thinking about checking out this afternoon and driving to Corpus Christi instead."

"Oh, you must have heard about the guy who got knocked off at the church."

"If you're not safe at church," Ruth said, "where are you safe?"

"We heard it was a random killing," I said. "Does that happen often here—some innocent person is walking down the street and someone drives by and blows him off the seawall?"

"Is that what the police said? I haven't seen the afternoon paper." Louis motioned for the waiter to bring three more drinks. "Galveston has a rough crowd, but when the cops use that 'random crime' excuse, it usually means they haven't got a clue."

"You think his murder was planned?" Ruth said, swirling the ice in her glass.

"Think about it—most are."

"But the guy wasn't from Galveston," I said. "He was here as a speaker at the Pelican Island Conference."

"If that's true, you have nothing to worry about." Louis grinned, and the hair strand flopped back over his eye.

"How's that?"

"If you don't have any enemies here, you're safe. Hey, I got an idea. I have a friend who just blew into town. He doesn't know many people. How about if we show you gals the town tonight? Have a little fun. Safe fun." He winked at Ruth.

I wanted to slug down my second drink and run away. Ruth's face went ashen. I took a slow drag on my cigarette and said, "Dinner?"

"Of course." Louis straightened his tie.

"We'll meet you and your friend here at eight." I stuffed out my cigarette and picked up my clutch. "Thanks for the drinks. Come on, Ruth, I have us scheduled to play tennis in a half hour." Since she was glued to her seat, I tugged at her arm and we left.

"You've come unhinged," Ruth said. "I'm not going out with some sleazy stranger."

"You're here to keep me out of trouble, remember?"

"That's true, and that's why we're going to stand up Louis and his friend."

"Still have your little gun?"

She clutched her purse to her chest.

"I thought so. Go back to my parents' house for a couple of hours so Mom won't get suspicious. Meet me at the hotel room at five. We'll dress in our best vamp outfits. Then I'll go over the game plan."

Ruth started to protest, but despite her revulsion at the idea of going out with Louis and friend, she couldn't resist a covert operation.

"I don't have a vamp outfit," she said, smiling.

"Look in my mother's closet—the one where she keeps her Hollywood stuff."

"Fun," Ruth said.

CHAPTER NINE

While I mulled over my wardrobe, I considered the unfortunate circumstances that had befouled my trip to Galveston: two threatening letters, slashed tires, and a body in the trunk of my car. I was no fool. They had to be connected. But why me? What was I not supposed to find out concerning the conference? I was no different from the dozens of other reporters here.

I pulled out my red pencil skirt, held it up to my waist, and looked in the mirror. That skirt with my white sweater and heels was as vampish as I could get. I threw the skirt on the bed when a horrifying thought flashed through my mind. It wasn't possible. Please don't let it be possible. I sat down on the corner of the bed and stared out the window.

But I was different. No other reporter had a grandfather who had been murdered in this hotel.

"THAT WAS EIGHTEEN YEARS AGO," RUTH SAID. "Your mom's skirt is too long, and it makes me look fat."

"Is that the best you could do? I wouldn't call that suit a vamp outfit. It looks more like something you'd wear to church. That was in my mother's closet?"

"Yes, and it still had tags on it. I think it's new. Her Hollywood stuff smelled like mothballs. And I didn't want to wear my own clothes. No telling what we'll be up against tonight. Besides, your mother's too busy to miss it. She's giving the caterer a hard time. She's insisting on lobster thermidor. He suggested something more local like oysters Rockefeller or shrimp cocktail. She won't budge. The poor guy is ready to quit. Back to your theory. This can't be related to your grandfather's murder."

"Why not? The case was never solved. Maybe someone thinks I know something. After all, I was one who found him."

"But why wait until now to rub you out? You've been to Galveston many times since then."

"But not as a nosy reporter. And we didn't come to the island much after the murder."

"I think you're grasping at straws."

"It's all I can come up with."

Ruth turned around and struck a Miss America pose.

"That won't work. Let's go. We have enough time to hit the thrift store."

The phone rang just as we were walking out. Ruth snatched it up. She mouthed, "It's for me." Her cheery look turned sour. "How long will that take? But I need her there immediately. We're scheduled to open in a few weeks." She began to fume. "Just give me the phone number and I'll call her."

I rushed over with a fountain pen and notepad. Ruth scribbled down a number and hung up.

"What was that all about?"

"That was my secretary. Lauren, the nurse, had to go to Atlanta, a family emergency. Damn! Just when things were working out so well."

"I'm sure everything will be fine."

"You're right. I'll give her a call tomorrow. I've never been to a thrift shop. I hope no one sees me."

AN HOUR LATER, WE STEPPED INTO FAYE'S FASHIONS, a secondhand store on Mechanic Street. Ruth had a good point about not wearing our own clothes. The last time I was on assignment, I ruined my entire wardrobe. Finding a tart outfit for me was easy. I have the body for it. Any tight, low-cut top and skirt with a slit up the side would work fine. Dressing Ruth was a different story. Finding a sexy outfit for someone who stands four-feet eleven inches and weighs ninety pounds isn't easy.

"I'll never find anything here." Ruth shoved aside dress after dress.

"It's only for one night."

"All these outfits are garish, not a sexy piece in the entire lot. All the sizes are huge."

"Let's look in the girls' section."

"Funny."

"We could find a smart two-piece outfit and go for the hot, young temptress look."

"You're a barrel of laughs."

We were running out of time when she found a red-sequined dress just the right size. I draped a white-feathered boa over her shoulders. "You look like a first-class tart."

I found a royal blue sleeveless dress with huge white polka dots. The skirt flared from the waist, a wide white belt hooked in the front by three gaudy rhinestones. The bodice was little more than a bustier with a strap around the neck. A large white flower was pinned over the right breast. I found a black beaded sweater to throw over my shoulders. Faye wrapped up our clothes, and we wore our party-girl costumes out of the store.

BY THE TIME WE REACHED RUTH'S CAR, we'd received three whistles and a throaty growl from guys lingering in the doors of the downtown bars. Ruth had a sneezing fit and threatened to throw the boa in the gutter.

"Just keep it away from your face. Drape it loosely over your shoulders."

"Why don't you wear it?" she sniffled.

"Because without it, you look like a majorette. Here, I'll give it a good shake to get rid of any dust."

Ten minutes later we were sitting at the Balinese Room bar scanning the room.

"They're late," Ruth said. "We should go to the ladies' room for a few minutes. We don't want to look too eager."

"Yes, we do. We're fast women—women who are ready for a good time, women who are hot to trot, women—

"Okay, I get the picture. Oh my God! Look! Don't look!"

"What! Is my Dad here?"

"No. The guy with Louis is shorter than me!"

I turned to see a man the top of whose hat came up to Louis's shoulder. Without his platform shoes, he wouldn't have reached his friend's elbow.

"You get the short guy," Ruth hissed.

"It doesn't matter. I'm taller than Louis, and you're taller than the midget. We'll just stay seated the entire evening. No one will notice."

"Howdy." Louis straightened his shoulders and adjusted his tie. "This is my good buddy, Buddy Leach. These two good-looking gals are Sydney and Ruth."

"Hello," Ruth and I said.

"My pleasure," Buddy squeaked, sounding as if he's just sucked a lung-full of helium. He kissed my hand, and then reached for Ruth's. She pretended not to notice and threw one end of her boa over her shoulder and sneezed.

"It's our lucky night," Louis said. "There's a great band playing, and I feel like dancing. Buddy can cut a rug. Can't you, Buddy?"

"Fred Astaire Dance Studio." Buddy placed his hand over his abdomen and swiveled his tiny hips. "Mambo master. Won three dance competitions this year."

Ruth looked at me and flared her nostrils.

Buddy grabbed Ruth's hand, jerking her off the barstool. He placed her hand in the crook of his elbow. "Dinner awaits, my dear, and then who knows?" He rose up on his toes and whispered in her ear. "Nice dress. Real classy."

Louis and I took up the rear, and soon the four of us were seated at a booth. We ordered drinks and Louis started the conversation. "What do you gals do? I mean, like, jobs."

Damn. We were so into our costumes we didn't think about what stories we were going to tell the boys. I knew, however, that Ruth would follow my lead.

"I'm a sales clerk at Neiman Marcus and Ruth is a beautician." The kick she threw caught me in the knee, causing a reflex that luckily launched my toe into the table leg and not into either man's crotch.

"I knew it," Buddy said. "You two had to have something to

do with fashion, wearing those stylish duds. Those look like real feathers, Ruth." He nodded at her boa.

"Dodo," Ruth said.

"I thought they were extinct," Louis said.

"They are now," she smiled.

Buddy laughed so hard, he got the hiccups.

Our waiter came over and we ordered. Ruth and I chose prime rib medium rare, Louis ordered the New York strip well done, and Buddy ordered a cheeseburger, cut the onions. He winked at Ruth. As the waiter turned to leave, Louis caught him by the arm. "Wait. Let's celebrate."

"Celebrate what?" Ruth asked.

"First dates," Louis said. "Bring us a bottle of champagne."

The band started up, and Buddy said, "Is that a cha-cha-cha I hear? Come on, Ruth. Let's go."

"But I don't know how."

"Easy. I'll show you."

She slid out of the booth, pinching my thigh hard enough to leave a bruise.

Before Louis could ask any more questions, I turned the conversation around to him. "Are you from Galveston?"

"Na, I'm from Biloxi. Been here about ten years doing different things. I started off working at Guelfi's Market, butchered a while. That got old. Couldn't get the meat smell off. Attracted every dog in down." He laughed. I smiled and gulped my martini. "Then I went to work for the cannery. Cutting fish is much easier. You wouldn't believe how hard it is to take the meat off a cow's rump. With fish, once you get the hang of filleting, it's a snap."

"Interesting," I said.

"It was, but I knew I was destined for greater things." He paused as the waiter set down our salads.

"Your destiny?" I prodded as soon as the waiter left.

"Oh, right. I work as an orderly at the hospital now. I figured it was my knife-wielding talent that got me the job. You know, a natural progression."

I was speechless. I was certain the job of an orderly didn't involve dismemberment.

"Gotcha," he laughed. "You should see the look on your face.

Everybody falls for that joke. To tell the truth, my brother-in-law got me on at John Sealy Hospital. Benefits are good, and I get to know what really goes on in town." He raised his eyebrows. "Know what I mean?"

Now we were talking. It was time to play the vamp. I batted my eyes and set my chin in the palms of my hands. "No, Louis, please tell me. What sorts of things go on in Galveston?"

"Well, I used to hate getting assigned to work the night shift in the emergency room. But, it's the hottest place in town on Saturday nights."

"Were you working the night they brought in that guy who was murdered and then stuffed into some woman's trunk? But I guess they sent him right to the morgue."

"You guessed wrong." He leaned over and lowered his voice. "You see, two fishermen had drowned the day before and the morgue was full. Anyway, they had to do some body shuffling, and this Roland guy stayed with us in ER for a couple of hours."

"You said that you don't think it was a random killing," I whispered, "that Roland must have had enemies." I realized I was sounding too much like a reporter so I added, "how exciting." For effect, I shook my shoulders and squealed. "Nothing exciting ever happens at Neiman's except when we have a lingerie sale." I winked, and Louis choked on his drink. "Did you hear something about the murder?" I continued.

"Did I ever?" he leaned even closer. I could smell the bourbon from his Manhattan and see the bit of cherry stuck between his teeth. "The ME, that's the medical examiner, started his investigation right there in the ER, that's emergency room. I mean he didn't start...you know, the cutting part, but he did the EO, that means external observation. He had to start before the body got too cold and stiff."

"RM," I said.

"What? Oh, yeah, rigor mortis."

I prayed that Ruth and Buddy stayed on the dance floor for a few minutes longer. This was good stuff, and I didn't want Louis to be interrupted. But I didn't hold out much hope. Out of the corner of my eye, I could see what looked like a wrestling match between Ruth and Buddy.

"Go on," I said.

Louis continued, but he wasn't telling me anything I hadn't already heard from Detective Fidalgo. This was not the local gossip I wanted to hear so I nudged Louis. "Ewww, that sounds so disgusting."

"Yeah, but it gets better. At first, the ME thought the man was taken by surprise. You know, like they were having a discussion and the killer suddenly pulled out a gun and bam!"

"Stop it!" Ruth shouted.

Louis and I looked over to see Ruth pointing her finger at Buddy. He was smiling wickedly, but Ruth seemed to have things under control.

"That's not what happened?" I asked Louis.

"No, seems this Roland guy put up a struggle before he got the lead. There were bruises on his knuckles and blood under his fingernails. Someone worked him over and then shot him."

The waiter came back with a bucket of ice and the bottle of champagne. He popped the cork and filled our glasses. Ruth and Buddy walked up, slightly out of breath. Ruth grabbed her glass and downed her bubbly.

"Cheers," Louis said, and the three of us toasted.

"Ruth's a fast learner," Buddy said. "That little filly's got the cha-cha-cha down pat. Hey, maybe we can work up a routine and enter a couple's dance contest."

"Sure," Ruth said. "I might just move to Galveston. Set up a little beauty shop here in town. With all the heat and humidity, I'm sure I could get a successful business going." She held out her glass for Louis to refill, and threw me a look that could kill a holy man and send him straight to hell.

"Chip off the old block, she is." Buddy was smitten. "All the men on the dance floor couldn't take their eyes off you, Ruth."

"I'm a classic beauty," Ruth said, emptying her glass again. "No matter how much I try to hide it, it simply shines through. It's something I've learned to live with."

"It might be because your slip is showing," I informed her.

She raised her glass for another refill. "Then I'll just run to the little girl's room and take it off."

Buddy drooled into his glass.

I took Ruth's glass and set it on the table away from her reach.

Our meals arrived and we dug in. It was difficult to get the conversation back to the dead man. Buddy began telling us about his failed attempt to become a Hollywood star. After mastering ballroom dancing, he had hoped to strut his stuff on the big screen, encouraged by the success of hundreds of dwarfs who had landed rolls in the Wizard of Oz.

"The dancing dwarf thing just never took off," Buddy bemoaned. "Not that I'm a dwarf; I'm just a little guy. Anyway, if you weren't part of the Oz crowd from back in the '30s and '40s, your credentials meant nothing. All those cha-cha-cha lessons. And all I can do now is impress the locals."

"Maybe you should take up ballet and try out for one of the mice in the Nutcracker?" Ruth said.

"Never thought of that," Buddy perked up. "I am fairly limber."

Buddy left the subject of his dance prowess and went on to tell us about another failed career. Once he took a job as a duct man for a heating company until he realized he was claustrophobic.

"Tell them about the time you got stuck and passed out," Ruth said. She reached across me for her glass of champagne, but I blocked her with my shoulder.

Louis ordered another bottle.

"That experience still gives me nightmares," Buddy said. "While I was out cold, some guy crawled in, stripped off my pants, and greased me down with butter. He looped a rope around my ankles and pulled me out."

The image of a naked, greased Buddy brought visions of a rump roast, sans thermometer, ready for the oven. It's a good thing we'd had dinner. "What do you do now?" I asked.

"I'm out of work. Louis told me there were a lot of opportunities here in Galveston. Besides dancing, I got many other talents." He held up four fingers and began reciting a litany of his gifts. "First, I can do algebra in my head; second, I have unbelievable eyesight; third, although I'm claustrophobic, I'm not afraid of heights, so I'd be great at doing crane work. I'm sure I have many more talents that haven't surfaced yet."

"That's only three," Ruth said.

"And, number four, in general, I'm a fast learner. I probably should have gone to college, but I was afraid that academia would stifle my creativity."

"If anyone needs to hire a tightrope walker who can think on his feet," Ruth said, "you'd be a shoo-in."

"Think there's an interest in that? Maybe I should work up a routine and contact Barnum and Bailey."

At this rate, we'd never get back on the subject of murder, and I certainly didn't want to arrange a second date.

"Ladies' room?" I asked before Buddy could demonstrate his ability to turn his head 360 degrees.

"Past the bar down the hall," Louis said.

I grabbed Ruth's arm and we excused ourselves. Once in the bathroom, I told Ruth to cut it out.

"What?" she said.

"You'll be sloshed before dessert."

"You'd drink heavily too if you'd spent half an hour on the dance floor with the cha-cha-cha master. He had my boa around my waist and started twirling me around. Then he tried to place his hands on my hips to show me how to get the motion. I almost slapped him."

"I heard you giggling."

"Of course I was giggling! I'm supposed to be a bimbo. Why I let you talk me into this, I'll never know? The things I do for you! I'm an idiot!"

"Not a bimbo—a vamp."

"What's the difference?"

"There's a big difference. Vamps have some class; bimbos have none."

"Really?" I could tell by the look on her face that she was rolling this bit of enlightenment around in her brain. After a couple of seconds, she said, "I couldn't be a bimbo if I tried." She adjusted her boa and started to walk to the mirror. Her hair was damp and she was red in the face, so I stepped in front of her.

"And another thing," she said. "I'm not going back out on the dance floor. This dress itches."

"Relax. No more dancing, I promise. Louis was about to let go of some good information. We were on the subject of Roland's murder. Let's go back. You can help keep us on track." I grabbed her by the shoulders to turn her around and pointed her to the door.

She pulled away and dodged me to get to the mirror.

"Look at me!" She pulled her compact from her purse and dabbed her nose. Then she paused. "Oh no."

"What?"

"I'm sweating. I can feel it running down my stomach."

"You'll survive. Let's go. Besides, we're supposed to have fun, remember?"

"That was before I was forced to cha-cha-cha with a midget."

"He's not a midget. He's just short."

"Oh, please!"

Buddy was licking catsup off his fingers when we returned to the table. "I've got an idea," he said.

"Wonderful," Ruth muttered.

"Let's blow this pop stand and go for a walk along the beach."

I had to admit, Buddy was becoming a pain in the ass. Louis came to our rescue. "We got another bottle of champagne coming, and I'm sure these gals aren't dressed for the beach."

"I'll second that," I said. "Louis, tell Ruth about what happened on your shift."

Louis began the story from the top, taking his time, adding finesse to the retelling. Ruth fidgeted with her boa. Buddy's eyes never left her face. We'd be here all night if I didn't hurry things along.

"Louis, dear. Ruth is squeamish. Skip over the EO and the RM part. You said Roland was attacked before he was shot."

"Right. Seems there was a scuffle."

"But who would do that? He wasn't even from Galveston."

"Pro'ly someone Roland owes money to," Buddy slurred. His eyes were still on Ruth, but they had taken on a look of red fish bobbers floating in water.

"Probably someone he forced to dance the cha-cha-cha," Ruth said.

"Doesn't matter." Louis was into his story and ignored Ruth and Buddy. "His murder could be linked to almost anything."

"Even the Pelican Island Project?" I asked.

Louis looked at me skeptically. "Who knows? Galveston does have a dark side, though. Not many talk about it, but everyone knows that there's sort of an underworld running this town." He looked around. "I've said too much. We're here to have fun."

I gave it one more shot. "I read in the paper that the mayor received death threats over it."

"What's new? Quinn's got a big mouth. He's always pissing people off."

"It just seems too weird to me. Galveston's giving me the willies."

"Yeah," Ruth said, looking over her shoulder.

"Don't worry, Ruth," Buddy said. "I won't let nuttin' happen to you. I'll stick by you like glue. You and me, that's how it will be. We're a dancing team. We'll make 'em scream." He paused. "I told you I had undiscovered talents." He took a cocktail napkin and began to write down his verse.

The waiter delivered another glass to Ruth when he brought the next bottle. He filled it, and she drank it down before I could grab it.

"It's a wild town," Louis said. "But like I said before, trouble won't find you gals. Trouble only starts when people start making waves."

"Like the mayor," I said.

"Maybe," Louis said.

Ruth hiccupped and sneezed.

A thud caused us to jump. It was Buddy, whose inebriated body had slid under the table and hit the floor.

CHAPTER TEN

While Louis carried Buddy out of the Balinese Room, I hauled Ruth to the car.

"How about tomorrow night?" Louis asked.

"Sure," I lied, shoved Ruth into the car, hopped in, and drove off before Louis could set a time and place.

"CHA CHA CHA CHA, CHAAAA CHA," Ruth had her boa wrapped around her hips as she danced up the hotel steps. My cousin was tiny, but she had never before had trouble holding her liquor. However, a martini, a bottle of champagne, and a night on the dance floor really sloshed her.

"I can do the cha-cha-cha. I can do the cha-cha-cha." She stumbled on the last step, and I caught her before her face made contact with the cement.

I wanted to take the stairs up to our room, but I feared Ruth would pass out before we made it to the fifth floor. It was almost one, and the lobby was empty. However, as we stepped into the elevator, two other couples joined us.

"I can do the cha-cha-cha. I can—"

I put my hand over Ruth's mouth as we started our slow trip up. The two couples looked as if they'd been partying too, so I wasn't worried about Ruth's state of intoxication.

"Hey," one of the guys said. "You two were at the Balinese Room tonight. Marie, that's that woman who was dancing with the midget."

Ruth's happy mood disappeared. She leaned her head on my chest and started to cry. We stepped off the elevator and ran smack into Blanche. "Don't you ever go home?" I asked.

"I'm working a double. Looks like you need some help."

I didn't argue. I did need some help. Ruth was beginning to sag like a bag of sand. Blanche helped me drag my cousin to my room.

"How's the sugar daddy?" Blanche said.

"What?" I asked.

"The man who was in your room. Showed both of you a good time?"

"I told you, he's my father."

"You should try uncle. No one believes that father crap."

I thanked Blanche for her help and advice and shoved her out the door.

Ruth was out cold by the time I took off her dress and put on her gown. I took advantage of her condition and tucked her in on the cot. Then I got ready for bed, switched off the light, and flopped down onto my nice, big bed. When my head hit the pillow, I felt as if I'd cracked my skull. I picked up the pillow to see if it was stuffed with rocks. It was indeed an ordinary feather pillow, but underneath it was a dark oval object. I jumped out of my bed and stood there looking at it. I poked it with my shoe. It didn't move. Feeling sure it wouldn't attack, I turned the light on. Sitting there, shiny and purple, was a well-formed eggplant. Scratched into its skin was the word "Beware." Jeez, what next? At this point, did I really care? I sat it on the windowsill, crawled back into bed, and fell fast asleep.

THE POUNDING IN MY HEAD CAUSED MY EYES TO POP OPEN. Sunlight had forced its way in between the blinds. Although I was careful not to drink too much last night, the cheap champagne must have done its work. As the pounding became louder, I realized that it wasn't accompanied by the usual headache. Ruth began to moan, and I mashed a pillow over my head. The pounding continued.

"Sydney! Sydney!"

"Dad? Wait a minute." I jumped up and threw on my robe.

"Uncle George?" Ruth cried. She rolled over, fell off the cot, and grabbed her head. "Oh, Lord."

"Go to the bathroom. There's some aspirin in my overnight bag. I'll take care of Dad."

I'd never seen Ruth crawl before. It was a sight to behold.

I opened the door. Dad leaned against the door jamb and surveyed the damage. Our vamp clothes were strewn all over the room, Ruth's boa draped over the lamp. The stale aroma of last night's alcohol was strong enough to freeze the lungs.

"I thought you were here to work." He walked in and picked up the boa.

"I'll order coffee. Sit down. We were working."

"Uh. There's a short cowboy in the hall with his imaginary horse."

"Ignore them; they'll go away."

"He wants an apple for his palomino."

"I'll add it to my grocery list."

"Been doing some gardening?" He nodded to the eggplant.

"Found it under my pillow last night."

"Most hotels use chocolates."

"I guess they ran out by the time they cleaned my room."

The sound of Ruth's retching drew our attention away from the nightshade.

"Sounds like Ruth worked overtime."

"What's up, Dad?"

"I needed a safe haven. Those three women are driving me nuts."

"Three?"

"Yeah. Since things are falling apart at the last minute, Frances called in reinforcements."

Ruth emerged from the bathroom, looking like I've never seen her—pale and with smeared makeup. She held a washcloth to her mouth.

"Marcella arrived late last night. Oh, hello, Ruth."

She turned, ran back in the bathroom, and slammed the door.

"On second thought," I said, "let's go downstairs for breakfast and give Ruth some time alone. I may have pushed her to the limit this time." I threw on a pair of slacks and a sweater, stuck a hat on my head, slipped my feet into my saddle shoes, applied lipstick, and grabbed the eggplant.

ON THE WAY TO THE RESTAURANT, I walked up to the front desk and sat the eggplant down in front of Mr. Chambers.

"Let me guess, you're on a special diet?" he chuckled.

I turned the vegetable around so he could see the message. "I found it under my pillow last night when I returned to my room."

"Someone doesn't like you. I'll just toss it in the trash."

"No, thanks, I've grown attached to it."

Over Belgian waffles and coffee, I told Dad about our adventure at the Balinese Room and Louis's assessment of the murder.

"That's an urban legend. There's no underground group running this town. Of course, we do have our share of shady characters."

"Well, Roland's murder was not a random crime. And he's not from around here. Do you think someone would be so anxious to stop the Pelican Island Development that they'd kill over it?" I hadn't told him about the threats or my suspicions about my unfortunate circumstances being linked to PoPo's murder. As I ran those ideas through my brain, they now sounded ludicrous.

"Stay out of it, Sydney." He leaned close and gave me one of his stern looks. "Write your story and stay out of this. Don't try to solve any murders. Understand?"

My dad stopped telling me what to do the day I moved to Austin to attend college. The deep creases around his eyes looked new. I attributed his bossiness to the chaos going on at home, so I tried my best to alleviate some of his vexation.

"Sure. I wouldn't think of it." The wheels in my brain began spinning furiously. That's exactly what I should do—try to find out what happened all those years ago when PoPo was murdered. I owe it to him. It's the least I could do; what little sanity I had came from the Lockhart side of my family.

"I mean it, Sydney Jean. If something happened to you, I'd be lost."

"You'd still have Scott and Mom. Oh, I see what you mean. I'll not give crime solving another thought."

Dad knew I was lying. Before he could say more, I changed the subject. "Do you think Mom can pull off this party?"

"Oh, there will be a party all right. Come hell or high water, I will not have this fiasco canceled again. We going to celebrate our anniversary, have a grand old time, and then forget about the damn thing! We might have to do it without a band or caterer, but there will be a party."

"I thought a band and caterer were already booked?"

"They quit. I'm not surprised the way your mother is so demanding. So, to make sure this damn thing comes off, I've ordered a case of hot dogs and a few cases of Lone Star. I figure I'll take my truck out to the beach this afternoon and gather some driftwood for a campfire. We can roast the dogs, and I'll turn the truck's radio on. We can dance on the beach to the Hit Parade. I told your mother a simple party on Stewart Beach was the best idea. Looks like I might get my wish." He motioned the waiter to bring more coffee. "Marcella is one sharp young lady."

"She seems to have won over everyone except Ruth."

"Understandable. Speaking of Ruth, they are wondering where she's been running off to. I don't know how much longer I can keep them from discovering you're in town."

"Tell Mom and Aunt Frances that Ruth has an upset stomach and she's resting in her hotel room."

"Right. That wouldn't be far from the truth."

I often wondered about my parents. They are so different. Dad is calm and levelheaded while Mom lives her life in constant chaos. I guess it's true that opposites attract.

Dad left to collect driftwood just as Ruth crept into the restaurant. She was walking slowly and wearing sunglasses.

"Dad and I had waffles."

She sat down. "Nothing for me."

"Not even coffee?"

"Okay, maybe coffee and some orange juice."

"How are you doing? Aspirin kick in yet?"

"I took four, and, no, they haven't kicked in yet." She scratched her waistline. "That sequined dress rubbed my skin raw. I've got bright red welts from my armpits down to my knees." She scratched again.

"Stop it. You'll make it worse. We'll find a drugstore and get you some lotion. Guess what? I just did you a favor."

"You decided to shoot me?"

"I told Dad to tell our mothers that you have a virus and aren't able to help them today."

"Did I hear him correctly, or was I hallucinating?"

"You mean hearing things."

"That's what I said. Is that Marcella woman in town?"

Ruth had softened. She used to refer to Marcella Wheatly as "that woman." "That Marcella woman" was an improvement.

"She is, but that's to your advantage. Because as soon as those aspirin work their magic, you and I will be back on the trail of a murderer, actually two, and you won't have to help with the party."

"No cha-cha-cha?"

"Not even a mambo."

"That was a dirty trick you played on me last night!"

"You knew what you were up against. I told you not to drink all the champagne."

"I'm not talking about that. I'm talking about the cot."

"You insisted I take the bed."

"I did?"

"You're a nice person."

"Damn right."

"By the way, I found this in bed last night." I held up the eggplant. "Know anything about it?"

"It's an eggplant."

"Besides that?"

"Nope. Were those strawberries on your waffles?" Ruth pointed to my almost-empty plate.

"Yep."

"Okay, I think I can handle waffles, and strawberries, and maybe some bacon, but nothing else. Now, tell me what happened last night."

"You drank Buddy under the table, literally. You're some party woman."

"Damn right."

WHILE RUTH POLISHED OFF HER BREAKFAST, I went to the front desk to ask about the room across the hall.

"The family is checking out," Mr. Chambers said.

"Wonderful. When can we move in?" I asked.

"That room is reserved."

"Hey, wait a minute. You were holding it for us, remember?"

"I left a note, but the night clerk must not have seen it. Sorry. Maybe tomorrow."

I was about ready to grab the snotty Mr. Chambers by his tie and drag him over the front desk, when Ruth walked up.

"Hello, Jasper."

"Good morning, Miss Echland. Sleep well?"

"Not very well. That little bitty cot is soooo uncomfortable." She rubbed the small of her back. "I had to take four aspirin. I insisted my cousin sleep on the bed. I just overheard you say that the bigger room is unavailable."

"Yes, it was a terrible mistake. My sincere apologies."

"I have an idea. Why don't you put those people in our room and let us have the bigger one?" She winked and dropped her voice to a whisper. "No one will ever know."

Jasper leaned down and in a whisper said, "I don't know why I didn't think of that. You're soooo clever, Miss Echland. Consider it done."

Jasper's devil smile earned a devil squint from me.

"I know I shouldn't ask, but how did you do that?"

"Like Abe Lincoln said, 'A drop of honey catches more flies than a gallon of gall.'"

"Did you remember that from your history class?"

"Nope. This new book I read."

I stuck my fingers in my ears. "I don't want to hear it."

"Very well." Ruth looped her arm through mine. "Come on, Sydney. We have work to do."

With the conference canceled, I needed to fire off a story to my editor. While I typed, Ruth tidied up the room and packed our stuff. A short time later, the housemaid knocked on the door and told us our new room was ready. I let Ruth do the moving, and I read through the final draft. Not bad, if I say so myself. I was ready to take it to Mr. Cahill's office and send it to Ernest by wire when Ruth came back fuming.

"I'm leaving! You can have that big, nice room to yourself."

"What brought this on?"

She flopped down on the bed. "I spoke to Lauren Patterson, the nurse I hired to run the Home. She's backed out. We're scheduled to open soon, and I don't have anyone to run the place. I've got to get back to Dallas today."

As much as I loved to hear those words, I needed my cousin with me. "Listen, today is Wednesday. Don't rush off so quickly. Call your secretary and tell her to contact an employment agency. Depending on your friends to find someone qualified to handle such an important position is asking for disaster. Let the pros handle it. By the time you get back to Dallas, you'll have several candidates to interview next week. Just don't overreact."

She sat up. "Maybe you're right."

"Come on. While I grab the rest of my stuff, call your secretary."

"I will! Sometimes, Sydney, you amaze me."

I wasn't sure if I was amazing or stupid—time would tell. I wheeled my writing table across the hall into a room twice the size of the cracker box we had been staying in. I knew immediately which bed was mine. One lone, flat pillow lay on top of the bedspread. On the other bed, three pillows were neatly fluffed up against the headboard.

"My secretary is calling agencies as we speak. What do we do first? I'm feeling chipper."

"Okay, first, we have to go to the police station and see about getting my car. Then, we go to the newspaper office and read through the old issues reporting PoPo's murder. Once that's done, we head back to the police station to read the police reports and finally out to Pelican Island."

"Beats calling caterers and making place cards. Except our first stop is the drugstore."

"HOW ABOUT CALAMINE LOTION?" RUTH HELD A BOTTLE, reading the label.

"That's for chiggers."

"Maybe that's what I have. No telling where that awful red dress was before it ended up at the thrift store."

"I'm sure it was the sequins. Here," I picked up a jar of medicated cream and handed it to her. "This might work."

"I don't have time to cut out lacy hearts!" came a voice from the next aisle.

Ruth and I immediately ducked. "Your mother!" she whispered. "What do we do?"

"The back door," I said. "Hurry!" We duck-walked down the lotion aisle.

"Now, Mary Lou," Frances said. "It won't take that long. I can make a pattern and we can trace the hearts. Think how cute they'll be on the tables."

"Frances is right, Aunt Mary Lou," Marcella said. "With both of us working, it wouldn't take that long."

Ruth sucked in a breath. "She called your mother, Aunt!"

"Quiet, they'll hear you. Keep walking."

"There won't be any tables if we don't find another caterer. I've got four days! I'm so glad you're here, Marcella. I thought I could count on my daughter to help, but she's in Austin playing like she's a reporter."

Now I was the one who sucked air. "Bitch," I hissed.

Ruth started giggling and stumbled. I grabbed her arm. "Hurry! They're walking this way. There's the door. Go!" I pushed her, and we dove out the back door. We were halfway across the parking lot when we heard someone yelling.

"Thief! Stop!"

"Oh, no!" Ruth cried.

I looked down and she was still holding the jar of cream.

"Run!"

We darted around parked cars, weaving our way through the parking lot. I looked over my shoulder, but the pharmacist had gone back inside, to call the police, I'm sure. I yanked the jar of cream from Ruth's clutches and threw it into the bushes. "Keep going," I yelled. We ran down the street and around the corner. It was a typical workday downtown with people milling around. A few stopped and stared, but most went on their way. At the end of the block there was an establishment with its door wide open. Darkness oozed out and spilled across the sidewalk. Cigarette smoke curled upward as if looking for an escape route. A tiny neon sign flashed "open." We ducked inside.

Ruth flopped into the first chair she saw. "My side is killing me. And look! I've broken my heel. These are brand new Ferragamos!" She slipped off her shoe and massaged her foot.

"Why didn't you leave the damn cream?"

"I forgot it was in my hand. You should be ashamed of yourself for calling your mother a bitch."

"We've got bigger problems. We're wanted women."

"No one's going to go to the police over a jar of cream."

"This is a small town, Ruth. I'm sure that guy got a good look at us—a tall redhead and a tiny blonde. We stand out like horns on a nun."

"Well, it's too late now. No use crying over spilled milk. Is there another pharmacy in town? I still itch."

"Shut up, Ruth."

"You shut up."

"We shouldn't have run away like that."

"Too late now."

"It's all my mother's fault. This damned anniversary party has been plaguing me for months. It started back in Hot Springs. I should have left that wedding picture at the hotel and let my mother go back to Hollywood. Scott would have followed, and Dad and I would be much happier."

"You don't mean that, Sydney."

Just then I saw a police car slowly cruise down the street in front of the bar. "Don't get too comfortable."

Seconds later, the car backed up and stopped. Two cops stepped out.

I tugged at Ruth's arm. "Hurry! Out the back door."

"Again?" Ruth hobbled along with her heel in her hand.

The bartender had been staring at us the entire time, mouth agape. Without saying a word, he winked and pointed his thumb to the back exit. Once in the alley, we ran several more blocks, stopping to catch our breath inside another doorway.

"Do you think the bartender will tell on us?" Ruth gasped.

"I doubt it. He didn't look like the type who enjoyed talking to cops. Let's wait here a moment."

"I can't go another step in these shoes."

"Stay here. I'll see if the coast is clear." I ran to the end of the alley. No cop car. I motioned for Ruth to follow. She defiantly held up her heel.

"Take your shoes off!"

"Are you crazy? I'll step on a nail and get ptomaine poisoning."

"Trust me, Ruth, that's not going to happen. Come on, we can't stay here all day."

Ruth hobbled over. We fast-walked down the street. "Act like nothing is wrong," I said.

"You're delusional. I'm telling you I can't walk any farther. My stockings are ruined. I'm going to find a place to rest. You go back and get my car. There, that office will do fine. Here are my keys."

We walked into the Wallace Insurance Agency. Three secretaries stopped typing and stared. Finally, a lady with a pearl chain hooked to the stems of her pearl-rimmed glasses said, "May I help you?"

"I had a little accident," Ruth said, holding up her heel.

"We were out for a stroll." I added. As soon as the stupid words slipped from my stupid mouth, I knew it was the wrong thing to say. I should have reached over the counter, grabbed the stapler, and stapled my lips shut. Instead, I made things even worse by saying, "We're looking for the library."

All three women exchanged glances. Finally, after what seemed like eons, Pearl Glasses gave us directions. I turned to leave, but Ruth had parked herself on a chair in the small waiting area.

"Let's go, Ruth."

"You go! Get my car and come get me," she hissed.

Pearl Glasses picked up the phone surreptitiously.

"Listen," I whispered out of the corner of my mouth. "I don't think she's calling the nearby cafeteria to place a lunch order." I nodded toward the secretary.

"What?"

I raised my eyebrows and glared. I was thrilled to see comprehension dawn in Ruth's eyes. She jumped from the chair, and we were out the door as I heard the woman say, "Excuse me, but I think we have a situation here."

In minutes, we were in another alley.

"That was close," Ruth said.

"This is all your fault. Look at me! Running from the police and hiding in a filthy alley!"

"At least you have both heels. I think I sprained my ankle."

"No, you didn't. Come on. The police station should be around the corner."

"Are we turning ourselves in?"

"Something like that."

CHAPTER ELEVEN

Ruth and I waited innocently as Detective Fidalgo caught his breath and blew his nose. He replaced his handkerchief in his pocket. "I haven't laughed so hard in years."

"I don't think it is one tiny bit funny," Ruth said. "Do you know how much a pair of Ferragamos cost nowadays? I doubt if I can ever find another pair like these."

"Stuff it, Ruth. Be happy we're not behind bars."

"You can say that again. If it wasn't for me still feeling sorry for you after all these years, I wouldn't hesitate to throw you two in the slammer."

"I was counting on your kind heart."

"I'll bet you were. I'll call Fred Porter and straighten things out at the pharmacy, but you're running out of favors. Any more trouble and you're done for, understand?"

Ruth and I nodded our heads like the good girls we were not.

"Good. I'll have a deputy take you to your car."

I didn't think it was a good time to ask to read the police reports, so I willingly left the station.

Ruth was resting on the bed with an ice pack on her unhurt ankle. There was no swelling, no bruising, nothing, but I let her play the victim just to keep her off my back. I plopped down on my own bed and closed my eyes.

"How can you sleep at a time like this?" Ruth quipped.

"I'm not sleeping; I'm thinking."

"How can you think at a time like this? There's nothing to think about, except that I don't have any pumps to match this outfit and I didn't bring that many clothes."

"My head is pounding, Ruth. Could you please just stop talking about your damned wardrobe?"

"That's not your head, stupid, that's the door. Answer it."

"No, they'll go away."

Whoever was knocking wouldn't let up.

"It must be my mother. She must have found out I'm here."

"Answer it!"

"No!"

We listened for a few more seconds.

"Sydney, Ruth, are you in there? The desk clerk said he saw you step into the elevator."

I turned and smiled. "I think I'll answer the door. Hold on, Marcella—I'm coming!"

Marcella walked in. I was surprised to see her in slacks and a sweater. I was used to seeing her dressed in smart, conservative courtroom attire. She actually looked relaxed.

"Ruth, are you okay?" Marcella asked.

"Peachy, just peachy."

"What happened?"

"She doesn't do well running from the law," I said.

Ruth smashed a pillow over her head.

"How did you find out I was here?"

"I overheard Ruth and your father talking when they were on the back porch rearranging the patio furniture for the party. I hope you don't mind."

"I don't care if the entire island of Galveston knows. I just don't want my mother finding out. By the way, thanks for coming and helping," I added.

"We were doing just fine without you," Ruth muttered.

Marcella pretended she didn't hear Ruth's rude comment. Years of practicing law must have given my half cousin a tough skin. "Your mother and Frances are a hoot. I've really been having a good time."

"How have you been feeling?"

"Much better. Thanks for asking. I took a short leave of absence from work. Jeff and I hired a law clerk, so things are running smoothly at the office. I keep in touch by phone. This is the first time I've taken any time off since I began practicing law. I was literally working myself into an early grave. If it wasn't for my dear sister here, I might not be around."

Other than knowing that Marcella was the daughter of Ruth's father, I didn't know much else about her. I wasn't even sure of her age, probably in her mid-thirties.

"Half-sister," Ruth harrumphed.

"Are my legal services needed again?" Marcella asked.

"Not this time. How's the party planning?"

"Not good. The only band we could find is a polka band from Yoakum, and no one is willing to cater a party for two hundred at the last minute. Your father's idea of beer and hot dogs on the beach went over like a lead balloon. The good news is that the country club is definitely booked."

"I thought they couldn't accommodate so many people."

"They're willing to squeeze them in. Apparently, since they just opened they want the business. You know, if they can impress two hundred people, they've got free advertising. The only problem is the kitchen isn't operational yet; otherwise, they'd cater."

"Hot dogs and a polka band at the country club. It's got a nice ring to it. It suits my dad well."

"Your mother is determined to find a high-class caterer. She has a menu in mind—boiled shrimp and bleu cheese as an appetizer, followed by lobster bisque, Caesar salad, then tournedos with Marsala sauce, with peach melba for dessert."

"What happened to lobster thermidor?"

"That too."

"My mother's hanging around with the wrong people—the ones who have money."

"Your dad really likes the idea of the polka band."

Ruth decided to come out of hiding. "I can't polka with a sore foot."

"How about the cha-cha-cha?" I said. "Just a few tiny steps and a lot of hip swiveling. You can handle that, can't you, Ruth?"

"Shut up!"

"Sounds like I missed out on a lot," Marcella laughed.

"I'll fill you in."

By the time I finished with the story of our escapades, it was getting late and I hadn't accomplished my three tasks. Marcella had checked in to the hotel and returned to her room. Finding a room was no problem now that the conference had been canceled. I gave serious thought to finding one myself. Ruth said she was ready for a nap. Thanking God for the time alone, I hurried out and hailed a cab to take me to the office of The Galveston Tribune.

Within ten minutes, I found the stories of my grandfather's murder. It had made the front page of the next morning's paper. The headline read, LONGTIME RESIDENT SHOT TO DEATH.

"James Robert Lockhart, retired businessman and current doorman at the Galvez Hotel, was killed Tuesday afternoon while working at the hotel. Witnesses saw a white Plymouth drive up to the front door. Several shots were fired. Lockhart was hit several times and apparently died instantly. His granddaughter, eleven-year-old Sydney Jean Lockhart, found his body within seconds of the shooting."

I WAS SHOCKED TO SEE MY NAME. I fought hard to keep the lump in my throat from turning into something worse. My parents told me very little of what had happened that day. After finding PoPo, I don't remember much except attending his funeral. It was another brilliant day, and the church was packed with people. I wore a navy blue dress and black patent-leather shoes. My mother and I had a big argument while I was getting dressed. She insisted I wear my hair pulled back with a matching bow. I refused. I wanted to wear my hair in a ponytail because PoPo liked it that way. I locked myself in the bathroom and cried until I thought I would choke. My dad finally stepped in and offered a compromise: no bow, no ponytail. I agreed quickly because I knew it would make my mother angrier.

There were a few follow-up stories during the next week, but the event gave way to other news. The last thing I read was a short piece on page three stating that there were still no leads concerning his murder. Except for resurrecting unwanted memories, my trip to the newspaper didn't offer any clues.

I left The Tribune and walked the few blocks to the police station. This time I didn't wait to be announced. I made my way to Fidalgo's office.

"You again. You just left."

"I know. I have two favors to ask."

"All you have is a lot of nerve." The detective was no longer in a laughing mood.

"Okay, one question and a favor. Can I have my car back?"

"We're finished with it," he said. "You'll need to have the trunk cleaned. What's your favor?"

"I want to look at the police report of my grandfather's murder."

"Why?"

"Just curious."

"It's public record."

"I know."

"Promise to leave me alone?"

"Sure."

"Right. Stay here. I need to get a release."

Fidalgo brought me to the records room, a dusty, dark corner in the basement, and handed me the folder. I made myself comfortable at a metal folding table. I opened the file and began reading. I was hoping for more details than the newspaper stories had offered. The first thing I saw was a photo of PoPo lying in the foyer. My breath caught, and this time I wasn't able to fight back the tears. I felt like I was eleven again—shocked, helpless, hurt, and angry. Eighteen years later his case was still unsolved. I vowed at that moment to change that. I blew my nose, lay the picture aside, and began reading the scant notes of the police report.

Several bullets had struck him, but the one over his heart had severed his aorta, causing a quick death. It had happened close to three in the afternoon—the time of day when people were checking in. There were several witnesses, but no one could identify the killers. The best report of what had happened came from a woman names Ellen Keys. I read her statement:

"My husband had just gone into the hotel to see if they had a room. I was waiting in the car. Suddenly, a car came speeding through the drive. There were three men; a guy in the backseat pointed a gun at the hotel's front door. I ducked and heard the shots."

I heard those shots too. Until this moment, all I remembered hearing was what had sounded like a car backfiring, but the woman was right, there had been a string of shots. The report went on: "Several witnesses reported having seen a white sedan, possibly a late-model Plymouth, leaving the scene. The license-plate number was not noticed."

How could no one have noticed the license-plate number? It was the middle of a bright, sunny day. The long, sweeping driveway of the Hotel Galvez provided enough opportunity for someone to have gotten at least part of the number.

The scene flashed through my mind, details I had forgotten. I was near the hotel, happy about seeing my grandfather. We'd planned a picnic on the beach for the next day, Saturday. In a letter he'd written me, he told me it was to be a special picnic, just the two of us. My birthday was around the corner. He had a surprise for me. I was playing a game in my mind as I rode my bicycle down the street to the hotel, trying to guess what the surprise might be. We used to do that quite often—play the three-guesses game. His gifts were not the ordinary kind— bikes, dolls, toys—not the kind that could be put in a box and wrapped, not the type of present I could hold in my hand. Early one morning, we walked out to the beach right before dawn. He pointed to the sky: a rare constellation was visible just above the western horizon. I remember being cold and how he draped me in his old sweater. It seemed like we were the only two people awake that morning. Another time, after an unusually low tide, he took me to the beach again to see hundreds of sand dollars that had washed up after a storm. I still have one on my desk at home. It sits on a dessert plate and is so dry and brittle that I'm afraid if I touched it, it would crumble into dust.

I was deep in thought as parked my bike in the rack. I saw the car speed by. I felt the panic, but didn't understand why, and until this moment, didn't remember. But now I recall seeing a car parked under the portico, probably the Keys' car. I remembered hearing the shots. I closed my eyes and let the memories flow.

I was the first person to walk into the foyer, an important fact that had been lost on me as an eleven-year-old. Soon others came running up. Somehow I moved from the foyer to the lobby. Then some woman had me by the shoulders.

"Are you all right, honey?" she had asked, her eyes searching for any signs that I might have been shot as well. She continued talking, but I couldn't concentrate on what she said. All I remembered was a smear of red lipstick on her front tooth. Then I heard a woman scream. Someone shouted to call the police, to call an ambulance. Someone else ordered people to stay away, go back to their rooms. Someone said, "It's that nice doorman. He's been shot." Someone else cried, "Oh my God, is he dead?"

After that the curtain fell. I don't recall how I got home, or if my parents came to the hotel. One moment, I was facing the woman (I can still feel her fingers gripping my shoulders) and the next, I was sitting in the police station answering questions. My mother was beside me. I asked her where Dad was. She said he was making arrangements. Making arrangements? I remembered thinking that was an odd thing to say. Now, whenever I hear those words, I think of funerals.

I replaced everything back in the folder and returned it to the clerk. I asked to speak to Detective Fidalgo.

"Find anything helpful?" Fidalgo walked in, stuffing the end of a hot dog into his mouth.

"There's not much there."

"Nope."

"The detective on the case, a guy named Warren Grant—"

"Dead, about five years ago. Heart attack."

"Who was the police chief back then?"

Fidalgo thought for a second and said, "Frank Mullins. He retired and moved to Florida."

"When?"

"Listen, I don't know what you hope to accomplish after all these years."

"Someone murdered my grandfather—"

"And you plan to find out who? The conference was canceled, so you're looking for something else to do?"

The look on my face stopped him dead in his tracks.

"Sorry," he said as his hands flew up as if to ward off my attack. "Wrong thing to say. I understand your frustration."

"No, you don't. Thanks for coming to my rescue earlier today." I spun on my heel and left without telling him that mustard was smeared on his mouth.

CHAPTER TWELVE

I picked up my car in the police lot and drove it to the Red Top Garage. Wally Brighton was standing out in front talking to a man who didn't look happy.

"You blew a gasket," Wally said. "It'll take a few days to get the part. I can have it to you by Friday."

"Damn wife. Told her she needed a car like I needed a hole in the head." He threw me a glare as if to say all women drivers were a nuisance, then turned and walked away grumbling.

Wally smiled when he saw me. "Miss Lockhart, what can I do for you today?"

"Afraid I need another car wash, Mr. Brighton."

"Looks pretty clean to me." He looked at the sky. "And with those clouds—"

I opened the trunk and motioned for him to have a look. He let go a shrill whistle. "Take this sporty number out on a hunting trip, did you?"

"Not exactly." I told him about the unfortunate occurrence that had befallen my car.

"If I were you," he said, "I'd trade this little beauty in for a black Ford, one that blends in. Seems this one attracts attention from the wrong kind of people."

I didn't tell him I was pretty sure it wasn't just the car that attracted attention. "I'll try to live with this one a while longer. Think you can get the stain out?"

"Might have to prime the trunk, but I'll do my best."

"I don't have time for the prime job. Clean it as best you can for now. How long?"

"I'll get right on it. You can have a seat inside and wait. There's still some coffee in the pot. Help yourself."

Since I was tired of racing all over town on foot, I took him up on his offer. The coffee looked like oil he'd drained out of someone's engine and tasted worse. I fished a quarter out of my purse and pulled a bag of peanuts from the rack and a Royal Crown from the cooler. Waffles always seemed to leave me hungry, and I could feel my energy ebbing. I made myself at home next to an old wood-burning stove. It had begun to drizzle outside, making the afternoon feel colder than it was.

As I watched the raindrops slide down the grimy garage window, I thought about everything that had happened since I'd arrived on the island. There was no longer any doubt in my mind that the threatening phone calls to my room had been intended for me and that the tire slashing had not been a random act of reckless teenagers. Someone wanted me off the island, but why? When I left the police station, I was bound and determined to investigate my grandfather's murder. Now, sitting here in this ordinary automotive shop, my resolve began to fray and I was unsure where to direct my energy. Maybe Fidalgo was right; maybe I should pack my bags and go back to my cozy little apartment in Austin. This was my favorite time of year. The trees were bare of their leaves, and I could see Lake Austin from my front window. I could put a few logs in the fireplace, cuddle up with my pets, and tap away on my Smith Corona. Maybe I'd write the novel that had been brewing in the back of my brain, or just do my job at the newspaper. I could ask Ernest to transfer me back to the travel-writing department.

Who was I kidding? My snack tamed the hunger pangs and dissolved my maudlin mood. By the time Wally's helper backed my car from the stall, I knew my next move—a move I wasn't looking forward to.

AFTERNOONS IN THE EMERGENCY WARD at John Sealy Hospital were quiet, as I had suspected. I ducked into the ladies' room, added an extra layer of lipstick, fluffed my hair, stuck a piece of gum in my mouth, and transformed myself, mostly in attitude, into Sydney the Vamp. I found Louis on his break in the cafeteria, cigarette and coffee in one hand, a racing sheet in the other. Hearing my heels tap on the linoleum floor, he looked up as I approached the table.

"Sydney! It's my lucky day."

"Hello, handsome." I smacked my gum and gave it a good, loud pop—a skill I had picked up from Patty Peters when I was a senior in high school. Popping Patty, we called her. She'd pop her gum every time Mrs. Murphy, our English teacher, addressed the class. Poor Murph never figured out where the sound came from. She'd pause, tilt her head, and continue until Patty popped again. Needless to say, Murph rarely completed her lessons.

"Hope I'm not bothering ya." I swaggered over, exaggerating the rhythm in my step—something I'd seen Marilyn do in her films.

"Bothering me?" He stood up and pulled out a chair. "Are you kidding? I was just thinking about you."

Fast horses and fast women; it figured.

"Sorry I ran off last night. Ruth was starting to wobble. She usually doesn't drink, well, not that much."

"Looked like she and Buddy were hitting it off. The little guy was out cold. I had to get the bouncer to help me haul him into my car. He was still there sawing logs when I went to work today. The secret is pacing."

"Pardon me?" I glanced at the racing sheet.

"Pacing. You know...the booze."

"Oh, sure, pacing. I got you." I sat down across from him.

"Can I get you some coffee? The hospital stuff is pretty rank, but I'm not picky."

"No, thanks. I just stopped by to thank you for a swell time."

He looked at his watch. "Break time is up. I gotta get back. My shift ends at eleven. What'd you say the four of us pick up where we left off last night? We could start at the Balinese Room and then check out some of the other local hangouts."

The last thing I wanted was another date with Louis. I'd hoped to get what I needed here in broad daylight with normal, everyday people around. But if another date was what it took to glean information, I'd do it, with a minor adjustment, that is. "I'm game," I said, "but Ruth is still nursing a hangover. I don't think she's up for another night on the dance floor."

Louis didn't waste any time. He winked and reached across the table. "Well then, why don't we let Ruth and Buddy fend for themselves? Tonight it will be just you and me, darling."

My stomach squirmed. Before he had a chance to take my hand, I faked a sneeze. "I'll see you at the Balinese Room at eleven thirty."

BACK AT THE HOTEL, I walked past the front desk, ignoring Mr. Chambers, who, I saw out of the corner of my eye, was watching me. My finger was a hair away from pressing the elevator button when he called, "Oh, Miss Lockhart?"

I turned, and he held up a slip of paper and smiled. "You're a very popular lady."

"Seems." I didn't wish to engage him in conversation so I took the note and headed back toward the elevator. Any idea I had about leaving town was gone. The message was from Ernest, telling me to stay put and follow the Roland murder. He thanked me for the story I'd wired, calling me a crackerjack reporter. His instructions were short and to the point. "Dig... deeper."

That's exactly what I needed to do. Instead of going to my room, I took the opportunity to pay Mr. Cahill another visit. The door to his office was open. The man sitting behind his cluttered desk did not resemble the neatly groomed and professional general manager I'd visited with on Monday. He looked like he'd been up all night.

"Mr. Cahill?

"Miss Lockhart, I didn't hear you walk in." He shoved some papers around and tugged at a muffler wrapped snuggly around his neck. "What can I do for you, Miss Lockhart?"

"Sorry to drop in unannounced. If you're too busy now, I can come back later."

"Not at all. Seems I've picked up a winter cold."

I felt bad for the man; he was overworked and ill, and I'm sure in no mood for the discussion I planned to have with him. Nevertheless, I plowed ahead. "Do you have a few minutes for some questions?"

"For you, sure. Maybe we should visit in the lounge. I could use a cup of hot tea. How about you?"

"Sounds good." I was grateful for the change of venue. I didn't want his staff overhearing our conversation.

Once we were seated at a quiet table, I wasted no time. "Tell me about that day." The pleasant look on his face disappeared. He knew immediately what I was referring to.

"I figured you'd want to know about that sooner or later. You probably don't remember much."

"Parts of it I remember all too clearly. Were you here that day?" The look of horror that spread over his face reminded me that talk of murder wasn't something most people considered casual conversation.

"Uh, yes. I was here."

"Did you see me?"

"I did." He paused and gazed out the window at the ever-changing gulf and then turned and smiled. "You were wearing a pink dress and your hair was up in a ponytail. You were in shock. Several people were milling around you. All asking questions. You just stood there...frozen. I didn't know at the time that James was your grandfather. In fact, I figured you were staying at the hotel with your family."

He seemed to have relaxed a little, so I went ahead with my next question. "How well did you know my grandfather?"

He sat there so long that I thought he wasn't going to answer. Finally, he said. "Well. He was one of the nicest men I'd ever met. We all liked him. We knew James didn't need the job. It was something for him to do after he retired. He was so good at greeting people. He acted as if this were his home and he were welcoming back old friends. Guests often commented on his pleasant manner. He loved to talk about Galveston. He was a wealth of information for curious tourists. He knew the town better than anyone and was the best person to give directions, always ready with an entertaining story about the town's history."

"That sounds like him." I wasn't sure about the next question, but the moment was right. "Mr. Cahill, do you think his murder was deliberate?"

The waiter walked up and set the tea service down. When he left, Mr. Cahill poured. I let the silence linger. He added cream to his tea, a couple of spoons of sugar, and took a sip. When he finally spoke, I was surprised at his answer.

"Maybe."

I thought he would say more, and when he didn't, I pushed. "Why?"

"For all of James's good qualities, and believe me there were many, he could be a little ..."

"Nosy?"

Mr. Cahill smiled. "You knew your grandfather well. You know, you look like him."

"I've been told that many times." I didn't add that his nosiness was also inherited. "You're the only person I've spoken to who hasn't been quick to label it random violence."

"I wouldn't go that far. It's just that the police couldn't find any reason why James might have been targeted. Their attitude was that he was just ..."

"A doorman."

"Right."

"Who would want him dead?"

Mr. Cahill shrugged. "I certainly can't answer that, Miss Lockhart. James was sort of like a goodwill ambassador. He knew everyone on the island."

Since he emphasized the word everyone, I took it as an invitation to drop a name. "Ever hear of the Boedecker family?"

"The Boedecker family?" He paused. "Sure, I've heard them. Old Man Boedecker, Warren, I think was his name, used to come to the bar quite often. I wish I could tell you more, but that was a long time ago." He checked his watch. "I promised the wife I'd make it home at a reasonable hour today. I don't relish sleeping with the mutt in the dog house." He signed the bill and rose to leave. "I'm truly sorry about what happened, Miss Lockhart. Please, take care." He hurried off before I could say another word.

Tea was not my favorite beverage. I pushed my cup aside, pulled out my notebook, and contemplated my next move. Louis was the most obvious person to drop the Boedecker name to. Then I thought about my father and wondered if he knew about PoPo's connections. They were as close as a father and son could be. Then a horrible thought struck me: What if Dad knew more than he was letting on?

CHAPTER THIRTEEN

"What are you doing sitting here in the dark?" Ruth plopped down, dumping an armload of packages on the floor.

"Shopping at this time of the afternoon? Aren't the stores closed?"

"Now they are. I had to be escorted out of the last shop, a cute little place off Grand Street. They specialized in petite sizes. I exhausted myself. So when I spotted another drugstore and stopped in for a jar of cream, I treated myself to a root beer float." She looked down at my cup. "Tea? Are you ill? Did you catch my upset stomach?"

"I'm fine. I just visited with Leonard Cahill, the hotel's manager."

"And?"

"And I'm becoming too suspicious for my own good."

"I've been telling you that for years. What did you find out?"

"That PoPo may have been the intended target after all."

"I've got to hear this. Let's go up to the room before Marcella comes waltzing in and sticks her nose into our business."

So as soon as we settled in to the safety of our room, Ruth insisted on a fashion show before continuing our conversation. While she opened her boxes, I made a quick call, hoping to catch Chuck at the office. The receptionist told me he was gone for the day, but when I told her I was a fellow reporter, she gave me his home number. While Ruth paraded her wares, each one more astonishing than the next, I dialed the number. It rang seven times. I was about to hang up when he answered.

"Yeah," he said.

"Chuck, this is Sydney. Sorry to call you at home."

"No problem. I was just fixing dinner. My first course—a bourbon and water. What's up?"

"Ever hear of the Boedecker family?"

"Are you kidding? Hey, what are you on to?"

"Nothing yet. I just found out that they were, or are, the muscle behind a lot of what went on in Galveston."

"You're right about that."

"How about now? Are they still active?"

"Yeah, but in a different way."

"What do you mean?"

"They've cleaned up their act, gone respectable. Warren Boedecker, back in the twenties and thirties, owned a small shipping company in town. Once the cash started to flow, he opened up a department store, then a couple of bars, and even an insurance company. Old Warren had the city officials in his back pocket, and when he wanted things done, like getting building permits, changing zoning restrictions, et cetera, he succeeded, usually overnight."

As I listened to Chuck's history lesson, I watched Ruth add accessories to the outfit she now had on: pearls, matching earrings, a dangly bracelet, all new. I gave her a thumbs-up. She'd also purchased two skirts, a suit, three dresses, each with a pair of matching pumps and handbags, a strapless gown made of icy-pink rayon, and a more casual tea dress, pale-gray gabardine fitted dress. She whistled a jaunty tune that I didn't recognize at first. Then images of Edith Piaf emerged.

"Shady, but not all that unusual," I commented.

"True, but there were a couple of times when he ran into roadblocks, and soon after the roadblock was found washed up on Stewart Beach or rotting on Pelican Island. As the city became, shall we say, more civilized, the law began nipping at his heels. When he died, his sons, Cleve and Monty, took over the business. Cleve still runs the family enterprise, but Monty died shortly after their father—a boating accident, I think. Since then Cleve has tried to stay within the law."

"Has he?"

"As far as anyone knows. How did you learn about the Boedeckers?"

"Excuse me a moment." I put my hand over the receiver. Ruth's whistling of "La Vie en Rose" had turned to singing. "Ruth, do you mind? I'm trying to have a conversation here."

"Go ahead, you're not bothering me. And don't worry, I'm listening to every word."

"Listen a little more quietly, will you?" I picked up a pillow and threw it at her. "I've been nosing around," I told Conrad. "What businesses does Boedecker still own?"

"Most of the same, but who knows? He is the C of M & C's Department Store."

As he said the name of the store, I noticed the same name on the boxes strewn all over the room. Suddenly Ruth's chipper mood disappeared, and she threw a shoe across the room.

"Thanks, Conrad, you've been helpful. Go enjoy your meal." I hung up and dodged a shoebox Ruth tossed over her shoulder. She picked up another spiked heel.

"Hey, watch what you're doing! You're going to put my eye out."

"I know I bought a pair of kitten heels."

"A pair of what?"

"Kitten heels, they're the latest style by a new French designer, Roger Vivier. They're not here." She studied her receipt. "That damn clerk rang them up, but I don't have them."

"They're not made from felines, are they?"

"Don't be silly. They're sexy, but sweet and innocent. That's just the look I was going for, French and sleek. Now I have nothing to wear with my Dior silhouette! I wanted to make a fashion statement for the anniversary party."

"I thought you shopped at Neiman's before you left."

"I decided I don't like what I bought."

"The party's not a fancy affair, Ruth."

"It's at the county club."

"That's not a sure thing. If things continue to fall apart, the party will be on the beach like Dad hopes."

"But the outfit was so French."

"I'll buy you a scarf and beret for your birthday. When you walk into a room wearing them, I'll shout, 'Ooh la la!' You should have brought the dungarees and flannel shirt you bought in Hot Springs."

"I threw the stupid dungarees away, and in case you forgot, the shirt has a bullet hole in it."

"You kept it?"

"Of course, otherwise my future grandchildren will never believe me when I tell them I took a bullet for you."

"Go back to the store tomorrow and get the shoes. It's no big problem. Do you want to hear what I found out or not?"

Her pouty face made its appearance, and I took that for a yes. As she folded her booty and replaced each piece in its box, I filled her in on what Conrad had told me.

"That's the store!" Ruth cried. "I knew something fishy was going on there."

"What do you mean?"

"Just intuition. The owners' portraits were on the wall near the front door—a huge oil painting of two guys with sinister smiles. I'll return tomorrow and do some investigating."

"At this point, there's nothing to investigate."

"Let's get back to your grandfather. What did Mr. Cahill tell you?"

"PoPo knew everyone in Galveston, and I'm not just talking about fine, upstanding citizens. He also liked to engage in a little gossip from time to time."

"That makes perfect sense," she said. "I remember your grandfather with a different yarn to spin every time I saw him."

"Yeah, but most of those stories were fabricated."

"Maybe they weren't. I remember him telling us about the ghost who lived in the swamps on the west end of the island."

"It wasn't a ghost; it was the goat man."

"It was a ghost."

"A moot point. Neither a ghost nor goat man killed him. Don't get me off track."

"Why are you so cranky?"

"I'm not cranky!"

"You and your detective have a tiff?"

"How could we have a tiff? He's hundreds of miles away. And he's not my detective."

"So, that's why you're cranky. Ever think about moving to Hot Springs? I'm sure they have a newspaper there you could work for. If you married the man, you wouldn't have to work. I could come visit and we could have lunch at the country club. We could go to the horse races. We could soak in the hot mineral baths. We could—"

I rolled over on the bed and pressed my pillow over my head.

"Sydney? Ruth?"

We both jumped and stared at the door.

"I'm not here." Ruth scampered to the bathroom in her stocking feet and closed the door.

"Just a minute, Marcella," I called. I pushed Ruth's boxes away and went to the door. "Come in. Ruth and I were wondering how the day at the Lockhart household went."

Marcella walked in and paused. Every chair was filled with boxes. Except for a narrow path, the floor was covered with them as well.

"Here," I said, "have a seat on Ruth's bed. She won't mind. Make yourself comfortable. I'm sure you had a busy day."

"Looks like you did, too."

"I worked. Ruth shopped. What's the latest?"

"RSVPs are arriving by the minute; mostly by phone since the party is two days away. And all but a couple of people have accepted the last-minute invitation."

"Probably out of curiosity. I'm sure they're all wondering how this insane woman can pull this off. How will they know where to go, if the venue is still up in the air?"

"A phone tree. Your mother is incredible. She and Frances are tireless. This afternoon, we had an assembly line going on the kitchen table. The phone would ring; Mary Lou would answer and write the name down, then hand it to Frances, who immediately wrote the name on the place card, then she'd pass it to me and I'd check the name off the list. When the phone wasn't ringing, your mother was making calls. She's very good at this; she should run a wedding-planning business. By the way, where's Ruth?"

"In the bathroom hiding."

Marcella hoped off the bed, trotted over to the bathroom, and knocked on the door. "Ruth, can you hear me?"

"No."

"Good. I took the liberty of making reservations for dinner at eight at Gaidos tonight for the three of us. We've all had a busy day. Dinner is on me. What do you say?"

"Count me in," I said. Then I raised my voice. "I'm not sure about Ruth. She might have a date with her new flame, Buddy."

The door flung open and the little blond fury flew out. "Not funny!"

"The Cha-cha-cha master?" Marcella asked.

"Go ahead, tease me! Gang up on poor, little Ruthie. I sacrificed myself to help Sydney, and this is the thanks I get." She grabbed her clutch, slipped on her pumps, and stormed to the door. "I'd rather have dinner with the goat man!" Slam. She was gone.

"Uh-oh, I may have overdone it," Marcella said. "I didn't want to make her angry. I was hoping to make her laugh."

"You've got to catch her in the right mood."

"I'll need your help for that," Marcella said. "You don't think it's hopeless that Ruth and I can be friends, do you?"

"Give it more time. At least she doesn't think you're trying to steal her fortune anymore."

"I guess you're right. Who's the goat man?"

"Don't ask."

"So it's just me and you for dinner, then."

"I wouldn't change the reservations too quickly. We're the least of the worst possibilities for her. She could have dinner with my family, dine alone, or join us. She'll be at the restaurant before we order, believe me."

"Good. Then after dinner we can come back here and have a girl party."

"No on that one. I've sort of got a date later tonight."

"Dixon's in town!" she asked.

Damn! I needed to get a grip on things. Just hearing his name gave me the tingles. Suddenly, I saw those bonbon eyes boring a desirous hole though me. The kind of look that made me feel nine and twenty-nine at the same time, made me doubt my every thought while feeling like I was the cleverest woman in the world. I just hoped my face wasn't as red as it felt.

"He's not here, thank God. I don't want my mother to get her insane claws into him. She'll pull out that infamous guest list of hers and start planning another wedding—mine. No, the date is ..." I hesitated. How much should I tell Marcella? I trusted her. It's just that I didn't want her to slip and say something to my parents about my antics. Dad's already warned me about minding my own business. "Well, it's not really a date. Let's just say I'm working late tonight."

"Oh, I understand. Sources. Say no more. I keep forgetting you're here on business."

You and everyone else, I thought. Maybe I didn't act professional enough. Maybe I should buy a briefcase, wear a Chanel suit, wad my hair into a twist, and stick a pencil in it. Visions of Rita Fredricks marched across the back of my eyeballs. The last time I saw the female gangster, she was on the floor of the infamous Ohio Club in Hot Springs leaking blood from a wound I thought I'd caused. Word from Dixon was that she had recovered and disappeared from the hospital.

"Sydney? Syd? Are you okay?"

Marcella shook my arm and brought me back to the present. "You had the funniest look on your face."

"Except for the hunger that's gnawing at my stomach, I'm okay. It's a bit early. How about if I change and we sip on a cocktail in the hotel bar?"

"I need to change, too. See you downstairs in half an hour?"

"Perfect."

MARCELLA WAS SITTING AT A TABLE IN THE CROWDED LOUNGE. She'd changed from her slacks and sweater to a casual black dress and pumps. I was still amazed at how much she looked like Ruth—taller and darker—but my two cousins were strikingly similar: same pixie features, same heart-shaped face.

Two martinis bookended a plate of boiled shrimp. "I took the liberty of ordering a little appetizer. I hope you don't mind. It's Wednesday night. Free shrimp cocktail. The waiter said these tasty crustaceans were alive and swimming in the gulf this morning. And after you mentioned you were hungry, my stomach started to growl."

"Let me guess. My mother forgot to feed you today. When she seizes on something, everything else is forgotten."

"Frances insisted we stop for lunch around twelve thirty."

"You had tuna sandwiches and canned tomato soup."

"How did you know?"

"That's about all my mother knows how to make. She thinks she can cook, but that's just another example of her being out of touch with reality."

"You know, Sydney, you're too hard on her. She's really pretty funny."

"Funny! My mother? Oh, funny in an odd sort of way."

"No, I mean humorous funny. Once we got the assembly line going, your mother began cracking jokes. She had us in tears."

The look on my face must have told volumes.

"Maybe I should mind my own business, but..."

"But..."

"Never mind."

"No, I'm a big girl. Tell me. You were going to say I'm being unfair to her, that she's really a wonderful woman."

"No, I was going to say that my mother and I fought all the time. All the time. I was always angry with her."

"Why?"

"I wanted her to stop seeing your uncle Martin. I knew he was my father, but it wasn't until I was about twelve that I learned the real reason he and Mom weren't married. This is just between you and me. She kept hoping he'd leave Frances and marry her."

I felt as if I'd been punched in the stomach. I hadn't given Marcella's feelings any thought. She was my uncle's illegitimate daughter whom he'd provided for, but I'd never really considered how her life had been affected by that.

"I'm sorry. How callous of me. It must have been difficult."

"What I wanted to say was that I'd spent all those years blaming Mom, and now that she's gone, I'd give anything to have her back and do things differently."

If I thought I felt lousy a moment ago, the way I felt now convinced me I was wrong. Marcella was the most sensible, stable person I'd ever met, despite growing up in an unstable home. Then again, what did a stable home have to do with it? Look at Ruth and me. We had two parents, a house, a yard, a ranch, bicycles, Girl Scouts, and we plow through life like a couple of brainless dimwits.

"We're being too serious," Marcella said. "Let's talk about something else. Tell me about Dixon. I only saw him for a few moments in Palacios before I was taken to the hospital. I remember dark and handsome, not so tall."

"We're about the same height, when I'm not wearing heels."

I nibbled on some shrimp but couldn't take Marcella's advice about not being so serious. The woman sitting across from me, my half cousin, had lived a life I couldn't even imagine. She'd managed to prevail despite her difficult circumstances. She was staying at my parents' home doing what I should be doing.

CHAPTER FOURTEEN

Ruth must have been really angry with us. Marcella and I were finishing our dessert, and Ruth had yet to show her face. For once, I was disappointed. I had planned to have her follow Louis and me. I hadn't received a threat since I arrived two days ago, and as far as I knew my car hasn't been victimized, either. So, I figured I was past due for a visit with trouble. I had an hour before I had to meet Louis. Maybe Ruth was up in our room pouting. Marcella paid the bill, and we drove back to the hotel.

"Your prediction was wrong," Marcella said as we parked in the lot.

"She's probably in our room."

"I don't see her car in the lot."

Marcella was observant. I looked around. Ruth's Caddy was easy to spot, and I felt a twinge of worry.

"She might be at your parents' house."

"I doubt it. I'll ask at the front desk if she's been in."

The desk clerk was a woman I'd never seen before. I walked over and said, "Excuse me, but have you seen my cousin? She's staying with me." I put my hand up to my chest and said, "She's blond and about this tall."

"Oh, you mean Miss Echland. You must be Miss Lockhart. I saw her earlier this evening, rushing out of the hotel."

"Where could she be?" Marcella asked. "Does she have friends in Galveston?"

"No, she doesn't."

"Should we worry?"

"Let's go upstairs. Maybe she left a note." I knew that wasn't the case. The desk clerk was right. If Ruth was in the hotel, the staff would know.

My room was dark. The clothes boxes were still where Ruth had left them two hours ago. I was about to ask Marcella to be my tail for the evening, but someone had to stay here in case Ruth called. As if reading my mind Marcella said, "Don't worry. I'll wait up. If she doesn't show soon, what should I do?"

"Call Dad, but don't let Mom or Frances know what's going on. I'm sure she'll be back soon." I considered calling Louis and canceling, but what good would that do? I changed and left a few minutes early to drive by my parents' house to see if Ruth's car was parked out front.

It wasn't, but all the lights were on. I saw Mom and Aunt Frances busy at work at the kitchen table. A pinpoint light glowed in the backyard. Dad was having a smoke under the pecan tree. I looked closer and saw that someone was with him. It was probably Dave Rowlings, the next-door neighbor. Lacy Rowlings wouldn't let her husband smoke in the house, either. I sped on by before Dad could spot my car. Well, at least if Marcella had to call, she wouldn't wake anyone up.

LOUIS HAD MY MARTINI READY when I sat down on the barstool. He leaned over as if to kiss my cheek. I had the feeling Louis had arrived early and the Manhattan sitting before him wasn't his first.

"Mind if I have one?" I dodged his lips and pointed to his pack of Camels on the bar.

He lit two and handed me mine. "How's Ruth?"

"She's asleep," I lied. "She'll be as good as new in the morning. What do you do in Galveston for fun, besides hang out in the Balinese Room?"

"That's what I plan to show you. Drink up." He killed his Manhattan in one swallow.

"Where are we going?"

"Don't worry that cute red head of yours. Let Louis be your guide. The Balinese Room is swanky, but I know an exotic locale that'll knock your socks off. It makes the Blue Parrot in Casablanca seem lame. I'll pay the tab, make a trip to the little boys' room, and we'll be on our way."

Damn! I wanted to catch the names of a few places so I could call Marcella and let her know my itinerary in case I ran into trouble. Instead, I was on my own. When the bartender wasn't looking, I poured my martini into the vase of flowers, which sat at the end of the bar. I was munching my last olive when Louis returned. He gawked at my empty glass. "I'm ready if you are," he said and offered me his arm.

Once outside, I insisted we take my car. Louis had the passenger door of his Dodge, which had seen better days, open and was waiting for me to crawl in. "No way. I might not have a classy car like yours, but I won't have my date driving me around."

I reached into my clutch. "I meant to buy a pack of cigarettes before we left. I'll be right back."

"I'll get it. Stay right here. What brand?"

"Luckies."

As soon as Louis walked back into the Balinese Room, I popped the hood of his car, snatched the distributor cap, and tossed it over the seawall.

LOUIS WAS IN HIGH HEAVEN DRIVING MY CAR. Despite the cool evening, I let him put the top down, and we cruised slowly toward downtown. The bars that were closed during the day were hopping. We drove down Strand Street. For all my time in Galveston, I'd never visited this area of downtown after dark. The neon glowed with a naughty twinkle, and if I squinted my eyes, the glow turned to pulsating. There were people on every corner, laughing, smoking, arguing, and a few sucking on something in brown paper bags. It was what I imagined a night in the French Quarter of New Orleans might be like.

"Wild, huh?"

"Scary," I said.

"Don't worry. I know my way around."

I decided to see how much he really knew. "Ever heard of a guy named Boedecker?"

Louis slammed on the breaks, and I almost flew out of the car. "What's wrong?" I cried.

"Uh, I almost hit a cat. I thought you were new in town." He threw me a too-suspicious look.

"I am, but Ruth and I were shopping at Boedecker's Department store this afternoon. There was this portrait of these two guys hanging by the front door. The sales clerk was one of those chatty types. She told us that Boedecker came from a notorious family."

"You notice things, don't you?" Louis said. "Hey, I thought Ruth was sick."

Oh boy, I'm losing my touch. Louis was smarter than his sleazy appearance indicated.

"She is. I thought shopping would help, but it made her feel worse, especially after the clerk rang up her total. Writing that check was enough to send her back to bed." I needed to be careful. Despite Louis's suspicions, I pressed on and reminded myself that, while on this date, I was not a classy woman, that I was playing the part of a vamp, a not-too-smart broad. "The clerk said the Boedecker family used to be involved in gambling and bootlegging, but I guess that's a thing of the past."

I thought Louis was about to clam up, but he finally said, "I wouldn't know. That was before my time. All I know is that one of the brothers is dead, drowned in a boating accident. There's a space in front of the old Tremont Hotel. I'll park there."

We walked down Strand Street for a couple of blocks and turned onto a side street, then into an alley, and into a packed parking lot.

"Up there," Louis said, pointing to a set of rusty stairs leading up the side of a red-brick building and into a dark hole rimmed in blue neon. The name was written in red neon script over the door.

"Ruby's of..."

"Rubaiyat of Omar Khayyam," Louis informed me. "Like I said, exotic. You'll love it."

A short man wearing a fez met us at the door. "A buck each," he said and stuck out his hand. Louis peeled off two bills. The doorman drew back a red brocade curtain and we walked inside. It's what I imagined a joint in Cairo would look like. More blue neon glowed over the bar. In the middle of each round table, tent-shaped lanterns with camel cutouts twinkled. Arabic posters, illuminated with gallery lights, lined the walls displaying desert scenes. The waitresses wore harem pants and midriff tops covered in gold, jingly disks. A gauzy scarf draped from ear to ear hid the lower half of their faces. On a small stage stood a guy dressed in a galabeya and a turban, a common grass snake draped over his shoulders. The word "cobra" was printed on the side of a basket sitting next to his feet. A sweet smell of incense competed with the aroma of a beer-soaked floor. Louis was right, the place was exotic, but in a sinister sort of way.

The snake charmer and his fake cobra left the stage and a jazz ensemble replaced "The Snake Charmer" tune with some livelier melodies. Louis and I danced whenever a swing number played, clasping hands for a twirl. My date took the opportunity to hold on to my fingers with a grip that told me he was afraid I'd fly into the crowd and disappear. After each dance, I'd wriggle my fingers loose. Whenever a cheek-to-cheek number began, I rushed off to the ladies' room to powder my nose. As the evening progressed, Louis got that romantic look in his eye. The couple sitting at the table next to us didn't help matters much. They were lip-locked, coming up for air long enough to gaze into each other's eyes.

On one of my forays to the restroom, I called Marcella to find out if Ruth had shown up. She hadn't. I couldn't waste much more time with Louis. I needed to get what I came for and find my cousin. The bar was now crowded, and the music was too loud for conversation so I suggested we go for that stroll to cool off. As we walked down Strand Street, Louis grabbed for my hand. I acquiesced. "Galveston's a fun town," I said.

"How long are you staying?" Louis let go of my hand and slipped his arm around my waist. I smelled his hair tonic, a stench of old grease and molasses.

"Ruth and I have to be back at work in a couple of days. Austin's a drag. We may have to make Galveston a regular weekend trip."

"See, I told you Galveston isn't a bad place. Every town has its Boedeckers. You just gotta know how to get around."

"Hey!" I stopped suddenly, dislodging Louis. "You don't think they had anything to do with the murder?"

"You're certainly fascinated by the seedier side of Galveston."

"Working as a clerk in a department is boring. Besides, I'm on vacation."

"Let's go then. I'm ready for a little action." Louis rushed me over to my car, and we hopped in. He squealed out of the parking place, and before I could protest, the engine was purring like a puma. I wanted to chastise him for being too reckless with my convertible. Instead, I cried, "Wheeeee!" and threw my arms into the air. My performance deserved an Oscar.

I became curious when we left the downtown area, concerned when we neared the outskirts, and damned angry when we ended up on Stewart Road on the west side of the island where streetlights would have stood out like a beam on a rat's butt. A stroll on the beach near the seawall where people were in shouting distance was fine. But if Louis's idea of a little action involved parking in the boonies, he had another think coming. Just as my mood went from bubbly to bad, the refreshing salt air changed to a pungent stench. I covered my nose.

"It's Petri's Pig Farm. The smell will go away when we turn down the next road," Louis informed me.

"Speaking of next road—"

"You're in good hands, honey."

I didn't like being in anyone's hands—okay, maybe Dixon's, but that was by choice. I reached in my clutch for my gun, a present from my detective, when I saw a house up ahead. It was lit up like a bordello with red lights blazing from the foundation to the roof. Cars were parked up and down the road for a hundred yards in each direction.

"The last of the best," Louis said, as he squeezed my precious sports car between two pieces of junk each resting on four tires.

"A gambling hall?"

"Just wait and see."

Despite the crowd of cars outside, the place was fairly quiet—no music blaring, no rowdy customers lingering.

"Does this place have a name?"

"Not really. Locals refer to it as Washington's. Best fried catfish and hush puppies in the county."

"It's a restaurant?"

"Yep. Come on, let's go. I'm starved."

The front porch resembled any front porch in midtown America. We walked in, and I couldn't believe the size of the place. A cavernous room seemed to go on forever. It reminded me of the cartoon where a person enters a small teepee and once inside discovers an enormous palace. Washington's lacked the elegant ambiance of Gaidos, but the aroma wafting from the kitchen was heavenly.

Louis must have noticed my astonishment because he laughed. "The place is bigger than it looks. The back rooms aren't lit up like the front of the house, so when you drive up you don't notice how the place spreads out. Every time they outgrow the place, the owner just adds another room to the back. Come on. I want you to meet a friend of mine."

We walked up to a table with at least a dozen people crowded around. Judging by the number of beer bottles, the party had been going on for some time.

"Cleve, this is Sydney Lockhart," Louis said.

A huge man stood up, picked up my hand, and with a flourish, kissed it and bowed. "I finally have the pleasure to meet the young, beautiful, hotshot reporter from Austin. I'm Cleve Boedecker."

I gasped and looked around to see how Louis would respond to my deception, but he was gone. Boedecker sat back down and his three hundred pounds spread evenly over his six-foot-plus frame and seemed to meld comfortably into a hefty, but agile man. The glare coming from his bald head formed a suspicious halo.

"Join us, please. Can I call you Sydney? I'd introduce you to the rest of my guests, but considering their condition, they wouldn't remember you in the morning anyway. But I think you know this beautiful, young lady sitting next to me."

As he leaned back in his chair, my perky little cousin came into view. She sat with her arms folded, a smug look frozen on her beautiful, young face.

"Where in the hell have you been?"

"Following you around town, where else? Someone's got to watch out for you."

I made myself comfortable across the table from my host and Ruth. Cleve Boedecker snapped his fingers, and three waiters materialized.

"Bring Miss Lockhart a Lone Star and a plate of catfish, pronto. She looks hungry." He smiled broadly.

"How about my cousin? I hope you fed her as well, Mr. Boedecker?"

He threw his head back and let out a chortle that caused every head in the place to turn. "You're not only young and beautiful, but smart, too. I tried, but she insisted she wait for you."

CHAPTER FIFTEEN

It took you long enough," Ruth said. "I'm starved!" She pulled her compact out of her purse, fluffed her hair, and applied a layer of lipstick, something her manners normally would never have allowed her to do in public. But this was no ordinary evening.

A waiter placed two Lone Stars and two enormous plates of catfish and French fries in front of us. Ruth handed the bottle back to the waiter and said, "I don't drink beer. I'll have a martini, dry, extra olives."

The astonished waiter glanced at Boedecker, then back at Ruth, and stammered, "We don't serve liquor ma'am." He sounded as if he alone were responsible for the establishment's lack of class.

"Then I'll have a glass of red wine," Ruth huffed.

I took a long drink of my Lone Star and scanned the others at our table. They'd gone back to their conversation and didn't look the least bit interested. "Okay, first, how do you know me, and second, did you kidnap my cousin?"

"He most certainly did," Ruth said. "I stopped at a stoplight and these two guys jumped into my car."

"How many times do I have to tell you to lock your doors?"

I was proud of my cousin. The first time she was kidnapped was just two months ago, and the experience had caused her to faint. Now she sounded as if abduction were a mere annoyance, something comparable to a broken nail.

Ruth simply harrumphed.

"That wasn't supposed to happen," Boedecker said, "and I must sincerely apologize. Sometimes my employees become a little heavy-handed. It comes from their old-school mentality. Louis works for me. When you started dropping my name this evening, he became suspicious. He said he also noticed your cousin," he nodded toward Ruth, "following you as you left the Balinese Room. He called me from the Rubaiyat and reported your interest in me. I simply told him to bring you here so we could talk. You see, I'm as interested in you as you are in me. Again, I'm sorry for the inconvenience." He reached into his jacket pocket and pulled out an envelope and from it unfolded a newspaper article—my article—the one that ran in The Statesmen yesterday afternoon. "You have a way of accurately reporting the facts while adding your own innuendoes."

"You have a problem with that?"

"Not at all. It's entertaining. I'll add this to my scrapbook. I like to keep a collection of articles written about my innocent little town."

"Innocent, my foot," chimed Ruth. "I paid way too much for a pair of Viviers at your department store, a pair of pumps that never left your store, I might add."

"You have excellent taste, Miss Echland. We're all friends here. May I call you Ruth?"

"No, you may not."

"Your shoes have been delivered to your hotel room, and your check was torn up to make up for my clerk's incompetence."

"So you've read my article, but how did you know who I was? My accidental meeting with Louis at the Balinese Club was planned. Why?"

"Like I said, we'll talk later."

"But why the deception? Couldn't you have called me at the hotel instead of having Louis bring me here?"

"What I have to talk to you about is very private."

I looked around the table again.

"These people don't matter."

"This doesn't have anything to do with my grandfather's murder, does it?"

"Eat first. We'll talk business later when these so-called friends roll out of here. Enjoy your catfish before it gets cold. I'll send over a bottle of Bordeaux from my collection. Right now,

I have a few phone calls to make." With that, he left the table.

"You scared him off with that blunt question," Ruth said.

"Don't be silly. I have a feeling he doesn't scare easily."

"If I eat all this food, I'll get fat," Ruth said, tasting a French fry.

"Don't worry; I have the feeling the night will be busy. You'll need your strength."

"You're right." Ruth snapped her fingers and another nervous waiter appeared. "Catsup, please." She smeared tartar sauce over her fish. "Don't look at me like that. I didn't get to dine at Gaidos like you and that Marcella woman. I hope you enjoyed your meal."

"You declined the dinner invitation."

"Some invitation. While you and Marcella were chumming it up at the restaurant, I was sitting in the car."

"You should have come in."

"I know when I'm not wanted."

"You sat there all evening?"

"My life is as exciting as a wet pillow."

"Blanket."

"Who cares?"

"Then you followed me and Louis downtown? Where did they nab you?"

"Just on the outskirts of town."

"You're taking this well."

"Thanks to my sunny disposition." She looked around the room. "Buddy isn't with him, is he?"

"No, I haven't seen the little guy all evening."

"Why you let Louis bring you out here, I'll never understand."

"Neither will I. He must have been tailing me from the beginning. Now that I think of it, he was probably the one who slashed my tires. All this time, I thought the meeting at the Balinese Room was happenstance. Boy, was I a fool."

Ruth looked around. "This place is huge. Maybe you're right. Half the town is here. Where's my wine?" She started to snap her fingers again when she gasped and turned white. I thought she was choking on a French fry. I was about to slap her on her back when she pointed.

"We've got to get out of here, now!"

I started to turn around to see what had caught her attention when she clutched my arm.

"What!"

"Oh, Sydney! Please don't turn around."

"What!"

"It's your dad. He's sitting at a table in the back room—in the dark back room."

"Mom must be here too. Let's go. I'll deal with Boedecker later. I don't want to deal with my mother now."

"I'm pretty sure Aunt Mary Lou isn't here."

"Why?"

Ruth released her grip and gently patted my arm. "Because Uncle George is with Lattie the Lush, and it doesn't look like they're having a business meeting."

My mouth fell open, but my vocal cords refused to corporate with my brain. My parents might have a stormy marriage, but I never had any doubt that they cared for one another, even during the time they were separated. Before I could bolt, Boedecker returned.

"Enjoying your wine, Miss Echland?"

"We want to go back to the hotel at once!" Ruth said.

"But you haven't finished your meal, and we haven't had a chance to talk."

Ruth and I needed to get out of here quick before Dad saw us. "It's getting rather noisy in here. Think we could discuss business elsewhere?"

"Absolutely. I have an office in the back. I think you'll find it nice and comfortable."

"No! I mean, I'm not going into any back room with you," I said loud enough to cause heads to turn. My innuendoes didn't seem to faze our host.

"I agree. We need a quiet place to do business. My driver is out front. We'll take a little ride."

"Good idea." I wasn't sure how to get out of this situation, but I knew for certain I wasn't getting into any car with Cleve Boedecker. I prayed that Ruth wouldn't scream, and as I reached for my clutch, I knocked the glass of wine into her lap. I had my cousin up out of her chair and we rushed off to the ladies' room.

"What are you doing? My dress is ruined!"

"Shut up. Listen. We only have a few seconds," I hissed.

There was a woman in the stall so I did my best to make the incident look legitimate. I pulled several towels from the rack, soaked them with water, and dabbed at the red stain spreading across Ruth's dress. "A good dry cleaner can make this look new."

"It is new!"

The woman came out, washed her hands, tut-tutted at what she probably assumed were two inebriated women, and left. "Come on. Out the window before Boedecker gets suspicious."

The window was chin-level to me, which meant it was above Ruth's head. I cupped my hands together. "Take off your heels first."

"You've lost your mind."

"It's been known to happen. Up! Up! Before someone comes in."

The overload of adrenaline pumping through my blood gave me a bit too much strength, causing me to fling my ninety-pound cousin out the window. I heard a thud, followed by swearing, and was relieved to know I hadn't killed her. I tossed out her shoes and then climbed on the trash can and crawled out after her.

"Look at me! I landed in mud! I'm filthy!"

Filthy was an understatement. "You look fine. The mud masks the wine stain. Quit dawdling and put on your shoes. My car's parked on the road. Damn! Louis has my car keys."

"And how do you suggest we get out of here? Walk? Hitchhike? We're miles from nowhere," she cried, removing her ruined nylons.

"We're in a parking lot. We have dozens of other cars to choose from."

"You're not serious."

I picked out a nice black Ford and told Ruth to stand watch. I was under the dash, twisting the wires together when I heard, "Hello, Sydney."

Louis!

I shot an evil glance at Ruth. "You were supposed to be watching!"

"He sneaked up on me."

Now was not the time to be nice. I pulled my gun out. "I should shoot you, you weasel, but I don't have time to hide your body."

"Now, Sydney, take it easy."

"You double-crossed me!"

"I was following orders."

"Give me my keys."

"Boedecker had me drive your car back to the hotel."

"Get in this car, front seat. Ruth, you drive. I'll sit in the back."

"I don't think this was part of the plan," Louis said.

"Change is good," I said. "Now get in."

As we drove past the front of the restaurant, several waiters rocketed out the door like ants after cookie crumbs.

"Duck!" Louis followed my orders. Ruth didn't have to; she could barely see over the steering wheel. We quietly sped away. About two miles later, when I was sure no one was following, I started the third degree on Louis.

"What did you hope to accomplish by slashing my tires?"

He started to turn around. I jabbed my gun hard on the thin bone shielding his medulla oblongata.

"Ouch!"

"Who was the woman who made those threatening phone calls?"

"I—"

"And no wonder you knew so much about the condition of Roland's body since you're the one who plugged him."

"Now wait one minute, Sydney. I didn't kill anybody. You know me—I couldn't do a thing like that."

"I know nothing of the sort, except you work for Boedecker."

"Okay, I'll admit I do a little job for Cleve every now and then, but I'm not a killer."

"Uh-oh," Ruth said. "We're being followed."

"Step on it!"

I pulled my gun from my purse, rolled down the window, and

fired a few shots into the air. I was sure Boedecker didn't expect me to have a gun.

"They're slowing down. Keep driving."

"You gals are making a big mistake," Louis cried.

All of a sudden the car jerked to the left and my gun flew out of my hand and out the window. Then the car jerked to the right and I landed on the floor, banging my head on the armrest. When I crawled up to see what was going on in the front seat, Louis had his hands clinched on the steering wheel while Ruth attempted to dislodge him with an elbow to the nose. We came dangerously close to landing in the ditch on the right side of the road, and then on the left and then the right again. If these antics continued much longer, we'd end up rolling our stolen car.

I did the only thing possible; I grasped Louis by the throat. With his right hand, he reached back and helped himself to a handful of my hair. I buried my teeth into his shoulder. I guess Ruth thought that was a good idea because she copied my maneuver and sunk her choppers into Louis's left hand. He finally let go of the steering wheel, and Ruth managed to keep us on the road. But with one hand free, he grabbed me by the arm and jerked me over into the front seat then he grasped me by the throat. As we grunted and squeezed one another's jugulars to see who'd pass out first, Ruth grabbed her spiked heel and pounded his spine.

"Stop! Stop!" Louis wheezed. "Can't we all just get along?"

"Pig!" Ruth yelled.

Louis was certainly a pain in the butt, but "pig" was an unusual word choice. The car swerved again, bumped, and became airborne. When it landed in a cornfield, the three of us ended up a tangled mess of arms and legs. I fell against the passenger door and it flew open. I tumbled out head-first with Louis now holding onto my legs. I heard scampering and snorting, and the next thing I knew, a wet, slimy appendage poked my ear. Before I could sort things out, a light from above illuminated the scene and I looked directly into Cleve Boedecker's eyes. The man burst out laughing. "No one appears to be hurt," he called over his shoulder. "Help the ladies out and drive them to my house. And get that pig out of here."

CHAPTER SIXTEEN

W ell, I couldn't very well run over the stupid thing," Ruth
said. "It came out of nowhere and just stood there in the
road with a stupid look on its face. Sit still. You have more corn
husks in your hair."

"Stop pulling so hard," I said. "I felt a bump before we left the
road."

"Oh, that. It was only a mailbox. I can't for the life of me figure
out why they put those things right out on the side of the road
for people to run over. You know it would serve you well to cut
this mass of mad hair into a sweet little page boy."

"I cut my hair short when I was thirteen. I looked like I had a
frizzy, red helmet perched on my head."

We were sitting in one of the bedrooms of the Boedecker
house. Cleve had allowed us some time to dust off the road dirt
and told us to come downstairs when we were ready. I used
the phone extension and called the front desk at the Galvez to
leave a message for Marcella telling her that Ruth and I were
okay. Explaining what we'd been through in the last half hour
would have to wait.

"What do you think they're going to do with us?" Ruth asked.

"Nothing."

"You overreacted again; you've been doing that a lot lately.
The man just wanted to talk to you. Isn't that what you wanted,
too?"

"We needed to get out of that place. I guess I panicked."

"I tried to bring this up before, but you wouldn't listen.

Considering all the trouble you've caused, I should have insisted."

"What are you talking about?"

"This book I just read."

"Not another book. What is it this time? Ten Tricks to Avoid Trouble? Ten Ways to Swerve for Swine?"

"You joke. If I'd hit that pig, we wouldn't be sitting here."

"Sitting here is not such a good place to be."

"See there, negative, you're always negative. This book will help in that regard."

"Ten Benefits to Positive Thinking?"

"You're close. The guy who wrote it is very knowledgeable. He invented libraries."

"Say that again?"

"Libraries! Libraries!" Ruth stomped her teeny foot. "It's called How to Win Friends and Influence People."

It's a good thing I'd lost my gun; otherwise I would have blown my brains out. "That's not a new book, Ruth. It's been around since the mid-1930s, and that's a different man. Andrew invented libraries, as you so said, and Dale wrote the book."

"Don't bore me with erroneous details."

"Erroneous? Did you pick up that word from reading books by the library man?"

I ducked as Ruth's Ferragamo flew toward my head.

"Obviously you haven't read it. Part one is called 'The Fundamental Techniques in Handling People' and there is a section specifically for you. It is entitled 'If You Want to Gather Honey, Don't Kick Over the Beehive.' It's about this killer named Two Gun Crowley."

"You're comparing me to a killer?"

"He was too hotheaded and he misunderstood other people's intentions. That got him into big trouble."

"Can we talk about this another time?"

A knock on the door spared me the lesson on optimism, and death by shoe.

"You girls ready?" Louis called. "Cleve is waiting in the library."

"You'll feel right at home," I told Ruth. "While Boedecker and

I talk business, you can read the dictionary."

I threw open the door and was happy to see that my date was in worse shape than Ruth and I were. He had a goose egg over his left eye, and his arm was in a sling. "You're a swell date, Louis. You really know how to show a girl a good time. Come on, Ruth, we don't want to keep Cleve waiting."

Boedecker's house was a rambling ranch decorated with modern art, contemporary furniture, and newfangled gadgets I didn't recognize. We walked into the foyer and my mouth fell open. The decor took a turn back six hundred years. It was decorated in modern medieval. It smelled of freshly oiled hinges and brass cleaner.

"So, tell me, Louis, how are you related to the Boedecker family?"

"How did you know that?"

"You told me your brother-in-law got you the job at the hospital. Unless you lied about that, too."

"I haven't lied about anything. My sister, Marie, was married to Monty. They both died when their sailboat hit bad weather out in the gulf."

We followed Louis from one wing into another, and finally ended up outside a set of dark-paneled doors. He placed his hand on a glass doorknob and paused. "I have to warn you. Cleve has...a strange hobby."

"Is he a cannibal?" Ruth asked.

"Not that I know of," Louis said, eyeing Ruth up and down. "But he likes little things."

Ruth shuddered and stepped closer to me. Louis let us in and then vanished. Boedecker was hunched over a table, peering into what looked like a microscope. In his right hand was a scalpel, and he was slicing and scraping away at an object the size of a BB.

"Come in, ladies, and have a seat. Miniatures," he said. "I carve them. Have a look around while I finish up here."

On the far side of the room, an entire village in miniature sat on a table. Ruth and I sauntered over. "Oh, how cute," Ruth said. "Look at the tiny people; the sailboats, the beach umbrellas, and even a little poodle." On the wall behind the table, rows of bookshelves reached from floor to ceiling, and every inch of space was covered with more miniatures. One shelf held all the U.S. presidents from Washington to the newly elected Eisenhower; another displayed the monarchs of England.

"What I have on the table is my latest project. It's Galveston Island in all her wee splendor," Boedecker said and held up the object he was carving. "Been working on this all day." He walked over and, with a pair of tweezers, sat a tiny starfish on the beach right under the poodle's nose. "When you're my size, you learn to appreciate small things."

"You're a talented man, Mr. Boedecker, but my cousin and I would like to leave, so let's get down to business."

"Oh, look at this," Ruth chirped, "shoes, tiny shoes."

"How could I own the best department store in Galveston and not have fashion in miniature, Miss Echland?" He turned to me. "Both your cars are safely parked at the hotel, and the one you stole has been returned. The owner will probably wonder about the dents, though." He adjusted a miniature man lounging on a miniature chaise under a miniature umbrella. "You've been under the impression that I'm some sort of bad guy."

"How silly of me," I said. "You were chasing us."

"You stole a car."

"You kidnapped us."

"You shot at us."

"You took a hatchet to two of my tires."

He looked genuinely surprised by that last accusation, but he didn't bother defending himself. "It's true my father had something of a reputation for being unscrupulous, a reputation that I have been trying to make up for ever since he died. Once you hear my story, I hope you'll understand. Let's back up and start over. I may have been a little presumptuous and forceful in arranging our meeting tonight."

"Mickey Mouse, Minnie, Goofy." Ruth seemed to have forgotten our misfortune. She was lost in Boedecker's miniature world of make-believe.

"Listen, Sydney, like I told you before, I'm just a businessman, an honest businessman. But you and I do have something in common."

"I'm listening."

"We are both concerned about James Robert Lockhart's murder."

I didn't know what I'd been expecting, but it wasn't the mention of PoPo's death. "Why are you so interested?"

"Because your dear grandfather was a thief. He stole a valuable and very rare coin from my family. Until now, I'd given up ever finding it. I have reason to believe you know where it is." "You've got some nerve, Boedecker." I stood to leave. "Why would my grandfather steal a coin? And how could I possibly know where it is?"

"Sit down, Sydney. It's a long story." He turned off the light of his scope and opened a cabinet door. "Nightcap? How about a glass of sherry?"

"Sure, why not?"

"Let's get comfortable by the fireplace. This may take a while." He pointed to a cushy sofa and seated himself in an extra-large lounge chair.

Ruth continued to wander around the room. I took my sherry and had a seat.

"James and my father were close friends," he began. "My father was a wheeler and dealer, and your grandfather was who Dad went to for advice." Boedecker sipped his sherry. "James had a knack for investments. I'm not exaggerating when I said he was probably responsible for my family's financial survival after the stock-market crash in '29. I owe him a lot."

"PoPo? But he wasn't a wealthy man."

"He could have been, but he was content with his simple life. I remember when he'd come to visit. My brother and I enjoyed being around him. He had this calm type of charisma that put everyone at ease."

"Yes, I know exactly what you're talking about."

"Anyway, my father collected rare coins." He heaved himself out of the chair, walked back behind his desk, and reached toward what I thought was an air-duct panel. He lifted off the frame, and underneath was a safe. "I don't show this to many people." The dial spun under his fingers, and moments later he placed a small, black leather case on his desk. He unsnapped the latch and held it up for me to see. "This was his most cherished and valuable collection."

I walked over for a closer look. There were about two dozen small, shiny coins, all in pristine condition. I pointed to the only empty slot.

"He was obsessed with owning the entire collection of Indian Head five-dollar gold coins. There was one coin my father couldn't acquire, as you can see. The Indian Heads were only minted between 1902 and 1928. That's what makes them so valuable. Each coin alone is worth a lot of money; together, the collection is worth close to forty thousand. The only coin he didn't have was the 1904. That coin alone was worth twelve thousand." He glanced over at his miniature world. "I guess obsession sort of runs in the family. Thankfully, my desire to carve historical figures does not require the purchase of rare items."

"How does my grandfather figure into this?"

"I'm coming to that. A man from Houston, Elliot Hardy, owned the 1904 coin, but wouldn't sell. Your grandfather was negotiating with Hardy on behalf of my father, but despite your grandfather's charm, Hardy wouldn't part with the coin."

"You're not saying my grandfather stole it?"

"That's exactly what I'm saying, but he didn't steal it from Hardy; he stole it from my father. The last time James went to Houston to try to purchase the coin he brought with him a satchel of cash—almost fifteen thousand dollars to be exact. He was given a little extra in which to negotiate. My father believed that if Hardy were presented with the cold, hard cash, he'd sell. Well, it didn't work. James returned to Galveston without the coin and without the money."

My ears began to ring. I sat my sherry down on the table and pounded my head with my fist. "Did I hear you right?"

"On his way back, the satchel was stolen from him while he was at the bus station. At least that's what he claimed."

"Your father didn't believe him?"

"Oh, he did. He trusted James implicitly. James felt horrible.

He called the police, but the mugger was never caught. My father was convinced it was Hardy who was responsible for stealing the money. He had a reputation for being somewhat, shall I say, shady. Then Hardy was murdered and the coin was stolen."

"Now you're accusing my grandfather of murder?"

"No, it wasn't James. I'm ashamed to say my father was responsible—probably someone he hired. At least, that's what I suspect. I don't believe my father had intended to have Hardy killed. Since Dad believed Hardy had stolen the money, Dad wanted the coin, which he now felt he deserved. Whoever Dad hired to steal the coin from Hardy probably became overzealous and killed him as well."

"Talk about shady characters. Your father was responsible for Hardy's murder. He doesn't sound like a very nice man."

"He wasn't. I don't dispute that. He usually got what he wanted, one way or another. As far as he was concerned, Hardy got what he deserved for stealing the fifteen thousand dollars. My father got the coin. Case closed—that is, until your grandfather interfered. I don't know all the details. I wasn't privy to everything my father did."

"I find it hard to believe my grandfather would associate with people like your father."

"Your grandfather was not the type to make judgments against people. That's why everyone liked him. That's why he knew everyone. But he was a moral man. When my father showed James the coin, he became extremely upset. He wanted to go to the police, but well, you see, he couldn't very well do that. He'd be implicated in the crime."

"Your father threatened to blackmail his best friend?"

"Not directly, but the implication was there. James stopped visiting. Then it was my father who became very upset. He felt betrayed."

"He felt betrayed!"

"I know. I know. What my father did was wrong. Anyway, three months later, when my father died, we went through his safe and found the coin collection, minus the 1904 Indian Head."

"And you think my grandfather stole it?"

"I know he did. He left a note saying so."

Boedecker pulled an envelope from his desk drawer, drew out a piece of paper, and handed it to me. Written in my grandfather's eloquent handwriting were the words:

Dear Warren,

I couldn't let this go. I've got to make things right.

I'm going to the police.

Best intentions,

James

"James never had a chance to go to the police. He was murdered that afternoon."

"This is crazy. Besides, if that were true and he left his note telling you what he was up to, then you had a strong motive for killing him."

Cleve thought that was funny. "Yes, I did, but I had an alibi. I was burying my father at the time James was killed. Besides, why kill him if our intention was to get the coin back?"

"I still don't understand how I fit into this. I was only eleven at the time."

"You were the first one to get to James after he was shot."

"So?"

"So he might have told you something."

"He was dead when I found him. Don't you think I would have said something?"

Boedecker sipped his sherry and stared at me over the rim of his crystal glass. After a few moments, he seemed to come to a decision. "Possibly. You take after your grandfather, not just in looks, but in integrity as well. You understand—I had to find out. Listen, Sydney, you want to know who killed your grandfather? Find the coin, and you'll find his murderer."

"And if I refuse?"

"You won't."

"But why, after all these years?"

Boedecker smiled. "As bizarre as this mess might seem, I've spent my entire adult life trying to make up for my father's sins. I want to return the coin to the Hardy family, even after all these years. Make up for the trouble my father caused. I don't expect you to understand. You grew up with a grandfather, and a father, I might add, who were easy to look up to. Also, this has been hanging over my head for too long." Boedecker hit the button on his intercom. "Louis, my guests are ready to return to the hotel."

CHAPTER SEVENTEEN

D o you really believe that story?" Ruth said.
We were safely in our room, bathed and wrapped in warm robes. A thin sliver of light separated the gulf from the sky, a sign of a gorgeous day ahead.

"I'm not sure. The entire thing seems preposterous. Although, I'm discovering things about my grandfather that really surprise me. I can't see him cracking a safe and stealing a coin no matter what his intentions were. Boedecker is one weird man, but he seemed sincere."

"I don't know." Ruth was rarely at a loss for words.

"After eighteen years, where would I look for a rare coin? Talk about a needle in a haystack. There was no mention of the coin found on PoPo in the police report."

"Maybe it was among his loose change in his pocket."

"Probably not. A coin that rare would be in a case or holder of some sort."

"I can't think on an empty stomach. Let's either call room service or go down for breakfast. I'm not the least bit tired."

"Neither am I. Maybe we can come up with a plan after we get a good meal. I'll bring my notepad. Come on, get dressed." I opened the closet and stopped. My red pencil skirt lay on the floor; my gray slacks hung crooked on the hanger; my shoes had been tossed around. I turned and checked the chest of drawers.

"What is it?" Ruth asked.

"Someone's been in our room."

"Is anything missing?"

"No. I think that whoever was here was looking for something."

"The coin? Boedecker thinks you have it."

"Maybe. I wouldn't put it past him to have Louis do something like that when he brought our cars back."

THE BREAKFAST SPECIAL WAS WESTERN OMELETS with fried potatoes, bacon, and buttered toast. Since Ruth was watching her weight, she added a side of sliced tomatoes as an appetizer. While we waited for our meals, I made a list.

"We have two murders here," I said, making two columns on the paper.

"The murder of Maurice Roland and your grandfather."

"Is there a connection? Two murders eighteen years apart?"

"The connection, dear cousin, is you."

"The body in the trunk of my car. That could be a coincidence."

Ruth rolled her eyes.

"What does a keynote speaker for an island development project have to do with the disappearance of a valuable coin almost two decades earlier?"

I wrote James Robert Lockhart at the top of one column and Maurice Roland at the top of the other. "Cause of death," I said. "Gunshot, for both. Motive: stolen coin under my grandfather's name, question mark under Roland's. None of this makes any sense." I turned the page over and wrote my name at the top. "I need to start at the beginning."

The waiter brought Ruth's tomatoes, and she sprinkled each one with a nice coat of sugar.

I raised my eyebrows.

"It's for taste," she informed me.

"I checked into the hotel on Monday and immediately received two threatening calls telling me to leave. A few hours later, my tires are slashed near Pelican Island. The next morning, Roland's dead body is found in the trunk of my car."

"Then we were shot at last night."

"I can't link those incidents to the Hardy family. Why try to run me out of town or kill me if they think I have their coin?"

"Maybe they don't think you have it. Maybe they just want revenge for the murder of Evelyn Hardy, like Boedecker said."

"Elliott, not Evelyn. If that's the case, why me? Why not take their revenge out on Boedecker, and why wait all these years?"

The waiter brought our omelets, and Ruth ordered a side of sliced peaches. As the food began to refuel my body, I let the events run through my mind. One event continued to bother me, one I had no business trying to figure out. Ruth must have read my mind.

"Maybe they just happened to meet by accident. Maybe they really weren't together."

"Dad and Lattie the Lush? You said yourself that they looked intimate."

"Maybe I was wrong."

"What exactly did you see?"

Ruth closed her eyes. "A small table for two, a candle in the middle; your dad sitting on one side, the Lush on the other."

"Were they eating dinner?"

"No, drinking cocktails. Maybe your dad was by himself and Lattie just happened to come in and sit down."

"I can't see Dad going out there by himself. If he wanted a cocktail, he'd go to the Balinese Room."

"With all that's going on at the house, I'm sure he was out looking for a meal, and maybe he was tired of the Balinese Room."

"You're right. And he was probably escaping again. That makes sense. And Lattie's been known to follow him around, foist herself upon him." I was beginning to feel better. "Things aren't always what they seem. Dad would never cheat on Mom."

Ruth became quiet. She stopped eating and sat her fork down.

"What is it?"

"Except..."

"What?"

"I forgot; they were holding hands."

"How could you forget that?"

"Don't shout at me! Maybe Lattie was holding his hand."

"It takes two people to hold hands, Ruth."

As I popped the last bite of roll into my mouth, fatigue claimed my body. A dull pain started between my eyes, spread to the top of my head, ran down the back of my neck, and gripped my shoulder blades. I had two murders to deal with: one involved another story for The Statesman. The second? An anniversary celebration coming down in a couple of days, and a cheating father. There was only one thing I could manage to do.

"I need a couple of hours of sleep."

"I'm not tired. I might as well go over to Pee-in-a-Hat and see how things are proceeding, and I don't mean just the party."

"Great idea, but don't say anything to Dad about last night."

"Would I do that? Trust me. I'll have some answers for you by noon. Get some rest."

I WAS DEEP INTO A DREAM. POPO AND I WERE ON THE BEACH. It was late and millions of stars shone above. He was tossing coins into the ocean, laughing. He handed me a bag and invited me to join him. "You can't take it with you, dear girl." I reached into his bag and pulled out a handful of gold coins. They were so bright that they shone through my fingers. I was eleven again. As I flung them into the water, I felt as if all the burdens of a lifetime flew away as well. I threw a second handful of coins. Instead of landing in the water, they skipped across the surface and then took flight, joining the stars sparkling in the sky. "See there," my grandfather said, "don't ever underestimate yourself, Sydney. You put your mind to something and you can make it happen. Please remember that."

I woke up with a jolt. Looking around, I expected to see the room where I stayed when I visited my grandparents. The brown-and-yellow-striped curtains fluttering in the breeze, the afghan resting at the foot of the bed, my stuffed skunk on the pillow next to me. The memory of my dream began to slip back into the past. I wanted to grasp it, stop time, and live in that moment forever. But with the dream's disappearance came an intense desire to press forward. It was Thursday. I had less than two days to finish my second story and solve PoPo's murder. I couldn't do anything about my parents. Whatever was going on between them was none of my business. They were adults— well, my father was, anyway. I had my own problems.

The phone rang and I reached over, letting my hand rest on the receiver. The way things were going, whoever was calling couldn't be bringing good tidings. Against my better judgment, I answered.

"I'll be in Galveston this afternoon. Find me a room at your hotel. I'm too busy to make my own reservations. Thanks to you, I'll be staying alone."

"Scott." My head started to pound. "The party's not until Saturday. Why put yourself through two days of misery when you don't have to? Oh, I forgot, you live for misery."

"I'll ignore that crack. Mom needs me, since you're too busy to lend a hand."

"Mom has enough help. Ruth, Frances, and Marcella are here at her disposal. Not to mention Dad. She doesn't need my help or yours. She wants me around to give me a hard time and you to have someone to dote over her."

"I haven't met our new cousin yet. What's she like?"

"Like no one in the family. She's levelheaded, clever, patient, and sharp. And why blame me for you having to stay alone? Oh..."

"'Oh' is right. If Jeremiah didn't have to sit your pets, he could come with me."

"I really feel bad. I hate that he's going to miss the party." Actually, I was doing Jeremiah a huge favor by not putting him through the ordeal.

"I told him to put your animals in a kennel and he almost fainted."

"What do you two have in common, anyway? Jeremiah is compassionate and caring and you're—"

"What? What am I? Tell me."

"Never mind. Scott, have you ever...well, ever thought that things were... maybe not okay between Mom and Dad?"

I could have filed my nails and washed my hair in the time it took Scott to compose himself. When he blew his nose and caught his breath, he said, "I haven't laughed that hard since the time you fell out of the pecan tree and broke your arm."

"I'm serious. They haven't been the most stable parents, but I never thought they'd..."

"What, Sydney? You're never this wishy-washy. What's going on? Spit it out."

"Nothing. Nothing at all. I just didn't get any sleep last night and I'm not myself. Forget I said anything. I'll call Jeremiah and tell him to board Mealworm and Monroe. They won't like it, but a night or two won't hurt."

"Don't trouble yourself. When you make the reservations, I want a quiet room with a water view."

Click.

Being the gracious sister, I called down to the front desk and asked if there was a room available for my brother on the west side of the hotel on the second floor. The desk clerk asked if I would prefer a quieter floor since the late-night music coming from the bar across the street might be disruptive. I assured her that my brother was a heavy sleeper. Scott should know better than to boss me around.

I splashed water on my face, touched up my makeup, and dressed for serious business. Fidalgo told me not to bother him again, but I was after a story, and he was the man with information. Before I could slip on my pumps and hit the streets, the damn phone rang again. It sounded urgent, not the Scott type of urgent, but real-world urgent.

"Yes," I said.

"Sydney, glad I caught you. I'm on my way to the police station for the latest on the Roland murder. Big news. Meet me there."

"Conrad, what's happened?"

"Don't have time to talk. Just get your cute little butt down there pronto!"

If Chuck wasn't old enough to be my father, I'd resent his comment about my tush. I checked myself out in the full-length mirror. I have to say one thing for the old guy, though, he was right.

THE HORDE OF REPORTERS CROWDING on the steps of the police station told me that the news was bigger than I'd expected. A podium was set up on the steps and reporters were vying for the front row.

"Syd! Syd! Up here!"

I looked up and saw Chuck waving me to the front. "What's up?"

"Galveston's finest has made an arrest for the Roland murder. About an hour ago."

"Thanks for the scoop."

"No problem. Back scratching."

A short, chubby guy walked out of the station and up to the podium. The crowd went silent.

"At ten o'clock this morning, we made an arrest involving the murder of Maurice Roland."

"That was quick, Larry, are you sure you got it right this time?" A reporter shouted his comment and broke the tension of the crowd. The locals chuckled at the joke.

The police chief ignored the heckler. "The murderer turned himself in this morning."

"Name, do we get a name?"

"The man is local. His name is George Lockhart."

My notepad dropped from my hands, and I grabbed onto Chuck to keep from dropping to my knees.

CHAPTER EIGHTEEN

That man will do anything to keep from having this wedding. I should have stayed on that bus to LA. This will look bad for us at the country club. George is always thinking of himself."

When I walked into the police station, the entire Lockhart clan, except for Scott, was there, shouting, shoving, bossing the police around, and being a general nuisance. The only thing for me to do was to join in.

I've learned over the years to ignore my mother's postulations when she is upset. What little rationality she possessed under normal circumstances had vanished like the last bit of water gurgling down the drain.

Marcella had just hung up the phone when I caught her eye. She walked over.

"Are you sure you want to be a part of this family?" I asked her. "You don't have to decide now. Scott is on his way. Once you meet him, you can make a more practical decision."

"All families have their own unique way of handling trouble. Yours, including you, uses sarcasm and humor. But, I wouldn't be laughing if I were you."

"I know Dad didn't kill Roland."

"I agree, but he confessed."

Until that moment, I'd convinced myself that this was some silly mistake.

"Have you spoken to him?"

"Not yet. We all just arrived. I got off the phone with Hugh Norton. Your father asked me to call him. He's a friend of George's and a local attorney."

"There you are!" Mom said. "I thought maybe you vanished off the face of the earth. I was beginning to think I didn't really have a daughter, that the long labor pains were a figment of my imagination, that the redheaded, sassy girl who lived under my roof for eighteen years was a recurring nightmare."

"Oh, Mary Lou, you don't really mean that," Frances threw her arms around Mom more to keep her from attacking me than as a kindly embrace.

"Hello, Mom. I got here as soon as I could."

Mom gave me that all knowing look. "From Austin? You must have hired a DC-3 and flown right over. Your father has lost his mind. That's the only explanation I can come up with for what he did."

"When Hugh Norton gets here, we'll all sit down and find out what exactly happened, Mom. Just try to stay calm."

"Stay calm? My life's in shambles, and you stand there and tell me to stay calm! Frances, tell my daughter that her father has lost his mind!"

"You already told her that, dear. Sydney is right. Getting excited will not help matters. I'm sure this is all a big misunderstanding."

"Frances, my husband confessed to a murder. That's one hell of a misunderstanding."

Ruth came over and offered her own optimistic style of comfort. "Don't worry, Aunt Mary Lou. They go easy on people when they confess."

My mother let out a banshee scream and ran to the ladies' room.

"Oh, dear." Frances ran after her sister-in-law.

"I'm going to talk to him," I said. "Where's the person in charge?"

"That would be Sergeant Bordine over there," Marcella said. "You're going to have to turn on the charm. He's not too happy right now."

Ruth reached into her clutch. "Want my book?" Before I could say, "no," she had it opened and turned to a certain page. "It says here in part two, 'Six Ways to Make People Like You,' that when dealing with difficult people, you should start the conversation with a compliment." She looked over at the sergeant, who was glaring like a bulldog. "Maybe something like, 'you look very professional in that blue suit.'"

"I think you'd have better luck with a bribe," Marcella said. "You didn't hear that from me."

"Okay, here goes." I sauntered up to the sergeant's desk. "Hello," I stuck out my hand. "I'm Sydney Lockhart. Is Detective Fidalgo in?"

He ignored my offer of a handshake and picked up the phone. "The daughter is here." He laughed. "Yeah, that one. Right." He hung up the phone. "He's on his way. Is that your mother who's carrying on like a madwoman?"

I sort of enjoy bad-mouthing my mother, but when a stranger did it, that was another story. "That madwoman's husband, my father, has just been arrested. How would your wife feel if that happened to you?"

"She'd probably throw a party."

"Well, well, Miss Lockhart. Long time no see."

"I can do without the sarcasm. Can I see him?"

"Follow me." Detective Fidalgo and I walked down a dingy hall toward the jail. "You know, until you came to town a few days ago, Galveston was fairly peaceful."

"Surely you jest. I'm beginning to doubt that this island was ever peaceful. You wouldn't care to give me any of the details of this mess?"

"Nope. Here he is. You have fifteen minutes."

I looked inside the cell. Dad sat on the bunk. He had his fishing cap in his hands and he was fiddling with one of the lures. I went in and sat down.

"You'd think they would have taken this cap away from me. I could probably make a weapon with one of these hooks."

"Dad, what is this all about? I know you didn't kill that man."

"How do you know that?"

"Because I know you. Stop playing games. Tell me what happened."

"Is Norton coming?"

"He's on his way."

"I'll wait to talk to him. How's your mother?"

"She claims you confessed to the murder to keep from having the party."

"Every cloud has a silver lining."

"Did you know Maurice Roland?"

"Who? Oh, the dead man."

"George James, what the hell is this all about?" A high-pitched, grating voice interrupted us.

Dad and I looked up to see a small gray-haired man in a dark-blue rumpled suit. He looked as if he'd just crawled out of a rat hole. His thick glasses were flaked with dandruff, and his tie had a grease spot over the raised claw of a blue crab.

"Nort, come in and have a seat." The jailer scoffed and unlocked the door. "This is my daughter, Sydney. She was just leaving."

"I was not." I lowered my voice to a whisper. "Where did you find this guy?"

"Nort and I met a couple of years ago at the Balinese Room."

"I should have guessed." I stood up and shook the lawyer's hand. "I hope you have better luck, Mr. Norton. He's being obstinate."

"I need to speak to your father alone. I'll visit with you and your family later."

"Well?" My mother had a cup of coffee in one hand and a cigarette in another.

"Well, nothing, Mom. He didn't tell me anything. I didn't know you smoked."

"I gave her one of my menthols to calm her down," Ruth said.

The Lockhart family seemed to have taken over the entire waiting area of the city jail. I even recognized a few neighbors who had come to offer comfort and satisfy their curiosity. I didn't see the Lush, but it was still early.

"It was not my idea to move to Galveston. We should have stayed in Houston where things like this don't happen. Your father wanted to live in Jamaica. Imagine what would have happened there."

"At least they speak English here," Frances said.

Frances had her own way of following my mother's logic. I'd

given up years ago.

"Mom, let's sit down and talk about this."

"If you'd have come to Galveston when I asked you to, this wouldn't have happened."

"What happened this morning? Dad just woke up and decided to confess to a murder?"

"I wasn't there. Frances and I were at the country club. The chef and I were about to agree on the menu when I got a telephone call from your father. He was already at the police station. When he told me he'd been arrested, I'd assumed it was because of fishing without a license."

"They don't arrest people for things like that. They just issue citations."

"He's already gotten twelve citations."

"Oh."

"Did Dad know this Maurice Roland guy?"

"I've never heard of him. You're father has been acting strange lately."

"How?"

"Leaving the house without telling me, staying gone a long time, and not telling me where he went."

"He's always done that."

"Don't sass me. Lately, it's been different."

"Mom, please, give me something specific."

"The look on his face. He's hiding something. And he's been hanging out with Brewster Fallow."

"Who's Brewster Fallow?"

"He runs a bait shop off 61st Street. There's something fishy going on there."

Marcella, overhearing Mom's comment, snickered at the pun.

"What exactly is fishy about running a bait shop?" I asked.

"Nothing. It's what he did before he opened the damn bait shop."

"Which was?"

"He was in prison."

"For?"

"Killing a guy."

"Who did he kill?" I could conjure up dead relatives quicker than I could get information from my mother.

"I don't know. Some rich man from Houston. A guy named Ely or Evan or something. Wait, that was his first name. His last name was..."

I didn't want to hear this, but before I could stick my fingers in my ears, she said, "Handly. That's it, Evan Handly."

I didn't tell her that Evan Handly wasn't his name. It was most likely Elliott Hardy, the owner of the Indian Head coin.

"It was a big scandal. The man was found dead in his home in that fancy Melrose neighborhood." Suddenly, Mom burst into tears. "What's going to happen to my husband?"

Frances rushed over. "Now, now, Mary Lou, don't worry."

Ruth came over as well, "Here, Aunt Mary Lou, have another cigarette."

I left Frances and Ruth to tend to my mother and went in search of Marcella, who had obviously given up on listening to Mom and me. I found her with Detective Fidalgo.

"I was just telling Miss Wheatly that you all need to go home, and if you don't leave soon, I'm throwing all of you in jail." He turned and left.

"Don't worry. He can't do that," Marcella said. "He told me that he remembered you from the time your grandfather was killed."

"True, he was a young police officer back then. Listen, Marcella, I need a levelheaded person to talk to. Help me get my family out of here, and then we need to visit."

Once back at "Pee-in-a-Hat" Street, Marcella and I were able to slip away unnoticed. There must have been twenty people in my mother's kitchen. Ruth was passing out menthol cigarettes and Frances was mothering and doting. Marcella and I went to the only quiet place—under the pecan tree in the backyard.

"Now I have no doubt that Roland's death, my father's confession, and the murder of PoPo are all connected. I'm just not sure how."

"How did you come to that conclusion?"

I told her the story Cleve Boedecker had told me, and what

my mother had said about Brewster Fallow.

"Interesting. When did this Fallow guy get out of jail?"

"According to Mom, it was about two months ago."

"I say we go see the man about some worms."

"Uh-oh, let's leave through the alley. My brother, Scott, just drove up and I don't want to be here when he finds out that Dad's in jail."

The Green Bucket Bait Shop was nothing more than a shed with a water cooler hanging off a side window. The window in front had a zigzag crack, and tape had been applied to keep the glass from falling out. A moldy piece of cardboard with the word OPEN was nailed to the door. We walked in, and the smell of rotting fish made me gag. Except for the bubble of water through aquarium tubes, the place was quiet, not a soul in sight. Marcella pulled a hanky out of her purse and placed it over her nose.

"I've never fished before, and after smelling this place, I know I haven't missed anything," she said.

"Don't knock it, lady, unless you've tried it." The slam of a door preceded the raspy voice.

"Mr. Fallow?" I called.

"Who wants to know?"

"Nice guy," Marcella whispered.

"My name is Sydney Lockhart, and this is my cousin, Marcella Wheatly."

A skinny, dried-up-looking man of about seventy stood in the shadows. "Lockhart? You must be George Lockhart's daughter. You look like him. What do you want?"

"To ask you some questions. I'm sure you've heard that my father's been arrested."

He walked up to the counter, reached for a string hanging overhead, and switched on the light bulb. "That's got nothing to do with me."

A moment ago, I'd wanted a better look at Brewster Fallow. Now that I had it, I wished he'd turn off the light. His front teeth were missing, and his left eye seemed to have a life of its own. Although, my father was open-minded and didn't often judge people, I wondered how and why this old man and Dad had become acquainted.

"How about another murder, then? My grandfather's murder. Did you have anything to do with that?"

I hoped the shock of my statement would cause him to spill forth information. Instead, Brewster Fallow stared straight ahead, his tongue working manically along his upper gum line. "I didn't kill him."

"No, but you killed Elliott Hardy right after my grandfather visited him."

"That's what I was accused of, but I done my time. That's all in the past."

"Except that my grandfather's murderer was never found, and it seems that Maurice Roland's murder is linked to what happened eighteen years ago. I've heard you've been spending time with my dad."

"He comes in to buy bait."

"There's a bait shop two blocks from his house, and it doesn't appear you have a very large selection."

Fallow looked around as if seeing his place for the first time. "Your dad's a fine man."

"I plan to find out why he confessed to a murder he didn't commit."

"I can't help you."

"Tell me about what happened at the Hardy house."

"How do you know so much?"

"I had a little talk with Cleve Boedecker."

"The guy's an asshole. I got nothing more to say. Close the door on your way out." Brewster Fallow turned and left through the back door. I rushed to follow, but when I looked out back, all I saw was a pile of rusty crab traps.

"You spooked him," Marcella said. "What now?"

"Hungry? I think better with food."

"Lead the way."

MARCELLA AND I FOUND A BOOTH AT THE PEACOCK CAFE. The lunch crowd had disappeared, and we had the place to ourselves. We ordered two coffees and two blue-plate specials.

I pulled out my notebook. "I've spoken to three people who knew my grandfather and remember his murder: Detective Fidalgo, Cleve Boedecker, and Mr. Cahill at the hotel. But the person I haven't spoken to yet is the person who probably knows the most."

"Your dad."

"My dad. I say we eat and go back to the jail. Norton should be finished, and I don't plan to leave the jail without answers."

Our meal arrived and we sat in silence while we made quick work of our meatloaf. On our way to the jail, I spotted Hugh Norton shuffling down the street.

"Let's give the old guy a ride before he blows away," I said.

I pulled up to the curb, and Marcella rolled down her window. "Mr. Norton, can we give you a lift to your office?"

"My office is back in the other direction. I'm going for a stiff drink. You can join me, but the place is a bit rough."

"Let me guess, the Rubaiyat?"

He chuckled and hopped in the backseat. "Nice car. Is this the one with the body in the trunk?"

"Same car; body's gone," I said. "What did you find out?"

"Not much. You're father's one stubborn man."

THE RUBAIYAT WASN'T AS LIVELY COMPARED to the first time I was there. Since it was early, the character in the fez wasn't collecting a cover and the snake charmer hadn't yet arrived. We took a table in the corner under a poster of a silhouette of camels trudging across a sand dune. Norton ordered a double vodka and tonic. Marcella and I settled for two Royal Crown Colas.

After a deep swig, Norton said, "Your father didn't kill that man, that's for sure."

"Did he say so?" I asked.

"No, but after questioning him, it was clear that not only did he not know Roland, but he knew nothing about the details of the murder, or else he's a good liar."

I thought about Dad telling me that he didn't know why PoPo was killed. I knew he was lying. Is my father, in fact, a good liar?

"Why did he confess then?"

"He wouldn't tell me."

"Maybe he knows who did it and is protecting the killer," Marcella said.

"And risk spending the rest of his life in jail?" I said. "Oh, no."

"What? Wait, you don't think...?" Marcella said.

"That he thought the police would arrest me because of Roland's body in my trunk? No, that's not possible. I had an alibi; Dad knows that."

"Well, you'd better talk some sense into his thick head before it's too late. Even if he didn't kill Roland, confessing to a crime he didn't commit is a crime in itself." Norton finished his drink, threw some bills on the table, and stood to leave. "Besides, I can't defend a man who doesn't want defending." He tipped his fedora and left.

"To the jail?" Marcella asked.

"Boedecker first. The more information I have, the easier it might be to get Dad to talk.

BOEDECKER WAS FINISHING UP A TINY BEACH PAVILION when we walked into his library. "Miss Lockhart, what brings you here?" He snapped off his microscope light. "And who, may I ask, is this lovely lady?"

"This is Marcella Wheatly, my cousin—another cousin. We're here for some answers, Mr. Boedecker."

"Find the coin yet?"

"You know I haven't. I need information."

"I've told you all I know."

"What about Brewster Fallow, who went to prison for Elliott Hardy's murder?"

"Oh, that."

"You said you believed your father hired someone to kill Hardy. If he hired Fallow, then you must have known about it."

"I'd forgotten the guy's name. My father didn't discuss the details of his business dealings with me or my brother."

"Fallow got out of jail two months ago. My father was arrested this morning for Roland's murder."

"Is that so? You're wasting your time by coming here, Miss Lockhart. Find the stolen coin and you'll find answers to your questions and, most likely, the person who killed James. I know nothing about this Fallow guy. I have no more information for you. Care to join me for a cocktail?"

I thanked Boedecker for his offer and his uselessness. Marcella and I left, having accomplished nothing.

We drove back to town. I was getting nowhere fast. Finding a coin that disappeared eighteen years ago, discovering the man who killed my grandfather, and figuring out why and how this was connected to Maurice Roland and my father's confession was turning my brain to mush.

"Boedecker knows more than he's letting on," I told Marcella. "He was so eager to get me involved and now he's backing off."

"I agree. It was odd for him to drop this in your lap. Keep an eye on him, though. I've got an idea," Marcella said.

"I'm all ears."

"Let me talk to George alone."

"If Norton couldn't get him to talk, how do you plan to do it?"

"Norton's a washed-up old lawyer who should have hung up his shingle years ago. I didn't get where I am today by backing down to clients who refuse to talk."

"Sorry, I didn't mean to underestimate you. Give it a try. I need to sort through things. With everything that's happened, I'm not thinking straight."

"Drop me off at the jail and you go back to the hotel. I'll take a taxi back. You look a bit haggard."

I left Marcella at the jail and drove around for a while, letting my mind wander through the maelstrom of murder. Clouds drifted in, putting a damper on the beautiful day. Along with the clouds came that ominous rolling fog that changed the mood of everything it covered, me included. What was going on in Galveston eighteen years ago? My grandfather had befriended one of the city's most notorious citizens, given him advice that kept him from financial ruin, and when the guy's greed turned to crime, PoPo had tried to fix the situation by doing the honorable thing, all of which got him killed. I found it hard to believe that Boedecker caused so much trouble over a stupid little coin. True, the complete collection was worth forty thousand. What really irked me was that Warren Boedecker had come out clean, Elliott Hardy had died, PoPo had died, and Fallow had gone to prison. Why didn't he roll over and point the finger at Boedecker?

I should have gone to check on Mom, but I wasn't ready for the turmoil of the Lockhart household. I went back to my room and hit the sack.

CHAPTER NINETEEN

I woke to a sun well up and already into the business of warming the day, and to Ruth well into a late-morning dream. The phone rang and I snatched up the receiver and pulled the phone into the bathroom to keep from waking her. It was Marcella calling to report. Although she hadn't been successful getting Dad to talk, she did manage to get him released on bail. I told her I'd be over later, and then I dressed quietly and left. I grabbed a cup of coffee and decided to pay the slippery Mr. Fallow another visit. To keep Mr. Fallow from noticing my car and scurrying out the back door, I parked a couple of blocks away.

The OPEN sign was still there, but the place was deserted. I took the opportunity to snoop around. The shop was crowded with more than a dozen concrete tanks with hoses trailing out in all directions. I peered into one and was surprised to see it empty of any fish life—just dank water with a fine layer of algae growing up the side. I looked in the next one, empty too, and so was a third. The fourth housed a few sad-looking minnows. Maybe there had been a recent surge in demand for bait, but I doubted it. I stepped to the back of the shop and opened an icebox. Inside were four containers of night crawlers. Brewster Fallow was not getting rich selling bait, that was for sure.

I checked out the counter and saw that he'd returned after Marcella and I had left. A half-eaten bologna sandwich sat on a chipped plate next to a cup of coffee. I felt the cup. It was warm. I poked the sandwich. The bread was soft. Whatever had distracted Fallow from his lunch had happened only a short time ago. The cash register drawer was half-open. I counted four dollars and some change. Then I heard the back door squeak open and then close.

"Mr. Fallow?" I called. "Brewster?" I walked to the rear of the shop and pushed open the screen door. An old Ford was parked in the driveway. "Anyone here?" I called. No answer, so I went back inside to wait. Maybe he had to run a quick errand, or maybe, as Marcella had said, I had spooked him again. I continued my inspection of the tanks, and when I peered into the last one, I knew for certain that waiting for Fallow to return was a waste of time. I hurried out the door and into my car, and I was out of the neighborhood in a flash. I was sure that Brewster Fallow didn't accidentally stumble into his own fish tank and drown, judging by the bloody water and hole in his skull. I was also certain that whoever had left through the back door was the killer.

I DROVE TO THE PLEASURE PIER AND PARKED ON THE SEAWALL. The seagulls were out in number and squawking their eerie sound, a sound I enjoyed more than any other. For me, it was a mixture of innocent pleasure along with a bit of melancholy thrown in at the last second. When I was little, I often thought the gulls were calling me to join them for a flight over the beach, only to feel sad when I didn't sprout wings and take flight. That's what I felt like doing now—catching the vortex of a whooping-crane flock and migrating to Canada. Only it was two months too early for the birds' flight north. The cranes weren't going anywhere, and, unfortunately, neither was I.

The stench of dead bait from Fallow's bait shop still lingered in my nasal passages. I walked out onto the pier, inhaled the salt air, and listened to the gulls and the sound of my heels tapping on the wooden planks, hoping my racing heart would not explode from my chest.

Except for a few fishermen, the place was uncomfortably quiet. The fog had become heavy, wrapping me in a blanket of light mist. I could no longer see the end of the pier, and all of a sudden, I felt too vulnerable for my own good. Even the seagulls had stopped calling, or maybe they'd left to find a better stretch of beach.

I pulled my jacket around me, leaned against the rail, and tried to fit this new puzzle piece into the insane events that now dominated my life. Whoever killed Fallow must have done so only minutes before I arrived and had been in the back of the shop when I walked in. I'm lucky he didn't kill me too. When I fled the shop, I'd intended to drive straight to the police station and find Fidalgo, but I couldn't steer my car in that direction. Being connected to one dead body was enough. However, if I didn't report the murder, Fallow could lie in that fish tank for days before anyone found him. I was certain the man who'd killed Roland was probably the same guy who'd plugged Fallow. Delaying the report would only make the situation worse for everyone, especially Dad.

I lingered a bit longer, rehearsing in my mind what I would tell Fidalgo. The wind picked up, creaking the old pier. Someone coughed. In the distance, I heard footsteps. I turned, but couldn't see a damn thing through the fog. I was not the kind of person who had premonitions—that was Ruth's department—but at that moment, I felt as if something was wrong, very wrong. I listened for the clang of bait buckets and fishing gear to go with the footsteps, but whoever was strolling in the fog was not there to cast a line. Then the footsteps stopped, and for a moment, all I heard was the slow, gentle wash of the waves. They seemed to crest and hang for a moment before falling as if they weren't sure they wanted to be here, either. Someone could easily walk up, toss me over the rail, and no one would ever know until my body washed up on the beach. The footsteps sounded again. This time I distinctly heard two different footfalls, one near and one in the distance.

I usually think of myself as a relatively intelligent person, but at the moment, I felt void of all mental prowess. I'd given the killer a perfect opportunity to do me in. He'd probably followed me from Fallow's shop.

I slipped off my shoes and crept back toward the seawall. The footsteps in the distance picked up the pace. Then I heard an unmistakable sound from the person closest to me. It was the click of a gun's safety release. I froze. The shot split inches from my head. Another shot rang out, this one from a different gun. The guy nearest to me turned and ran. A scuffle ensued, and for a moment, I considered jumping over the pier rail, but I wasn't sure if I was over water or sand.

Suddenly someone grabbed my arm.

"Don't scream. Keeping walking and don't say a word." We walked together in silence until we reached the seawall. The headlights of the cars driving down Seawall Boulevard illuminated the street, causing the mist to turn yellow like sparklers dancing throughout the air. He opened the car door and pushed me in and then came around to the driver's side. Once both doors were locked, he grabbed me and pulled me over.

"What the hell are you doing here?" My heart raced.

"Keeping you alive, what else?" Dixon kept me from any further bitching by planting his lips on mine.

CHAPTER TWENTY

Dixon's motel room at the Sea Side Inn didn't smell much better than Fallow's Green Bucket Bait shop. One twin bed, covered with a dingy yellow bedspread, was nestled in the corner of the room. The lampshade had a burn hole in the side. The cabinets nailed to the opposite wall, a two-burner stove, and pint-size icebox made up a tiny kitchenette. Water dripped from the tap in the stained sink.

"I could get you a room at the Galvez," I said, looking around. I decided the bed looked cleaner than the tattered chair, most likely a hostel for a family of fleas, and sat down.

"I'm keeping a low profile. The place isn't that bad. Besides, I get free coffee in the morning from the owner, Mrs. Swainy." Dixon took off his jacket and draped it over a kitchen chair, straightening the shoulders. He loosened his tie and went into the bathroom for a washcloth. He sat down next to me and wiped the sand from his shoes.

There were many things about this Hot Springs detective I liked, one being his tidiness, another his classy style of dress, but, even though he had possibly just saved my life, I wasn't sure how I felt about him showing up out of the blue. The last time he arrived unannounced, he found me dancing with a goat in an alley in Palacios, Texas. That encounter really ticked me off, not because of the embarrassment over the goat, but because I fainted when I saw him. This time, I was more curious than angry. Maybe it was the kiss and feeling his heart racing when he held me. Maybe it was the relief from not being killed.

Or maybe I just liked having him around.

"What are you looking at?" he said.

"You missed a spot. There, on the side of your shoe. Looks like seagull droppings. How long have you been here?"

"Arrived last night."

"Did you see who tried to kill me?"

"Who could see anything once the fog rolled in? I spotted you cruising the boulevard, going in the opposite direction. I did a U-turn just as you pulled up to the curb by the pier. I parked several yards behind you. Another car pulled in between us. I thought nothing of it at first. The driver sat there a while. I sat and watched. Then he got out and walked to the pier. I didn't like the way he held his hand in his pocket. I've been a cop too long not to know when someone's packing heat. And I've known you too long not to know that you attract trouble like mud to a pig. Excuse the metaphor. That's when the fog grew heavy, and I couldn't see beyond the hood of my car. Does that always happen here?"

"It's life on the Gulf Coast. You get used to it."

"We have fog in Arkansas, but it knows its place and doesn't get out of hand." His shoes were shiny clean, and he tossed the washcloth in the sink. "Come here."

I had to slow my internal processes to keep from falling into his arms immediately. Once we parted for air, he said, "I think you're glad to see me."

"That surprises you?"

"Yes and no. I expected a dressing down for the unannounced visit."

"That will come later. Right now, there's a dead man in a fish tank over at the Green Bucket Bait Shop, my dad's confessed to a murder he didn't commit, a crazy fat man thinks I know the whereabouts of a valuable coin that disappeared over eighteen years ago, and someone wants me dead."

He just smiled.

"What?" I asked.

"I'm the detective. I'm the one who's supposed to come home at the end of the day telling all about my life of danger."

"I'm just a fun sort of girl."

"And you wonder why I show up all the time. I never have this much fun in Arkansas, at least when you're not there." He nuzzled my neck.

"We don't have time for this."

"You're right. Let's go see the dead man in the fish tank."

BY THE TIME WE PULLED UP IN FRONT OF THE GREEN BUCKET, I had caught Dixon up on the week's most important events. We parked and sat in the car to soak up some neighborhood atmosphere. I had hoped to see the street swarming with police cars so Dixon and I could cruise on past and I could forget I was ever here.

"What brought you to the bait shop to begin with?" he asked.

"Mom said Dad had befriended Brewster Fallow, the owner of this thriving business. Brewster Fallow got out of prison two months ago. He was involved with events associated with my grandfather's murder."

"Tell me about it."

I started from the beginning this time. Dixon listened, never taking his eyes off the shop's front door.

"Interesting," he said when I finished.

"Okay, your turn. I know why you came to Galveston yesterday. You suspected I was in trouble. You kept out of sight and followed me around to get a feel for what was going on. But, there's something else. Spill."

"You're not going to like it."

"I'm a big girl."

"Your dad."

"My dad? How did he know about you? I've never mentioned you to my parents! Ruth!"

"Cool it, hon. It wasn't Ruth this time. I made contact first. I did a little digging into what happened eighteen years ago. Then I called your dad. I figured he knew more than he was telling. When I called the first time, I introduced myself as your overprotective friend. He laughed and said he knew you had a beau—he actually used the word 'beau'—in your life who you were keeping secret. I told him you're sneaky. He said I didn't know the half of it, and if I planned to stick around, I'd better get used to your sneaky ways. I told him I didn't like the body in the trunk story. I told him to call if things got out of hand. He called yesterday afternoon."

"Why is he willing to talk to you and not me?"

"That's obvious. You're his daughter. He's trying to protect you."

"From what?"

"That's obvious, too. From the guys who killed your grandfather. The same guys who want that missing coin."

"After all these years?"

"It must be worth a bundle."

"Twelve thousand back then, who knows how much it is worth today."

Dixon whistled. "If that was its value back in the 1930s, you can probably double that figure. But you're wrong about your dad talking to me. He hasn't told me much. I was as surprised as you when I found out he'd been arrested."

"You haven't been to the house yet? You haven't met my mother?"

"Haven't had the pleasure. Let's go inside."

"I have a lot more questions."

"Later."

I led Dixon to the fish tank in back. Brewster was still there.

"Nasty," he said. "Looks like the damage was done by a .38, which is what was fired at you out on the pier. We'd better call the police."

"What do we tell them?"

"The truth—you came here looking for Fallow and found him dead."

"But that was more than an hour ago. Won't they be a little put out that I waited?"

"Probably, but we'll explain that you were frightened, left in hysterics. It took me a while to calm you down."

"Is that what you call it, calming me down?"

He grabbed me and drew me close. "That's our story, hon."

"The detective on the case, Detective Fidalgo, won't believe that hysteria part. He knows me pretty well by now."

"Is there a phone in here?"

"Over by the register."

Dixon pulled his handkerchief out of his pocket, picked up the receiver, and dialed.

While Fidalgo's men combed the bait shop for evidence, I introduced the two detectives. Dixon and Fidalgo eyed one another like two bloodhounds, each sizing up their competition, deciding if it would be mutual respect or professional rivalry. Something connected between the two, a mere second's flash of insight. I was relieved to see that respect had won out.

"Please don't tell me you two planned on going fishing and just happened by here to buy some minnows." Fidalgo lit a cigarette.

"I'm here to get a story for my newspaper."

Fidalgo raised his eyebrow. A thin stream of cigarette smoke spiraled upward in front of his face.

"And to get answers for a more personal situation."

"What did you hope to find by talking to Fallow?"

I stopped and considered how much I should say about what Boedecker had told me. I figured Fidalgo knew about the Boedecker connection, but I wasn't ready to play my hand. I glanced at Dixon.

"My father did not kill Roland. Why he confessed is beyond me, but I don't plan to sit around and let him go to prison."

"What's your business in all this?" he asked Dixon.

"No business at all. I'm just here enjoying the beautiful weather."

"Sure you are. And I'm here on the isle of paradise looking for the Fountain of Youth." Fidalgo looked at me. "You didn't answer my question."

"A visit to Fallow seemed like a good place to begin my investigation. He and my father had recently struck up a friendship. And since Fallow had been released from prison, well, let's just say I was curious about why Dad was coming around to see him."

"Cut the crap. You know more."

"I certainly do. I know Fallow was involved with the circumstances surrounding my grandfather's murder. He went to prison for killing Elliott Hardy. I'm looking for some answers since my father is not talking."

"Let me handle things. If you keep nosing around, I'll find a reason to arrest you."

"It's a free country," I scoffed.

"I have an officer coming over to take down your statement. After that, I want you out of here."

Fidalgo joined his officers, and Dixon and I went outside where the air was breathable. Fifteen minutes later, I had given my statement, and Dixon and I left Galveston's finest to their wretched work.

"Do you get the feeling we're just one step behind something nasty?" I asked on the way to my car.

"Count your lucky stars. You could have walked in on the murder. Let's get out of here."

I turned off Seawall Boulevard with plans to drive to the west side of the island. Instead, I slammed on my brakes.

"What!" Dixon cried. He pulled his gun from his holster.

"Marcella! I forgot about her. I was supposed to meet her back at the police station." I looked at my watch. "That was almost two hours ago."

"I'm sure she's not still there."

"I need to find a phone and call my parents' house."

I located a booth near a beachside food hut. As I dropped in my nickel, I prayed Mom wouldn't answer.

"Hello."

"Aunt Francie, is Marcella there?"

"Hold on. Marcie," she called. "It's Sydney."

"No, wait!" Too late. I said another prayer that Mom didn't hear that.

"Hello."

"Can you talk?"

"Some," she whispered. "Are you okay?"

"Yes, I got sidetracked."

"I figured. I called Ruth to pick me up. If I didn't hear from you soon, I was going to phone the police."

"No need, since I just left the pleasure of their company."

"Whoops. Tell me about it."

"Later. How are things with Dad?"

"Better. Damn. I can't talk now." I heard her muffle the receiver. "Sure, Mary Lou, just don't panic. We'll call a plumber if we have to," she called. "Are you all right?" she whispered.

"Yes, good luck with the latest disaster."

"Gotta go," she said. "Be careful."

"Everything okay?" Dixon asked.

"Nothing beyond the usual chaos. Now, we were on our way out of town."

"Going?" Dixon asked.

"To visit Cleve Boedecker. I have a feeling he's got more to tell me, and I figured while you're here, I'd use your skills. Are you game?"

"Drive on."

CHAPTER TWENTY-ONE

We drove most of the way in silence. My mind wrapped around Boedecker and the events of eighteen years ago. Dixon's thoughts, I suspected, were of a more pleasant nature, considering the slight smile on his lips. "I have to warn you. Boedecker's a strange man, a very strange man."

"In what way?"

"You name it. His house can best be described as a museum of the macabre. It looks normal from the outside—a modern ranch. But as soon as you as walk in the front door, which squeaks by the way, you get a feeling of stepping into a funeral parlor, no, more like a morgue. He has a collection of medieval swords decorating the walls of the foyer. A knight in shining armor, minus the knight, stands by the staircase. A chain-mail suit hangs in a display case near the stairs."

"Weird."

"Then there's his office—floor-to-ceiling bookcases of miniature figurines he's carved himself. The room where Ruth and I cleaned up after our adventure with the pig in the field, probably a guest room, looked like, except for the low ceiling, Rebecca's room in Daphne du Maurier's novel. I haven't seen the entire house, so who knows what else lurks there."

"Sounds like some castles I've visited outside of London."

"Yeah, but you don't expect that sort of thing in Galveston, Texas."

"How far out is his place?"

"We're almost there." I drove past the pig farm and turned down 8-Mile Road leading to Boedecker's house.

"What's our story?"

"We'll play his game. He believes I can find his precious coin. I'll tell him I need more information. I'll tell him you're a dealer in rare coins and want to inspect his collection to see if his is legit. Think you can fake it?"

"Not this time. If he starts asking questions, I'll run into trouble. I know zilch about old coins."

"You're right. That won't work. How about this? You're a private detective I've hired to help me find the coin."

"Bingo."

I rang the bell. The door flew open. There stood Louis.

"Do you live here, too?"

"Sydney, what brings you here? Who is this?" The look of delight on his face turned to annoyance when he noticed Dixon. The bruises on his face were beginning to yellow. I didn't feel sorry for him. Did this man really expect there was a future for us?

"This is business, Louis. We're not here to see you." I pushed past him, and we walked in.

"So you're Louis," Dixon said. "Looks like you're healing nicely after the pig-in-the-field incident."

"I don't like wise guys. Cleve is having dinner. You don't have an appointment."

"I don't need an appointment. Your boss set that precedent when he had you trick me into coming to see him at Washington's. Besides, I'm sure he'd love to see me."

"Wait here." Louis snorted and disappeared down the hall.

"Louis the Balinese date?" Dixon asked, studying a sword.

"The same. Know anything about swords?"

"They were extremely useful for the Three Musketeers. Other than that, no, but these are impressive, and expensive. Think he has a torture chamber in the basement?"

"I hope we don't find out."

Dixon walked over to the chain-mail display and was about to open the case when Louis came back.

"Don't touch anything," Louis said. "Cleve said to wait in his library."

We followed Louis to Cleve Boedecker's miniature world. I hoped our escort would leave us alone for a few moments so Dixon and I could discuss our next move, but Louis remained.

"You a cop?" Louis said to Dixon. "You look like a cop." Louis eyed the bulge under Dixon's jacket."

"P.I."

"Let me see your license."

"I'll show it to your boss right after I tell him how insulting you are."

Louis did the smart thing for once and left.

"What if Cleve asks to see your license?"

"I'm covered there. I keep a fake. This room gives me the creeps. I feel like Gulliver in another bad adventure."

Suddenly, the wall between two bookcases on the far side of the room opened and Buddy Leech walked in. "Mr. Boedecker told me to offer you refreshments." The little guy was decked out in a tux that was, not surprisingly, too big. The cuffs of his pants were rolled up and secured with safety pins. The collar of his starched white shirt caught him just below the ears, making his round head look as if it were resting on a platter. "Ruth's not with you?"

"Couldn't make it, Buddy. She sends her regards. I can't say I'm surprised to find you working here."

"Buddy, as in the Balinese Room mambo master" Dixon whispered.

"I heard that," Buddy said. "Just because I'm short doesn't mean I can't hear."

"One of his many talents," I said to Dixon. "Glad you found a job, Buddy."

"Being a butler is beneath me. But I got other duties around here too."

"Like what?" Dixon asked. "Dusting under the furniture?"

"No, smart man. I'm Boedecker's footstool. Don't insult me. Just because I'm short doesn't mean I'm not sensitive. Now, what do you want? Booze, coffee, or cucumber sandwiches?"

I looked at Dixon, and he shook his head. "Nothing for us."

"Oh, come on. I gotta bring something. I don't want to look like I'm not doing my job."

"Scotch and water," Dixon said.

"A martini, small one, two olives," I added.

"Gotta make it hard, don't you?" Buddy smirked and disappeared through the wall.

"I feel as if I've entered the secret life of a circus family," Dixon said.

"It gets better."

Just then Cleve ambled in, smiling and gracious as always. "Sydney, my gal, nice to see you again. Louis tells me you brought in reinforcements." He had the audacity to walk over and kiss me on the cheek. Then he extended his hand to Dixon. "Cleve Boedecker. So you're a private eye."

"Ralph Dixon. Pleased to meet you, Mr. Boedecker."

"Call me Cleve. I hope Buddy has taken care of you while you waited. He's still a bit rough around the edges, but he'll get the hang of it. He's a fast learner."

"So I've been told," I said.

"Let's have a seat by the fireplace. What can I do for you?"

"Dixon's here to help, and I wanted him to hear your outrageous story."

"So Sydney has told you about my family and the unfortunate circumstances behind the missing Indian Head? But before we get down to business, I must ask for your credentials, Mr. Dixon. Not that I'm not a trusting person, but a businessman has to be careful. I hope you understand."

"Absolutely," Dixon pulled out his fake license.

Boedecker scrutinized it and said, "I hear it's easy to fake one of these."

"It is," Dixon replied. "You can contact my partner in Hot Springs, Arkansas, William Ludlow. Will that suffice? I can't give you names of past clients, though. That's confidential—I'm sure you understand."

"No problem."

While Dixon and I made ourselves comfortable on the sofa by the fireplace, Cleve went to his desk and picked up the receiver. "Phone number?"

I tried hard not to gasp, but Dixon looked calm.

"TriVeca 4924. Call collect."

We waited while the operator connected. Dixon gave my hand a reassuring squeeze.

"Mr. Ludlow?" Cleve asked. "This is Cleve Boedecker in Galveston. Do you know a man named Ralph Dixon?"

Although I couldn't hear exactly what Billy was saying, I could detect his slow, methodical manner of speaking. I first met Billy a few weeks ago when I was in Palacios, Texas, covering the New Year's Eve Ball. Before the orchestra had a chance to play "Auld Lang Syne," a dead man landed in my arms and I landed in jail. Billy was the young deputy who took pity on me. After Ruth and I solved the case and charges were dropped, Dixon discovered the police chief's corruptness. He then offered Billy a job on the Hot Springs police force.

"Let's just say I'm considering doing a little business with the man. Uh-huh. Uh-huh. Well, that's what I wanted to know. Thanks for your help." Cleve hung up. "Dixon/Ludlow Private Investigators. How long have you been in business?" he asked Dixon.

"About ten years. William joined me just a few weeks ago. Found the young man in Houston. He was with the police force for a while."

"That's what he said. Okay, I'm satisfied." Cleve handed Dixon his license and joined us by the fireplace. "I want that coin, Mr. Dixon. Sydney tells me she doesn't know where it is. I'm not sure I believe her." He grinned at me as if I were a naughty child. "But for the moment—"

The wall opened up. "One scotch and water and a short martini with two green bobbers." Buddy interrupted. "How about you, Mr. Boedecker?"

Cleve shot Buddy a look that would surely have stopped a stampede of charging elephants. Buddy, however, didn't notice. "Don't you usually like that sweet wine after dinner? I hear it's a winner." Then he turned to us. "I personally don't care for that syrupy stuff, myself. I gotta watch my weight, before it's too late."

"Sherry, Buddy. I'll get it myself. Go practice your poetry somewhere else. If I need you, I'll call."

Although Boedecker's stare bounced off Buddy, being dismissed appeared to have hurt the little guy's feelings. "Sure thing," he said, retreating through the hidden door. "I'll go see if I can find some silver to polish. Maybe some boots to clean. What I'd like is a job description." The wall closed before we could hear the rest of Buddy's discontent.

"As I was saying," Cleve continued. "That coin belongs to my family."

"Actually, it doesn't," I said. "You're changing your story. You told me the reason you wanted it was to return it to the Hardy family, the rightful owners."

"I am the rightful owner. My father paid for that coin."

"With money and murder," Dixon said.

Boedecker shrugged. "Nevertheless, James stole it from my father, from there the trail gets cold, but I knew James very well. The coin was not on him when he was killed. He would have told someone where he hid the coin, and that someone was most likely his granddaughter."

"I told you my grandfather was dead when I found him."

"Listen, Mr. Boedecker—Cleve—you're going to get nowhere accusing Sydney. We'll help you find that coin, but you're going to have to believe Sydney. Otherwise, we'll leave now."

Cleve walked over and poured himself a hefty shot of sherry. "James's house. Your father and mother live there now. It could be there. James didn't have a safe deposit box. I already checked."

"Most of my grandparents' furniture was sold when my parents moved in," I said.

"The attic, then. The basement. The garage."

"Maybe we should dig up the backyard."

"This is not funny, Miss Sydney."

"Do I look like I'm joking? What I don't understand is why now? Why are you looking for the coin now? You told me you'd given up finding the coin until I showed up. That's difficult for me to believe. You aren't the type who gives up. I'm surprised you haven't searched the house already."

Cleve sipped his sherry. His eyes darted from me to Dixon and back again. He let out a breath and seemed to come to a decision. "I did," he said. "Not me, personally. I had some guys search the house. It was right after James died. Nothing was found. Then—"

A bloodcurdling scream shot through the house, causing me to slosh my martini. Dixon jumped up and ran toward the door just as Louis dashed in.

"What the hell happened?" Boedecker shouted.

"It's okay, Cleve. Buddy was in the kitchen trying to clean a spot off the teakettle and he started a little fire. He thought he'd grabbed a can of polish, but it was lighter fluid. Everything's under control."

"Lord," Boedecker said. "I seem to attract every imbecile who sails onto this island. Is anybody hurt?"

"No, it was the cook who screamed. I told Buddy to stay out of the kitchen for a while."

"Maybe you should lock him in the basement."

Louis left assuring his brother-in-law/boss there would be no more interruptions.

"Can I get you another drink?"

"No, I'm fine. In fact, I think we should leave. I don't want to have anything to do with you. Searching my grandparents' house really pisses me off."

"Tit for tat. James stole the coin from our safe while we buried my father."

Dixon came back to the sofa with a wet cloth from the bar. "Here. Gin wouldn't leave a stain, but you don't want to smell like liquor. Sydney has a point, Cleve. What's in this for her?"

"Like I said before, find the coin and you'll find who killed James."

"That trail is almost twenty years old," Dixon said.

"Okay, I'll pay. Ten thousand dollars and your expenses. When that coin is added to my collection, it will be worth...well, let's just say, I won't miss the ten thou."

"If I find it, Sydney gets the ten thousand. My fee is fifty dollars a day whether I find the coin or not," Dixon said. "And, if I don't find the coin, you'll pay Sydney five thousand for her trouble."

"Agreed."

"Now," Dixon said. "Show us the collection."

CHAPTER TWENTY-TWO

Is that how you always operate?" I said as we drove away from the Boedecker house.

"Pull over. That side road up ahead."

I did as I was told, and when I cut the engine, Dixon pulled me to him. "This is how I operate, hon."

Although I didn't want to, I decided I'd better come up for air. "I'm not sure I understand. I'm not a fast learner like Buddy. You're going to have to explain it again."

With lesson two completed, we got down to business. "Do you believe that bunk Cleve tried to sell us?"

"Sounds like you don't."

"It's too far-fetched." I pulled out my compact and applied a fresh coat of lipstick. "I just happen to blow into town, and he's instantly inspired to search for the coin after all this time?"

"That part I don't believe. But the man does want the coin, and he's convinced you know where it is or can help him find it. He's probably right about finding James's murderer if we find the coin."

"Where do we begin this madcap hunt?"

"I have an idea."

"Let's hear it."

"You've got to face the music, hon."

I looked over and saw concern, and then humor, shadow his gorgeous face. "You're not serious?"

"The hunt begins with your dad. Besides, it's time I met the rest of the Lockhart family."

"You should quit while you're ahead."

I DROVE TO 305 PEE-IN-A-HAT AND COUNTED eight cars parked on both sides of the street. My parents' place looked like an evangelical tent revival on Easter Sunday. I recognized some of the cars: Frances, Marcella, Ruth, and Scott were here. The others most likely belonged to numerous people my mother had recruited to help with what was now mushrooming into a debacle. I found a place to park in the next block.

"Are you sure you want to go through with this? There's still time to back out."

Dixon put on his hat, cocked it, and grabbed my hand. "You're mother's going to love me."

"That's what I'm afraid of."

I pushed open the front gate. The noise spilling from the house was enough to warrant a disturbance-of-the-peace call from the neighbors. On second thought, the neighbors were probably inside contributing to the ruckus.

I opened the front door just a crack. Dixon gave me a slight shove, and there we were, standing in the living room of Mary Lou Lockhart, ex-almost-silent-film star, aspiring member of the new country club, the woman my father married one gin-soaked night a little over thirty years ago.

I was surprised to see that preparations for the party were still under way. That was probably at my dad's insistence. Being in jail would have given him a good excuse for not having to attend. There were four card tables set up in the middle of the living room, each surrounded by a bevy of women scribbling, sketching, cutting, pasting, and stamping out party paraphernalia in what appeared to be a well-organized assembly line. Scott was weaving pink and white crepe paper and wrapping it around four barber-type poles.

"I'll shape this wire over the pole and cover it with the crepe paper to form an arch," he said. "Then we can wrap this greenery over the top."

"I can't quite see it," Marcella said.

Scott screwed up his face. "Well, then, you'll just have to trust me."

"What are you going to use it for?" she asked.

"Mom and Dad will stand under it when they renew their vows."

"When we do what?" Dad yelled from the back bedroom.

"Shut up, George," Mom yelled back. "A man who just got sprung from the pokey has no right to complain about anything!"

"I don't see the logic," Dixon whispered.

"Don't bother looking. You'd stand a better chance of finding Boedecker's coin."

The phone rang from its cubbyhole in the hall. Mom ran over, yanked the receiver off the cradle, and listened for a fraction of a second. "No polka music! What do I look like, an eastern European peasant?" She slammed the receiver down.

"Aunt Mary Lou, the only other option," Ruth said, "is a string trio."

"What's wrong with that?" mother said. "I like strings."

"Except—" I heard Aunt Francie's angelic voice.

"Except what?" Mom screeched.

"Except the quartet is made up of three brothers."

"So? I don't care if they're Siamese triplets."

"They're ages seven, ten, and twelve. The ten-year-old has a sun allergy and must be in the shade at all times. But I hear they're prodigies."

"Well, look who's here! Sydney, I haven't seen you since you were this tall." Hattie Spencer must be in her eighties. She lives across the street and makes the best oatmeal cookies in the world. I should know—as a child, I'd eaten batches at a time. "And who is that handsome fellow you brought with you?"

The room went silent. All eyes left the party-favor making and found Dixon and me. Scott dropped his roll of crepe paper and knocked over a pole.

"Hello, Ralph," Marcella said.

"I know you," Aunt Francie chirped.

Ruth giggled.

Mother's head peeked out from the dining room, followed by her right shoulder, then the left, and finally, the complete Mary Lou Lockhart stood in front of us. She folded her arms and leaned against the doorframe. She was wearing a black hoop skirt and yellow blouse with a black and white polka dot scarf tied around her neck and black-and-white polka dot pumps. She looked at me, then Dixon, and then me again. Her eyes narrowed into slits, and she turned her glare on Ruth, Frances, Marcella, and then back to me. Her nostrils flared, her lips pursed.

Dad came up behind her and mouthed the word "run" to Dixon. Instead of heeding Dad's advice, Dixon placed his hand on the back of my waist. "Aren't you going to introduce me?" he said.

"Let me do the honor," Dad said. "Mary Lou, this is Ralph Dixon, Sydney's... friend. Ralph, this is my wife, Mary Lou."

"Am I the only one here who hasn't met this man?"

"I haven't, Mom," Scott said.

"Shut up, Scott," Mom said.

Dixon walked over and extended his hand. "Hello, Mrs. Lockhart, Sydney's told me so much about you."

"Well, she hasn't told me a single word about you."

"Shake the young man's hand, Mary Lou, otherwise he might think you're rude," Dad said.

As Mom reached out her hand, Dixon floored me. Instead of a handshake, he gently kissed her cheek.

Just when I thought things couldn't get worse, the back door slammed and Jeremiah waltzed in. "Hot damn! Who are you?" In his Panama hat, sunshades, flowered shirt, and yellow linen suit, he looked like a tropical dessert, a pineapple upside-down cake, maybe.

"You're supposed to be pet sitting," I cried.

"And miss all this fun? Don't worry. I brought the girls with me." And with that pronouncement, I heard nails clicking across the linoleum. Monroe flew into the room, caught sight of me, and grinned from one fuzzy ear to the other." Before I could yell "sit," she dashed under the card tables, toppling them and sending party favors flying. She leapt up, planted her pink-polished claws on my chest, and licked my face.

"Hey, everybody, my daughter's finally decided to show up and be useful!" Mom said right before slamming the bathroom door behind her.

"That went well," Dixon said.

DIXON, DAD, AND I STOOD UNDER THE PECAN TREE while the folks inside attempted to repair the damage. Monroe was sniffing every inch of the backyard, and Mealworm was sitting in the window of the back bedroom shooting daggers at me with her eyes.

"What did she say?" I asked Dad.

"She wants to cancel the entire thing again. At least, that's what I thought she said. It was hard to understand her blubbering through the door. I'd just managed to talk her into having the ceremony and party in the backyard after the country club canceled a second time."

"Because of your arrest?"

"Na, something about the plumber was behind installing the sinks. They did agree to cater, though."

"I can't believe Mom agreed to that."

"I told her since we weren't married—which we are, but I used her insane belief to my advantage—that we were living in sin and we'd better rectify the situation soon. Frances and Hattie are in there now. Everything will be back to normal chaos in no time. I'm surprised you two showed up. I expected you'd wait until the last minute."

"That was my idea," Dixon said.

"We've had an interesting morning, Dad."

"Sydney and I just came from a visit with Cleve Boedecker."

"I see," Dad said.

"We have a lot to talk about." I hugged him.

"I guess we do."

"You knew why PoPo was killed."

Dad pulled out a cigarette and lit up. "I wouldn't go that far. I was living in Houston at the time. Pop was always involved in one thing or another. But during that visit that summer, I knew something was wrong. Something was bothering him. Mom was worried. She asked me to come and talk to him. I should have left you in Houston and come alone. Had I done that, you wouldn't have found him in the foyer of the hotel, and you wouldn't be involved now."

"Start by telling me why this Roland guy was killed?"

"That I definitely don't know."

"Then why did you confess to his murder?"

"That's obvious—to buy a little time."

"Time for what?"

"Time to figure out what I was going to do."

"That was a pretty drastic move, Dad."

"After they found the body in your car, I was afraid they'd eventually arrest you. I didn't want you in jail again."

"How does Brewster Fallow figure in?" Dixon asked.

"How much do you know?"

"I've been talking to Cleve Boedecker. I'm sure you know him."

"Who in Galveston doesn't? Actually, Brewster contacted me," Dad said. "He wants to clear his name, start over. Claims he didn't kill that guy in Houston, Hardy. Claims he was set up."

"Does he know who did?" Dixon asked.

"No, but he aims to find out."

Dixon and I exchanged glances.

"What is it?" Dad said. "You know something."

"Maybe too much," Dixon said. "Fallow's dead."

"My God." Dad tossed his Lucky into the birdbath, and for a moment, the only sound was the sizzle when the water doused the ember.

Finally Dixon said, "There are two people dead, and I have a feeling that the closer we get to the truth, the uglier things will become. Sydney's been shot at, and whoever is at the trigger end of the gun isn't far behind."

The three of us looked up and down the street and laughed. With so many cars parked around my parents' house, following me would be impossible. Then Dad grew serious and gave me one of his "you-listen-to-me-young-lady" looks. "I think you should drop this entire thing, but since you won't," he turned to Dixon, "I'm glad you're here. It'll take both of us to keep her in one piece. What did Cleve Boedecker tell you?"

"Seems this started with Boedecker's father's greed." I answered for Dixon. "The man wanted a valuable coin owned by Hardy, and Hardy wouldn't part with it. But I'm sure you know that."

"Only bits and pieces, and I didn't know much until Fallow got hold of me."

"Boedecker thinks that PoPo had the coin, and Boedecker thinks I know where it is."

"That's insane," Dad said, then paused. "You don't, do you?"

"Dad!"

"I mean, your grandfather was always playing games—maybe he told you and you just don't realize it."

"You mean he gave me a hint? I've thought about that, but like I've said many times, he was dead when I found him."

"What does Boedecker plan to do now?" Dad asked.

"He hired me—us—to find the coin," Dixon answered.

"Think you can do it after all this time?"

"I think Boedecker knows more than he's telling," Dixon said. "I plan to nose around and see what I can turn up. How does it stand with the charges against you?"

"The police are idiots," Dad said. "They wouldn't have arrested me if they'd done a little checking first."

"You confessed." I reminded Dad.

"Yeah, I know." He smiled. "That must have been what confused them. I have an alibi that reaches all the way to Cuba."

I thought of Lattie the Lush and wondered if she was the alibi, but the smile on Dad's face was the usual benevolent father-type smile, not a lustful one. I wanted to ask him about his meeting at Washington's. We've always been able to talk, but now was not the time.

CHAPTER TWENTY-THREE

We left Dad to deal with Mom. I felt as if I'd thrown the poor guy to the lions, but he's used to that so I didn't feel guilty for long.

"Where do we begin?" I asked as Dixon drove down Seawall Boulevard.

"Find out who Roland was and why he was killed? This is the only piece that doesn't fit in this crazy puzzle. And find out who's shooting at you."

"I can think of two people who might know something about Roland."

"I'm listening."

"Chuck Conrad, the reporter at The Galveston Tribune. He may be able to put me on the right track."

"And the other?"

"That won't be easy—the mayor. Something about him seems odd. I can't put my finger on it. The man is a true politician from his charismatic smile down to his diamond-patterned socks. I'll go see Chuck; you can have a go at the mayor."

"I suggest we stay together. The next time a fog rolls in, which could happen any minute, the shooter could let loose another bullet."

"I keep forgetting that."

"Your dad's right. We need a company of guards to keep you alive. Let's go by the newspaper office and see if Conrad's there. Then I'll drop you off and go after the mayor. You stay put until I come back. Understand?"

"Got it."

CHUCK WAS PUTTING ON HIS JACKET as I walked into the newsroom. A cigarette dangled from his lips and a frown creased his forehead.

"Rough day?" I asked. I walked over to the window and waved at Dixon letting him know I was okay.

"Every day in this business is rough. If you haven't figured that out yet, you will. What's up?"

"I need information."

"It's yours if I have it. It's past time for my cocktail hour. You can buy me a drink and we'll talk."

"I'm supposed to stay put until my...friend comes to pick me up."

His cigarette slipped out of his mouth, and he looked at me as if he had me figured all wrong. I jumped in before a wisecrack slipped out as well. "I've been shot at twice. I've got to be careful."

Now the look of disappointment changed to dismay.

"Okay, let's go, but if I get shot, you'll have a posse of lunatics to answer to."

"My favorite bar's just down the street. Makes this old Galveston boy feel like he's just stepped into a souk in Marrakech."

"What do you like best about it?" I smiled. "The waitresses in harem pants or the Arab with the grass snake?"

"You get around."

THE AFTER-WORK CROWD WAS SPILLING INTO THE GOOD OL' Rubaiyat. Bing crooned from the jukebox. A woman who'd seen younger, kinder days, had her cheek pressed against the glass and her eyes closed as if her powers of wishful thinking could cause Bing to materialize. A couple stared in silent concentration over a pool game. A low-hanging bulb over the table pierced the blue haze of their cigarette smoke. Vying for attention, a single beam of sunlight, coming through a dirty window, illuminated unsettled dust that danced a slow waltz across the room.

Chuck and I sat at the bar.

"I fail to see the attraction of this place," I said.

"That's it—that's the attraction," Chuck said. "The fact that the place is seedy and at times downright scary. I'll have a bourbon and water."

I motioned to the bartender, who was entertaining a couple of women at the other end of the bar. My request for service was met with annoyance.

"A bourbon and water and a martini," I called.

"Out of olives," the bartender called back.

"Then I'll have it without."

He snorted and pulled two glasses from the shelf.

"Wipe them off, will you, Doug?" Chuck said.

Doug snorted again, but we had our drinks in somewhat clean glasses.

"Okay, what do you want to know?"

"Roland. Who was he? Why was he killed?"

"Did you ask your father?"

"Funny. He didn't kill Roland."

"Yeah, I know."

"You do?"

"I know your dad, not personally, but I know of him. He's not a murderer."

"Thanks. What about Roland?"

"From what I could gather, the man's from Houston. The police are tight-lipped on this one."

"Because of the Pelican Island Development?"

"Not sure. Probably because the mayor's demanding they keep a lid on this."

"I'm trying to find a connection between Roland and my grandfather."

"That's a long string."

"Yeah, but it's got to be there."

"All I know about Roland is what came across the wire for his obit. He was a developer who played a role in building some of the casinos in Las Vegas. He also had his hand in some Lake Tahoe businesses several years ago. His company has been around for several years. Graduated from Stanford with a degree in engineering, married Cindy Porter in '38, has two boys in high school. Took a break from the real world and served in WW II from '43 to '45. Board member of his Rotary Club. Has gotten away from the planning stage of development and moved into sales, where his talent lies. The mayor knew he'd have opposition on his hands with the project, and he wanted someone who could handle the heat at the conference, someone with charisma. Looks like he found what he wanted with Roland."

"Has Roland's company ever built anything in Galveston before?"

"Not that I know of. It would be easy to find out. Just call and ask."

"What's the name of his company?"

"Briscoe, Roland, and Cooper. The office is downtown on Medical Way." He pushed his jacket sleeve back and looked at his watch. "Whoa, gotta go. I've got an appointment before I rush to cover a story on the mainland. Lucy doesn't like it when I'm late."

The look on my face must have spoken surprise.

"Just because I'm old and crabby doesn't mean I can't get a girl."

I threw a couple of bucks on the bar. "I didn't say a word. I'm sure Lucy is lovely."

"She is. And hungry too. I promised her filet of tuna."

"You cook?"

"Lucy thinks I'm a gourmet. All I have to do is turn the screw on the can, and she start's purring."

"You don't look like the type who'd own a cat."

"I'm full of surprises. Let's go. I'll walk you back to the office before your friend gets worried."

WHEN WE REACHED THE NEWSPAPER BUILDING, Chuck gave me permission to dig around on his desk. Roland's company phone number was written on a notepad somewhere under his pile of rubble. Since the newspaper was closed, he used his key and let me in the back door.

"You can use my phone to call, but Roland's office is probably closed as well."

"I'll try anyway. Thanks for your help and give Lucy my best."

"Actually, I won't mention you. Whenever I drop a woman's name, the little vixen goes on a tear and shreds my drapes. She's the reason I'm single. At least, that's what I tell myself. Thanks for the drink, and good luck. Let me know tomorrow how you came out."

A newspaper office is never closed. The presses run well into the night. I could hear the rumble and clanging of the huge printing press. The smell of ink and paper filled the stairwell. I pushed open the door leading to the third floor. Even though it was just after five o'clock, the blinds were closed and the office was dark. I felt around for a light switch and came up empty-handed. After a few moments, my eyes adjusted and I made my way through the maze of desks to Chuck's. I snapped on his lamp and began to rummage through his papers. I needed to get Roland's phone number and get out to the front of the building before Dixon showed up. If I wasn't there to meet him, I knew he'd think the worst.

I found the notepad under a snowball paperweight. I shook the glass dome, and as the hula girl danced in swirling glitter, I wrote down the number in my notebook. Just as I turned off the lamp, the stairwell door clicked. I jerked around. No one was there. Not good. I slung my bag over my shoulder and ducked behind Chuck's chair. I listened. All was quiet, but I wasn't taking any chances. I felt around and grabbed the paperweight, then crawled around Chuck's desk and over to the next one. I paused. Still quiet. The door to the elevators was only a few feet away, but I didn't want to rush toward it only to find it was locked. Then I heard footsteps, soft footfalls, as if the person had slipped off his shoes. Surely, the guy had seen me before I snapped off the light. Since his intention was for me not to see him, I was sure he wasn't a florist following to present me with a bouquet of carnations.

I ran a lineup of possibilities through my mind: Louis, Buddy, Boedecker. No, it had to be someone else. Boedecker wanted me alive to find his coin. And the other two morons worked for him. It couldn't be the mayor unless Dixon mentioned that I was at the newspaper office. I decided to play his cat-and-mouse game, as if I had any other options. Someone stumbled into a trash can and swore under his breath. I ducked and crawled among the desks. The floor creaked. I paused. Heard nothing and continued. When I neared the door, I pitched the paperweight across the room and then ran.

Taking the stairs several at a time I could feel the briny taste of freedom that awaited me on the other side, but when I pushed the door leading to the alley, it didn't budge—locked! The door of the third-floor stairwell above banged shut. There were fewer than forty steps between me and doom—thirty-nine, to be exact. If I'd planned to stay in this business, I needed to keep a supply of guns around. My pursuer crept down one flight and paused. I heard a rattle. It sounded like he'd tried the second-floor door, and then I looked up just in time to see an arm pointed down at me. The guy wore a black glove and in his hand was a gun. I dove under the stairwell as a shot rang out, spraying plaster down from above. Then the oddest thoughts ran through my mind. The anniversary party would have to be canceled again, this time on my account. My funeral would take place instead. Who would care for Mealworm and Monroe? Probably Jeremiah. Surely he wouldn't allow Scott to dump them at the pound. I should have made out a will with provisions for my pets. How would Dixon react to my death? One week of mourning for every week we'd known one another? That seemed fair.

The shooter crept down to the last flight of stairs. In a few seconds, he'll realize he'd missed his target, and then Sydney Jean Lockhart would no longer grace this planet. I considered whether anything in my bag could be used as a weapon: hairbrush, lipstick, wallet (which didn't contain enough money to buy my way out of this one), notebook, fountain pen, and address book. I grabbed the only item with weapon potential and lay down, exposing my legs in the manner of a dead woman. Surprise was on my side. I felt a teeny bit better.

The guy had replaced his shoes for which I was thankful. I counted his steps. At twenty-three I rose up, and feeling like an idiot, readied my fountain pen. Twenty-four, twenty-five, twenty-six. Pause. He was now on the first-floor landing. He rushed down and stopped again, studying what he could see of my prone body, no doubt. I saw the gun before the rest of him. The brain has a remarkable capability to stuff dozens of thoughts and actions into a split second. When the masked figure edged over the rail and showed himself with me expecting to see the face of the guy who wanted me dead, and him expecting to see blood oozing from my chest, the fright that took us both was enough to trigger what happened next. The pen stabbed and the pistol shot at the same time. His aim was high, blowing a hole in the plaster several inches above my head. Mine was low, spreading a dark stain across his crotch. I threw the fountain pen at his stocking-covered face and caught his shin with the toe of my shoe. I lunged for his legs. More shots rang out. He pitched forward but managed to grab the stair rail and fling a kick of his own at my face. I ducked, and he caught me on the shoulder and ran back up the stairs, leaving droplets of blood in his wake.

"Sydney!"

"I'm here! Stop shooting!"

The door flew open, wood splinters and doorknob remains scattering.

"He's getting away—up the stairs!"

Dixon glanced over every inch of my body and then ran after him. "Stay put!"

I followed.

The blood trail led us to the second floor. Dixon crouched down and reached for the doorknob. I squatted behind him.

"You hit him," I whispered.

"Not enough to stop him. See who he was?"

"Don't know. He wore a stocking over his face."

"I'm going to open the door. Stay low. He's had time to reload. I told you to stay put. You never learn, do you?"

"Neither do you. Now quit yapping, and let's go after him before he gets away."

Dixon pushed open the door. Instead of shots, we heard furniture crashing. The guy had chosen to run rather than fight. We dashed after him. The door to the lobby slammed shut. Sirens sounded and quickly grew louder. Once in the lobby, we followed his trail through a maze of hallways to the other side of the building and into another stairwell. We saw him at the door. He turned and fired. We dove back down the hall, and as soon as the door shut, we followed. Back down the stairs to the first floor, and it was clear where we were heading. The presses were running and seemed to be keeping pace with my beating heart.

Dixon threw open the door. It was like entering the entrails of some giant creature whose stomach was digesting its last meal of rocks. The deafening noise brought back memories of a harrowing night in Hot Springs not too long ago. It was the sound of a locomotive clacking over the tracks as the engine bore down upon me, my foot caught in the railroad ties because of the red spiked shoe I'd slipped on my foot moments before the cops raided the casino.

Dixon grabbed my hand, and we weaved and darted through the machinery. The few guys manning the presses were so intent on their work that we went unnoticed; so had the man we were chasing. He glanced over his shoulder, caught sight of us, and fired again. When he turned, he ran smack into a press, dropping his gun, which he didn't bother retrieving. He headed for the back door when one of the press guys noticed him and called out, "Hey, buddy!" A lot of good that did—moving lips with no sound. The press guy reached up and pulled a cord and several red bulbs lit up throughout the room, alerting the rest of the crew. Everyone looked around for the trouble. All eyes landed on us. The guys shouted and waved for us to stand still, to stay where we were. Dixon ignored them, and since he still had hold of my hand, so did I. We headed for the door and were about to follow our prey when a mountain of a man wearing a black apron and visor stepped in front and blocked our way. The guy slapped Dixon's gun from his hand. It flew over my head and discharged. Everyone froze.

The back door flew open, and in came a flurry of cops. Dixon stuck his hands in his pockets and shook his head in dismay.

CHAPTER TWENTY-FOUR

I should escort you two to the edge of town and point you to the bridge." Fidalgo's voice sounded sweet, but he looked as if rigor mortis had recently set his facial muscles and frozen his jaw, so I figured he wasn't too happy.

"Did you find the guy's gun?" Dixon asked.

"Yep. We'll check for prints."

"You won't find any. He was wearing gloves," I said.

"And a stocking over his face," Fidalgo echoed my words of a few moments ago.

"That's right," I said. "He was an amateur."

Both Dixon and Fidalgo turned and stared.

"He was a terrible shot. He stood a few feet in front of me and missed twice."

"Any idea who it was?" Fidalgo asked.

Dixon and I exchanged glances. I had yet to tell Fidalgo about my contact with Boedecker and the fact that he had Louis follow me on the night that Ruth and I had a run-in with the pig. Dixon and I somehow agreed telepathically that now was not the right time. I also had a feeling Fidalgo wouldn't have been surprised if I told him my suspicions.

Knowing he wouldn't get any more information, he said, "I'll check the hospital."

"He won't risk being found out," Dixon said. "I don't think he was hurt that bad. In fact, my shot didn't slow him down." Dixon rose to leave. "Speaking of guns, did you find mine?"

"Give the detective his gun," Fidalgo told one of his officers. "My advice is to leave this thing alone, or next time, you two won't be so lucky. Let us do our job." On his way out, he turned to Dixon. "Since, you're here, try to keep her out of trouble."

"In case you haven't realized it, my girlfriend has a mind of her own. A damn good one too."

"WHEN DID I BECOME YOU GIRLFRIEND?" I asked as we stood across the street from the police station.

"When we were standing over the body of Ellison James sprawled in your bathtub at The Arlington Hotel." Dixon inhaled and passed me his cigarette.

"We hadn't yet been introduced."

"That sort of experience needs no introduction."

"As far as you knew, I could have been married and the dead guy could have been my husband."

"You weren't wearing a ring, and neither was he."

"Boyfriend and girlfriend then?"

"You were too classy for the likes of him."

"And you could tell that even though he was not wearing any clothes?"

"It was his hair. You wouldn't date a guy with a pompadour."

"True."

"I thought I told you to stay put."

"Which time?"

"At the newspaper office with Conrad."

"We went around the corner to the Rubaiyat. His idea."

"I can't trust you."

"You can when it counts."

"When's that?"

"Now." I slid my arms around his neck and hushed whatever sarcastic remark was about to slide from his lips.

We finished the cigarette in silence and walked to my car.

"What did you find out from the mayor?"

"The guy's slick, like you said. He talked a blue streak and didn't say a damn thing. When I pressed him, he reminded me that I had no authority here. He said that with a pleasant grin on his face, and then told me he was late for an appointment and ushered me out of his office."

"That's his standard excuse. Was the gun the same one that was used to shoot at me on the peer?"

"A .38. Whether it was the same .38, I don't know. Did you learn anything from Conrad?"

"Nothing helpful. Just what he'd read in the obit. I've a feeling the mayor and Roland go way back, though, or at least have some sort of connection. The mayor needed Roland to push this project through. Roland had the reputation for being able to make things happen, and the mayor knew he'd meet with opposition. I think we can remove the mayor as a suspect. Unless something went wrong."

"Something went wrong all right. Roland is dead, and you came close to following in his footsteps. Let's go to my motel room."

"Mine is much nicer."

"Yeah, but I have a present for you in my suitcase."

"YOU REALLY EXPECT ME TO WEAR THIS?"

"I do. I should have outfitted you with one of these a long time ago. Keeping a pistol in your purse hasn't worked too well."

"The only reason I lost my gun was because Ruth swerved to keep from hitting that pig."

"Pig notwithstanding, this will at least keep you from having to dig in your purse to find the gun. Here, let me show you how to put it on."

"That's a great line, Dixon. I think I can figure it out. It looks like yours."

"It's a little different. It's made for a woman. I ordered it from the department."

I slipped my arm through the opening, wrapped the belt around my chest, and fastened the buckle.

"It's a little loose. I'll tighten it." Dixon took his time adjusting the strap in back. "How does that feel?"

"Awkward. And heavy."

"You'll get used to it. Wear a sweater or jacket and you'll be well covered." Dixon slid my new .22 into the holster and adjusted the straps again. "It should be snug, but not too tight."

"I feel like Annie Oakley."

"You look like a million bucks. If I weren't so hungry, I'd suggest we play a game of cops and robbers. But I've been in town for two days and I have yet to pass one shrimp down my throat. Any ideas where to go?"

"I do. Only one place. Gaidos. It's been around for more than forty years. It's got a reputation for fantastic shrimp. Trust me."

"Oh, I do."

GAIDO IS AN OLD GALVESTON FAMILY that got started in the restaurant business when tourists began flocking to the coast once the island recovered after the Big Storm. They built their restaurant on the seawall, named it after themselves, and are first in line when the shrimp boats dock in the harbor. In case you're not sure where you are, huge windows overlook the gulf. The aroma wafting through the dining room lets you know that the chef knows what he's doing.

We were lucky and were given a table in the corner. We started off with a plate of boiled shrimp and two martinis. The pinkish red crustaceans looked too good to eat, lying on their bed of crushed ice, snuggled in little lettuce leaves. I peeled one, dipped its headless body into the spicy cocktail sauce, and slipped it into my "boyfriend's" mouth. "What do you think?"

"Nice."

"Rumor has it that shrimp consider it an honor to give up their lives to become part of Gaidos' shrimp cocktail."

The waiter came by and we ordered two plates of shrimp scampi and a bottle of white wine. When he left, I asked, "What next?"

"We need to dig deeper into Roland's background. And the only way to do that is to visit his office in Houston. I'm leaving in the morning. I'm tempted to take you with me just to keep you from getting shot."

"Is that the only reason?"

"Peel me another shrimp, and I'll see if I can think of something better."

An hour later, we pushed our plates aside and toasted with a final glass of wine. The sun was setting as only it can do on the

Texas coast, painting the horizon with colors you won't ever find in a box of Crayons. A piano player and lounge singer began their evening entertainment, and a few couples sauntered out to the dance floor. Out of the corner of my right eye, I saw a flash of light. As if trying like hell to follow a spectacular sunset show, the storm brewing out in the gulf provided us with its own version of entertainment as streak lightning danced across the sky.

"Want to dance?" Dixon asked.

"Have we ever?"

"This is a good time to start."

"Dancing could lead to other things. And you have to get an early start in the morning."

"You're right. How about dessert and coffee?"

"That I can handle."

Dixon motioned to the waiter, and soon we were presented with two slices of banana cream pie, coffee, and brandy.

When the waiter left, Dixon asked, "What's on your mind? You've been drifting in and out all evening."

"It's Dad."

"You worry about him too much. He can handle things. The charges will probably be dropped tomorrow. He might find himself in trouble for the bogus confession."

"There's something else."

"You've got my attention."

I told Dixon about seeing Dad and the Lush holding hands at the restaurant.

"I just met the guy, but that doesn't sound like your father. Are you sure you saw what you thought you saw?"

"Actually, I didn't see him. Ruth did."

"Well, there you go."

"She's flaky, but not about this. I'm going to come right out and ask him tomorrow."

"I wouldn't, not yet. Give things a chance to work themselves out."

"How did you get so smart?"

"I keep alert."

I got a surge of energy halfway through my dessert and coffee. I looked at my watch. "I have an idea."

"Change your mind about dancing?"

"No, I'm going out. It's not that late."

"Hey, I thought I was doing okay."

I place my hand under his chin and confirmed his thought. "You're terrific. I'm going barhopping."

"Wait just one minute."

"I know one person who might be able to give me some answers."

"Can't it wait until tomorrow?"

"I figure this person is easier to find after the sun goes down, and is much more talkative in the evening. I may even be able to kill two birds with one stone."

"The Lush?"

"The Lush."

"I'm going with you."

WE WERE PARKED ACROSS THE STREET from the Rubaiyat. We'd just left the Balinese Room. The Lush wasn't there. And unless she was with my dad, this is the most likely place.

"Wait in the car," I told Dixon. "I'll be okay. I need to do this by myself."

"She doesn't know who I am."

"Are you kidding? Since Mom met you this afternoon, the entire town knows who you are. You'll be close by. What could happen?"

"You mean besides getting shot, stabbed, poisoned, or kidnapped?"

"If she's in there, I'll come out and wave. Besides, I have my gun."

Dixon buttoned my jacket and nuzzled my neck. "And later, I'll help you remove it. And then we'll dance."

"And then we'll dance."

CHAPTER TWENTY-FIVE

It took me just two minutes before I spotted Lattie at a table with a group of people. True to my word, I went back outside and waved to Dixon once again. He was leaning on my car, fedora tilted, feet crossed at the ankles, looking too good to be true. I went back in and ordered tonic water with lime. Lattie's table was near the ladies' room. I took my drink and moseyed by, pretending not to see her. I don't exactly blend in with my height and long red hair, and sure enough, I'd just passed her table when I heard, "Sydney, Sydney, what are you doing here, girl?"

I turned and feigned surprise. I placed my hand over my eyes to get a better look at who was calling me.

"Sydney, darling. It's me. Lattie Lavelle. What are you doing here?" she asked again.

"I'm with some friends." I pointed to the other side of nowhere.

"Well, I should hope so. This is no place for a single woman alone," then quickly added, "I'm here with friends too. Sit down and I'll introduce you."

"Oh, I don't want to intrude."

"Don't be silly. We're all one big family here on the island."

Whose family? I wanted to ask.

"What are you drinking?"

I held up my glass. "I just got a drink. I'm fine."

She reached up and pulled the sleeve of my jacket. I jerked back a bit. Still self-conscious about wearing the gun and holster, I needed to be careful. "Sorry," I said. "I almost tripped. It's packed in here."

"It's like this every Friday night. Nelson, get up and find the lady a chair. You've got the manners of a warthog."

Nelson quickly did as he was told, and I had a seat between Lattie and a guy who was comatose. His chin rested on his chest and a trickle of drool seeped from the corner of his mouth. His eyes were open.

"Sydney, this is Marge." Lattie pointed to a lady who must have been pushing eighty. The only thing that kept her face from falling into her lap was the pancake makeup that had cemented in place her wrinkles and sags. "And this is her husband, Beanie." Beanie had either taken better care of himself, or was about thirty years Marge's junior. He wore a signet ring with a diamond the size of a prune. More diamonds studded his wristwatch, which lost their luster when I noticed the dirt under his nails. If I had to guess, Marge was the financial backer of Beanie's jewelry. Even in her advancing age, the way she held herself spoke of Old World class.

"Nelson and I went to school together, didn't we, Nelly?" Lattie blew him a kiss.

"Class of 190—"

Lattie's elbow met with Nelly's solar plexus, momentarily knocking the breath out of him. "Oh, Sydney's not interested in old history," Lattie interrupted. "And this guy," she pointed to the drooler, "is Roger Hawthorne III. We just call him Thorny. He's from England and has a title."

I turned and gave Thorny another once-over, looking for the slightest sign of royalty. His suit was expensive but had seen better days. He had a frayed, red satin hanky peeking out of his jacket pocket. I stared at his chest for a moment. Not seeing it rise, I asked, "Is he okay?"

"As right as rain," Nelly said in a poor imitation of an English accent. Then he slapped Thorny on the back.

"What? Huh? What, I say?" Thorny sputtered to life. "Had a bit of a wink-wink, did I?" He looked around and wiped the drool from his chin. "Stand one on me." He raised his hand to the bartender and then noticed me. "And who might you be, madam?"

"This is the daughter of my close friend. Her name is Sydney."

"Looks like me own granddaughter back in Sudbury." Then he snorted once and his head fell back into position, eyes open. I turned away before the drooling began.

Nelly shoved his way to the bar to pick up the round of drinks Thorny had ordered. Beanie attempted to get Marge out of her chair for a spin on the dance floor.

"How's your poor father?" Lattie said. "The Galveston police are such nincompoops. Your father wouldn't hurt a fly."

Since the Lush had brought up the subject, I dove right in. My lip quivered, my eyes squinted shut. I pulled out a tissue and pretended to bawl. "I...I can't believe this is hap—hap—happening. I don't know who to turn to."

"Dear, dear," Lattie scooted closer to me and threw her arm around my shoulder. The smell of bourbon was strong enough to pickle my eyes. "You can talk to Lattie, now."

"I'm being such a fool. I know things will work out. It's just that, Dad and I have always been able to talk, and now, he's like a different man. I'm so worried. I've been with him all day trying to get him to talk to me and finally I just gave up." I picked up my fake cocktail. "And this won't help."

"A little bird told me that things will clear up in a day or two."

I wondered if that little bird smoked Luckies and wore a fishing cap covered with lures.

"I sure hope so. After all, he can prove that he was with others at the time Roland was killed. But what worries me is why he confessed in the first place. He said he was protecting me, but I have an alibi too. No"—I drew in a deep breath and squared my shoulders—"there's something else. I just know it! But I shouldn't be telling you all this."

Nelly sat everyone's drinks on the table and picked up my hand. "I can cut a pretty fine rug, young lady. Care to find out?"

"Oh, good Lord, Nelly, can't you see the girl is upset? Run along now and try your luck with one of those dames at the bar."

Nelly let go of my hand, grabbed Thorny under the arm, and pulled him to his feet.

"Wha? Wha?" He raised he hand. "Stand a round—"

"No, no, Hawthorne, you just did that. We're going to charm the ladies at bar." The accent was back. "Tally ho, and God save the Queen, and all that rot." The two old codgers stumbled away, and Lattie said, "Now we can talk, darling." She took a tall swig of her drink. "Your dad's been troubled lately."

"I know. This murder and the anniversary mess, and just last month I was in jail. Oh, I'm such a burden to him."

"You are not! He is so proud of you, Sydney Jean Lockhart. He can't speak your name without smiling ear to ear." She hiccupped and another wave of bourbon-scented breath stung my eyes. She swigged again, draining her glass. The next one was ready and waiting thanks to Thorny standing another round. "I happen to know"—she put her finger to her temple—"the little bird again, that the trouble started a while back."

"Are you talking about Brewster Fallow?" If she was surprised at my knowing this, she didn't show it. She plunged right ahead.

"Brewster Fallow, that snake. They should have kept him in jail."

"You knew him?"

"I've been around Galveston a long time, darling."

"You must remember when my grandfather was murdered."

"Tragedy, real tragedy. They never found who did it."

"I have a feeling Fallow knew, and that's why Dad was spending time with him."

"I shouldn't say this, but Brewster Fallow got what he deserved."

"You think he killed my grandfather?"

"I've said too much."

I covered my eyes and began blubbering.

"Oh, dear, dear, please don't do that. It's just best to let sleeping dogs lie."

"I can't. I just can't"

"Listen, honey, back a long time ago, Galveston was a rough place. The town was run by a gaggle of gangsters, and anyone who crossed them seemed to disappear."

"My grandfather, he was one of those who disappeared?"

"I'm afraid so."

"Things don't seem much better today if you ask me. I've been here less than a week and two men have been killed. I know all of this is connected and I plan to find out how. I just don't know where to go to information."

The alcohol was taking its toll on Lattie. Her eyes seemed to move in opposite directions.

I had decided it was time to leave when Lattie whispered, "The hotel."

"What?" I asked.

"The hotel."

"The Galvez?"

"Be careful."

She leaned forward, and I plucked her glass out of the way but wasn't quick enough to keep her face from falling onto the table. I placed her sweater under her head as a pillow and hurried out before the rest of the party returned.

MY DETECTIVE WAS PACING UP AND DOWN the street, looking anxious. I rushed over.

"I was seconds away from coming in after you. Any luck?"

"Maybe. I think I know who was leaving me the threatening phone messages when I first arrived at the Galvez. Come on before anyone sees us."

I told Dixon about the conversation with Lattie and how she warned me again about the goings on at the Galvez. "That's where we need to look. That's where PoPo worked; that's where he was killed; Maurice Roland's body was dumped across the street at the church. It might be a good idea if you checked in."

"And leave Mrs. Swainy and the free coffee?"

"I'll make it up to you."

"Deal. If it was Lattie who made those calls, then she knew you were coming to Galveston. And she would have only found out from your Dad. So, he must have known. Who could have spilled the beans?"

"Are you kidding? Scott knew, Ruth knew, and Jeremiah also. No, I trust him. Actually, I don't think it was my family. Scott is too wrapped up in his own life to tattle on me. Ruth would have told me by now."

"You could have been spotted driving around, a tall, beautiful redhead, cruising in a red convertible."

"I had the top up. No, it was not happenstance. The first call came in just minutes after I walked into the hotel. Lattie knew I was coming and that I was staying at the Galvez."

"Someone from the hotel. You had reservations."

"But who does Dad know at the hotel?"

"I don't know if I want you staying there."

"Ruth will be with me."

"That's supposed to put me at ease? The lovely girl can't drive two blocks down the road without getting kidnapped."

"I'll keep her with me, and we'll be careful."

"Arrange for a room for me. I'll check out of the motel in the morning before I leave for Houston. I should be back tomorrow afternoon. It's late. Drop me off and we'll take a rain check on the dance. Unless—"

"A rain check is fine. Remember, we're in Mary Lou Lockhart's territory. If my car was to be seen at your motel, it would be all over town by noon."

WHEN I GOT BACK TO MY ROOM, I was surprised to find Ruth neatly tucked in and snoring just like I left her this morning. I pulled the phone toward the bathroom and put a call through to Dixon's room at the Sea Side Motel to let him know I'd arrived safely.

"I'm here, safe and sound. Ruth is here too, so don't worry. I'm about to get into bed."

Dixon started laughing.

"That's funny?"

"I just thought about Grady."

"Grady Broussard? The Arlington Hotel's detective?"

"Yeah, I remember him telling me about your tattered and charred PJs after your night at the Highway 27 Fish Camp."

"I almost blew myself up. I had no idea how powerful that moonshine was when I threw it into the stove."

"You should have kept those PJs as a souvenir. At least let

me see them. Seems like everyone else got a glimpse."

"They were nothing special."

"That's not what I heard?"

"Typical pink-and-white-striped man-style PJs. Trust me, you didn't miss anything. See you tomorrow night."

The receiver hadn't even reached the cradle when Ruth popped up. "He asked what kind of PJs you wear? Syd, don't let this guy get away."

"You're great at faking those snores."

"Aren't I though? Where have you been? It's late."

"Just so I can eliminate you as a suspect, did you tell Dad I was coming to Galveston?"

"Moi?"

"Oui. Answer the question."

"No, Miss Bossy. Not until you were arrested and I went to get him."

"I wasn't arrested. I was in for questioning." I walked over and sat down on the bed. "Ruth, think, how did Dad respond when you told him I was here? I mean, despite the fact that I was at the police station."

She sat up in bed, fluffed her pillows, and leaned back. "He just sat there and—what's the word—pondered, like he always does. One never really knows what he is thinking."

"I think he knew I was coming. The Lush knew I was coming too."

"That hussy!"

"I spoke with her tonight."

Ruth said in a whisper, "Did you ask her about seducing your father?"

"Who said she seduced him? You said they were just holding hands."

"Just holding hands? Well, one thing usually leads to another."

"Shut up and listen. She was sloshed and I took advantage of her condition. I told her I was trying to help my father and was getting nowhere with information. It was clear she knew something. She warned me about this hotel, and I'm certain she was the one who left those threatening phone calls right after I arrived. Before I could get anything else out of her, she passed out."

"Gee, your father is really mixed up in this, isn't he?"

"Afraid so. Dixon's going to Houston in the morning to find out more about the dead man Roland. I plan to nose around the hotel, and I'll probably need your help."

"Fun. Oh, I promised Aunt Mary Lou I'd be at the house early to help."

"What's left to be done?"

"Last-minute things. Well, actually almost everything because of the changes she made."

"I don't want to hear it. Tell Mom you got a relapse of that virus."

"There's something else."

"Spit it out."

"You should probably know that Jeremiah brought your pathetic poodle and that crazy cat to the hotel."

"Oh, no. They have a no-pet policy."

"Jeremiah snuck them in. He wanted to leave them at your parents' house, but your Mom wouldn't hear of it after Monroe plowed through the living room. But he said not to worry, he'd keep them hidden."

"How do you hide a white standard poodle with pink nails and a loud, cranky cat? I'll be so glad when this anniversary debacle is over. Come on, get up and get dressed."

"We're going to the bar?"

"You wish. We're going to see a lady about a hurricane."

I had almost forgotten about Asherah's rendezvous with her goddesses at midnight. The Lady Who Walks by the Sea's boathouse was easy to find. There were a handful of floating homes docked at Pier 41. Most were dark except for a dim light here and there. The one on the end rocked listlessly under a purple glow. I parked across the street, and Ruth and I watched as the women begin to arrive. Asherah was busy placing candles along the deck railing. Whispers mixed with the creak of their steps as they crept along on the dock. All nine women were dressed in purple robes, and each carried what looked like a football.

"This is probably a big waste of time, but my curiosity got the best of me."

"It's too mysterious for me, Syd. No telling what these women are up to. Voodoo, black magic, human sacrifices. It gives me the willies. Let's get out of here."

"Soon. There's no harm in sitting here and watching for a while."

Once all the goddesses had gathered on Asherah's boat, they formed a circle around her and held hands. Then Asherah handed each one a candle and led them in what sounded like a chant or prayer. One by one, with candle in hand and the object in the other, they carefully climbed from the boathouse into a motorboat with Asherah at the helm. Under a half moon, they puttered out toward Pelican Island.

"I'd love to see what they're going to do. Come on, let's go."

"Go! Are you mad?"

"Probably."

I drove down Harbor Side Drive to the bridge construction site where just a few days ago someone had slashed my whitewalls. I parked next to a bulldozer and cut the engine.

"They should be coming around the bend shortly."

The storm clouds that had gathered earlier passed, carrying their fury elsewhere. In their wake, a light mist began to fall, covering the windshield with droplets that obscured our vision.

"I'm going to step out and to get a better look."

"Well, I'm not."

"Fine, wait here. Lock the doors."

I grabbed my flashlight from the glove box, turned up the collar of my jacket, put on my fedora, and made my way toward the water. Soon the lights of Asherah's motorboat shone across the channel. They tied up to the boat ramp and climbed out onto the island. The nine women followed Asherah in single file to the top of sand dune.

"What are they doing?"

I almost jumped out of my skin. "Ruth! Damn! Don't sneak up on me."

"Look! A fire! I told you—they're into human sacrifices."

"Looks more like a campfire to me."

We watched as they stood around the flame and raised their arms into the air. A soft murmur of voices slowly crescendoed into an increasing urgency that seemed to mix with the wind and carry across the water. Then, one by one, they tossed their objects into the fire—thud, thud, thud. Although, it was dark, I had a pretty good idea what the object was. When the ceremony was over, they lined up behind their leader, and marched back to the boat.

"Party's over, but one mystery is solved."

"It is?"

"I don't think we have to worry about hurricanes this season, Oya has just received an appeasement of ten roasted eggplants." I told Ruth about the campfire remains I'd seen on my trip to the island.

Less than an hour later, we were back in our room. "This day has felt like a month," I said. "I'm beat. Wake me by seven."

CHAPTER TWENTY-SIX

At three o'clock, I was jolted out of bed by someone calling my name and pounding on the door. At first, because of the sucking sound that accompanied the noise, I thought it was a housekeeper with her vacuum cleaner.

"Answer the door, will you?" Ruth huffed.

"Sydney! Sydney! Open this door right now!"

Sniff, sniff, snort, sniff.

"I don't know if you're ready for this," I said to Ruth. I threw on my robe and then threw open the door. Monroe, happy as a six-month-old puppy who believes the world is her amusement park and all people her caretakers, bounded in, jumped up, and licked my face. She bounced on my bed and then flew onto Ruth's. My dog straddled my cousin, pinning her down and showering her with poodle kisses.

"I told him he was making a mountain out of molehill." Jeremiah was dressed in his usual white robe with pink roses. Although he has a tendency toward, shall I say, a colorful, delicate style of dress, his body is more suited to lumberjack attire. His dark hairy legs, sticking out below fluffy terrycloth, looked as out of place as a scoop of vanilla ice cream atop a sirloin steak.

Scott dove for my bed and pulled the covers over his head. All I heard from underneath the sheets was, "—no sleep—damn music—damn cat—slit my throat—what did I ever do to deserve this—go home—drown myself."

"Bad night?" I asked.

Jeremiah came in and shut the door.

"Get—this—dog—off—me!" Ruth cried. "She put her tongue in my mouth!"

I looked at Jeremiah.

"I'll take the cry baby in your bed. You take the woman and dog," he said.

"You got the worse deal," I said. I pulled Monroe by the collar and managed to calm her. Ruth ran into the bathroom and turned on the shower. Jeremiah sat down on my bed next to Scott. "There, there now. It's all better." He patted Scott on the shoulder. "He's so sensitive," Jeremiah said to me. "Music was blaring from the bar across the street, and the family next door got a wee bit loud."

"Wee bit!" Scott flung off the sheet and sat up. "Wee bit! Mommy and Daddy have been fighting since ten. The kiddies woke up and joined in. What could one family have so much to fight over?"

"I can't believe you asked that question. Did you call and complain?"

"We're harboring two illegals. Remember?" he shouted. "I wanted to call the front desk, but Jeremiah wouldn't let me." Scott disappeared under the sheet again.

Ruth came out of the bathroom—a toothbrush surrounded by a mound of white foam was where her mouth used to be.

"I wouldn't worry, Ruth," Jeremiah said, "a dog's mouth is cleaner than a human's."

Ruth turned around and stormed back into the bathroom.

"I didn't know it was possible to scream with a mouthful of toothpaste," Jeremiah said.

"She's a woman of many talents. Listen, we can't all stay in this room. I'll call and see if I can get another one."

"The hotel is full. I heard the Humphrey Bogart desk clerk telling someone earlier."

"And that's another thing!" Scott popped out. "You've been hanging around the front desk ever since we checked in. Don't think I haven't noticed!"

Jeremiah cross his legs and lit a cigarette. "All I do is look, dear boy. You can't blame a man for that."

"Yes, I can!" Scott was up and in march mode. "Lord knows what goes on when I'm at work! You lounge around all day in that robe, smoking cigarettes and drinking white wine."

"I do the sheets and the cooking. You love my spaghetti carbonara."

"Sometimes I call the house and you're not even there!"

"Lower your voice." Jeremiah whispered.

I've never seen Jeremiah anything but calm and self-composed, which, during an argument, sends Scott into angry overdrive. My brother kicked the trash can, sending it flying. Monroe yelped and jumped into Jeremiah's lap, landing on the lit end of his cigarette. She let out a howl that would raise the Baskerville hound from the fen. Luckily, a small flame on poodle hair singes quickly and doesn't spread.

"Oh, you poor pup—"

Someone banged on the door and things went silent. Jeremiah held his finger to his lips. Ruth, sans foam, peaked out from the bathroom. Scott grabbed the sheet and held it in front of him. Monroe sniffed the door.

"Security. Is everything okay?"

"It's the house detective," Jeremiah whispered.

"Is there a dog in there?"

I grabbed my poodle and dragged her from the door and into the bathroom. "Keep her quiet," I told Ruth. I shoved them both in the bathroom and closed the door.

"Let me handle this," Jeremiah said. He answered the door a crack. "Hello. Sorry, we were playing Monopoly. My friend here just landed on Park Place, which I own, and have three hotels on that property."

"Isn't this Miss Lockhart's room?"

I went to the door. "Hi," I said. "This is my brother and his friend. We'll keep it down. Most of us are about to go bankrupt anyway. Jeremiah always wins. I don't know why we bother playing with him."

"Chickens," Jeremiah said.

The house detective took in Jeremiah's robe from bottom to top. Then craned his neck to see into the room. "If I have to come back up here, you guys will be on the street."

"You can't do that," Scott said. He was standing behind Jeremiah. "What about the fighting family in room 213? Did you threaten to throw them out?" Jeremiah turned and placed his hand over Scott's mouth.

"I understand," I told the detective, and closed the door. "Okay, here's what we're going to do. In a few minutes, I'll will go back to your room and see if all is quiet. Then, we'll sneak Monroe back."

"I think the dog should stay here with you," Scott said.

"I have work to do."

"What work? Mom and Dad's party is tomorrow night, and you haven't done a damn thing to help!"

"What more is there to do? If things continue to fall apart, Dad will get his wish and the party will consist of hot dogs and beer." Before he could argue, I slipped out. This was my fault for getting them a room on the west side of the hotel. Sometimes my ideas bite me in the ass. This was one of those times. I put my ear to the loud family's door. All was quiet. I seriously doubted that I'd get any sleep tonight. On my way back to the room, I heard a door down the hall click. Nosy people. Doesn't anyone sleep anymore?

I laughed to myself. I had to give Jeremiah credit. That Monopoly story was perfect. I'd have to remember that one."

"Psst."

I turned back and saw that the linen closet door was open a crack.

"Psst." Then a hand came out and waved me over. I've done many stupid things in my life, but answering that summons was not going to be one of them. I was ready to bolt when I heard my name.

"Miss Lockhart. It's me, Blanche." Her head was now visible.

"Blanche? What's going on?"

"I'm working the night shift."

"Night shift? What's there for a housemaid to do at three in the morning?"

"Okay, I needed to talk to you. I was about to knock on your door, but it sounded like you were having a party. Then I heard the elevator ding and saw the hotel detective headed down the hall, so I ducked in here until the coast was clear."

"Has something happened?" I walked over.

"I think you should know that the conference was canceled." She pulled me by the arm into the closet and closed the door.

"I know that, Blanche. Everyone knows that."

"No, I mean it was canceled before that guy was found in the trunk of your car."

"How do you know?"

"I overheard Mr. Cahill. He was talking on the phone. I don't know to who."

"What exactly did he say, and when?"

"It was the morning that guy was murdered. You remember, the one who ended up in the truck of your car."

"Ummm, seems like I do remember that annoying incident."

"Good. Anyway Cahill said something like, 'not to worry. I'll make sure they pull the plug on the whole thing.'"

"He could have been talking about anything."

"He was talking about the conference, all right. He was using the phone in the cloakroom and whispering like he didn't want anyone to hear." She smiled. "I saw him slink in there all sneaky like, and I thought I'd better see what was going on."

"You shouldn't have done that. What if he'd caught you listening?"

"I'm an old pro. Don't worry about me."

"Have you told anyone else?"

"Not on your life. And you didn't hear this from me. Understand?"

"Understand. Thanks, Blanche."

"If I were you, I'd start putting out the 'Do Not Disturb' sign."

"What do you mean?" Did she know my room had been searched?

"With all that's happened, you need to be careful. We have some housekeepers who open all the doors of the rooms that need to be cleaned whether someone is still staying there or not. They're not supposed to, but they do. Anyone could walk in."

"Thanks for the advice."

I peeked out. The hallway was empty.

"One more thing," Blanche said. "I have a house and a big backyard and a collie who gets lonely when I'm not around. Your poodle and cat can stay with me."

"How did you—? Never mind. Would you be willing to do that?"

"Absolutely. I love animals."

"Your husband won't mind?"

"Who, Mr. Comatose? He wouldn't notice if I built cages in the backyard and turned our place into a kennel."

"Can you take them now?"

"Be glad to."

"You're a lifesaver. My poodle, Monroe, is high-strung and spoiled, but she's easy to manage. It's my cat that will be difficult."

"Cats usually are. I'll bring my car around the back. Take the elevator to the basement and I'll meet you." She left the closet, and as I turned to follow, I noticed tracks of sand on the carpet where she'd just stood.

TEN MINUTES LATER, I WATCHED BLANCHE drive away with my pets. Monroe was smiling, happy to be riding in a car. Mealworm glared at me from her carrier, but she glared at me from anywhere, so I wasn't worried. Then, as I walked back into the hotel, the idiocy of what I'd just done dawned on me like a nightmare turned real. I'd given my two girls, the only sane members of my family, to a total stranger. I didn't even know where Blanche lived. I didn't even know her last name. She could have made up that story about Mr. Cahill in the closet. She could be the killer!

I ran up five flights of stairs, rushed into my room, found Jeremiah, Ruth, and Scott, bickering over who was the most miserable, grabbed my car keys, and flew.

"Where are you going?" they cried.

I didn't bother to answer. Blanche could be anywhere by now. She was driving an old heap, though, so she couldn't be far. At this time of the morning, not many cars would be on the road. I turned onto Seawall Boulevard, in the direction I'd seen Blanche head, and gunned it. There were no taillights up ahead. I looked down each side road as I sped by. Then I saw two oblong taillights traveling down 24th Street. I followed, but it wasn't her. I made a U-turn and headed back. The concern I felt moments ago had turned to panic. I should have told the group of whiners in my room what I'd done. Four cars on the road searching for Blanche and my pets were better than one. Too late now. I didn't bother to stop at stop signs, just squealed around one corner after another. Rounding 21st Street, I misjudged the curve and knocked over a garbage can, sending a family of alley cats up a tree. I took the next corner at thirty. The milkman stood frozen in my path. I swerved, missing him by inches. A scream and crash echoed behind me. I looked in my rearview mirror to see him standing in the middle of a puddle of milk and broken glass, but otherwise okay.

I peered down the next side street and spotted more taillights. I slammed my brakes, threw it in reverse, and followed. It was not Blanche. Oh, my God! She could be anywhere! I needed to stop, I needed to think, I needed to call the police. Time was running out. My girls could be alligator meat by now. Blanche could have driven them to the west side of the island, opened the door, and shoved them out. Monroe has never spent the night outside. She'd run back and forth looking for me—the only mother she's ever known. She'd whine at first and then when I didn't come, she'd whimper, then howl. Then she'd lie down on the side of the road and will herself to die. Mealworm, on the other hand, would have the time of her life.

I pulled over and stopped. I stepped out of the car and gulped cold, salt-laden air, and finally my brain began to unscramble. How far could Blanche go? This was an island, right? Oh, Lord, it was an island with a bridge to the mainland. "Stop it!" I told myself. I looked up to the sky to see if God was watching. The moon and stars had taken cover. "Get off your throne and do something, damn it!" The wind picked up and a sliver of moon peeked down at me from a misty cloud and in a brief instant, blinked. "That's better," I told God.

Then I heard a jingle, then two jingles, followed by a gnawing sound and some yips. I jerked around and there behind a fence was a white cloud bouncing a couple of feet above the ground. And trying to shove the cloud to the side was a brown, hairy bundle with a sharp, needlelike nose. I slumped back in the driver's seat, put my head between my knees, and sucked more air. Then I started my car and drove back to the hotel before Monroe noticed me. After all, I didn't want to spoil her fun. She didn't often get to play with other dogs.

When I got back, Larry, Curly, and Moe were sitting in the lobby. Cousin Moe was the first to respond. "Where in the hell did you go? You look like you've been chased by the goat man."

"Close," I said. "I was pursued by my imagination."

"Now that you've kept us up most of the night, I'm going to bed." Scott stormed off.

"Don't you ever feel like killing him?" I asked Jeremiah.

"Often. Here." He handed me a piece of paper.

"What's this?"

"While you were taking Monroe and Mealworm down to the basement, that housemaid Blanche came in and wrote down her address and phone number and said to give them to you."

CHAPTER TWENTY-SEVEN

The sun was showing its ugly face, as if I cared. I shoved the pillow over my head and rolled over. Ruth was dead to the world; her snoring was a true indication—she wasn't faking it this time. I took my pillow and swatted her. No reaction. I shoved her bed with my foot; she snorted and said something that sounded like, "Monopoly money." Or it could have been "maple honey." While I listened to her snore, I imagined ways to kill my brother. He was the reason I'd had only two hours of sleep, he was the reason I'd almost killed a milkman, he was the reason I'd ended up doing stupid things. Well, the main reason anyway.

I gave up trying to return to dreamland. Ruth had sucked the sleep right out of me. I had too much to do anyway. I showered and dressed and stuck my notebook in my bag. I hung out the DO NOT DISTURB sign like Blanche advised, and went down to the restaurant for coffee. The place was quiet. Who'd be up and around at this hour except neurotics like me? I took a seat by the window, hoping the early-morning sun would be kind and rejuvenating. The last look at myself in the mirror was enough to suggest a bag over my head might be in order. I was glad Dixon was on his way to Houston.

My parents' anniversary party was fewer than twelve hours away. Would I be around to help the happy couple celebrate? Would Mom cancel again if her only daughter's body washed up on Stewart Beach riddled with bullet holes?

I ordered the continental breakfast, and by the time I'd finished my second cup of coffee, I felt like I might survive, at least until noon. I took out my notebook and began scribbling. If what Blanche said was true, the conference had been canceled before Roland's murder. Surely, whoever was behind this didn't kill the man just to have the conference canceled. If that were the case, this situation was uglier than I suspected. And if Cahill knew, then he was mixed up in this.

I slathered some butter on my roll and took a bite. My brain, demanding my attention, stopped the muscle contractions in my throat, causing the roll to lodge. My coughing brought a couple of people to my table. One guy slapped my back and was ready to throw my glass of water in my face. I raised my hand and waved him off. When I finally caught my breath and shooed away my rescuers, I wrote Cahill's name down on the list of suspects for Roland's murder. And then, I saw Cahill walking my way, as if he'd sensed my thoughts. I laid my napkin over my notes.

"Miss Lockhart, are you okay?"

"I'm fine. It went down the wrong pipe." I sipped my water and tried not to look suspicious of the man standing over me. "Please, sit down."

"I think I will. Excuse the casual attire. I didn't leave the hotel until around four. Today's my day off, but my assistant manager called in sick." He'd traded his suit and tie for a button-down shirt and a cardigan with a high shawl collar. I took solace in knowing that at least someone else looked worse than me this morning.

"Speaking of being sick, how's the cold?"

"Cold? Oh, yes. It must be better. I haven't had time to worry over it. Last night's wedding reception became rather rowdy. Around eleven, we had to pull three guys out of the pool. Normally, that wouldn't be a problem, but they were still in their tuxes and so drunk that we were afraid they'd drown. Then the maid of honor, sister of the bride, grabbed the singer's microphone and announced that she and the groom had been sleeping together for two months. She was drunk too. The bride took what was left of her wedding cake and flung it across the stage. The food fight ended with four people arrested, including the bride, who'd stripped off her dress and ran down the seawall in her slip.

Her father was also thrown into a squad car for slamming the groom's head on the piano keys."

I envisioned my parents' party taking a similar route.

"Then," he continued, "around three, a disruption broke out on the fifth floor." He paused. "That's where your room is, right?"

"Yes, but I was dead to the world and didn't hear a thing. Seems like you're here around the clock."

"Sometimes I am." He caught my eye and held it for a moment. "After twenty-three years, I've come to think of this hotel as my own."

I detected a slight harshness in his tone. Was it a warning? "Have some coffee," I said.

"Good idea." He waved over the waiter, and we soon had a fresh pot.

"I'm surprised you're still here," he said. "With the conference canceled."

"Roland's murder, remember? My editor wants me to stick around."

"Of course. Turn anything up yet?"

"The police aren't letting go of much."

"Wait," he said. "Was that your father who was arrested?"

"A misunderstanding. Things are almost cleared up."

"Good to know."

He finished his cup and was about to leave, or so he thought.

"I've spoken to Cleve Boedecker."

Cahill lowered his eyes. "Cleve Boedecker? You must be on to something."

"I am."

"Well, be careful, whatever you do. One person's already been murdered."

"Two, if you count my grandfather."

He patted his lips with his napkin. "Yes, that's true. Thanks for suggesting the coffee. It's just what I needed. Now I have a banquet to finish planning. Then I have a meeting downtown in—" he looked at his watch "—a couple of hours. You know where to find me if you need anything."

With that, he was gone. Watching him hurry away, I noticed he moved across the room like a rat looking for cover. All I got from this conversation was a feeling, but that was enough.

I had spent a good half hour rearranging my notes when I caught Ruth in my peripheral vision. Black sweater, bright-green flared skirt, black Ferragamos with green tiger stripes and matching belt. She grabbed an unused coffee cup and saucer off a table and joined me.

"What's with the casual look today?"

"I don't look too slouchy, do I? This was the best I could do since I got very little sleep last night. Those damn housekeepers were making so much racket cleaning the rooms that they woke me up." She opened the coffee pot, sniffed, and held it up. As if by magic, a waiter with a fresh pot appeared. "What did you eat?" she asked, her nose almost in my empty plate.

"Continental breakfast."

"I'll have that," she said to the waiter. "Does that come with bacon?"

"No, ma'am."

"Then I'll have a side of bacon. How about waffles?"

"It's a continental breakfast, ma'am. Rolls, fruit, juice, and coffee."

"Good, I'm not too hungry. Just add the bacon and an order of waffles." She looked at my butter dish. "And we'll need more butter."

I looked at her ninety pounds and wondered how she managed to maintain a size four petite. "You must have the metabolism of a hummingbird."

"People are always telling me I eat like a bird."

"You missed the point. Never mind. Have you called Mom and told her you're not coming today?"

"Yep. I gave her the virus-relapse story, but Scott will probably tell her the truth."

"Don't worry about Scott. We have a lot of work to do."

She waved over the waiter again. "Add two scrambled eggs."

After Ruth fueled, I suggested a walk along the seawall, where we could talk without being overheard.

"I'll need a scarf for my hair. I'll meet you out front by the fountain."

"Make it fast. Out front by the fountain is not my favorite place."

Even though it was a cool January day, the sun shone as bright as that awful day eighteen years ago. I looked down the drive and saw that car speeding way, swiping the oleander bush. The bush had survived; my grandfather hadn't.

"Here," Ruth said. She handed me a scarf. "You'll need this. It's breezy out."

"How do you manage to find matching shoes, belt, and scarf?"

"It's a talent."

"Come on, let's walk and talk this over."

I filled her in on what Blanche had told me and about my suspicions concerning Leonard Cahill.

"You think he killed Roland? And that he was the one who searched the room?"

"I don't know. What I'm sure of is that Boedecker's involved and that there's a connection between PoPo's murder and Roland's. We have to find that connection. Hopefully, Dixon will come back from Houston with something helpful. In the meantime, we keep looking. Here's what we know: PoPo had the coin, at least that's what Boedecker said. The coin was probably what got him killed. Then the coin went missing. Not much was done to find it until a couple of months ago. Then Boedecker starts to stir. The conference was scheduled to be canceled before Roland was killed. The mayor made the announcement that the cancellation was because of the murder. Also before all this happens, Brewster Fallow, who was convicted of the Hardy murder, comes back to town and contacts Dad. Then Fallow is murdered."

"Don't forget about someone searching the room."

"Right, and finally, the Lush hinted that the link was here at the hotel, and Blanche confirmed that by telling me that Cahill is up to something."

"Why would Blanche rat on her boss?"

I smiled. "I wondered that too, and then it all became clear this morning. The eggplant left on my bed, the sand Blanche left on the carpet in the storage closet. She's part of Asherah's little group. It was just too odd when she showed up last night at the hotel at three in the morning. I'd wager that there's a purple afghan along with a bunch of fairy accessories hanging in her closet. When she realized I was sticking around to delve deeper into the situation, she thought I might be able to shine some light on what was really going on and stop the development project."

"You checking in must have started everything."

"I don't think so. The dominoes started to fall before I arrived. The warning calls—I'm convinced they were from Lattie—came as soon as I got here. Slashing my tires, however, doesn't sound like something Lattie would do."

"You think the Lush is involved with the murder?"

"No, in her wacky mind, she was trying to help. Dad knew I was coming and that I'd start nosing around. For some reason, he confided in her, and she thought she'd help by trying to scare me away with the phone calls."

We'd walked nearly a mile. The aroma of fried clams was no match for the beach smells. The Clam Shack had just opened, and already there was a line out front. Ruth looked at her watch. "Kind of early for clams," she said.

"Evidently not. The Clam Shack has quite a following."

"Since we only had the continental breakfast, and we've been walking for hours—"

"You know, Ruth, you could pack enough food in that tiny body to keep a Clydesdale happy. Say no more. We'll split an order. There's a bench. Grab it and I'll order."

"Let's split an order of fries, too," she called. "And I'll have a Royal Crown."

We spread our midmorning picnic on the bench between us. "Did you get tartar sauce?"

"Right here." I handed her a cup. "Have you heard from your secretary at the Home?"

"Things are running according to plan. We have two mothers checking in this week."

"That's a good thing you're doing, Ruth. You really pulled it off."

"There's a lot more work to do. Sometimes I wonder if I've bitten off more than I can chew. I don't want this project to consume all my time. You need someone to look after you."

"Find someone to run the place for you."

"I will. When we wind things up here, I'll put an ad in the paper and start interviewing people. I won't hire just anyone. Whoever takes the job has to have many talents—a good nose for business and the ability to handle books. They have to be organized and, of course, circumspect and sympathetic."

"You've given it a lot of thought, haven't you?"

"You didn't think I could do it, did you?" Her cocky grin told me I didn't have to answer.

"I'm proud of you. Any more thoughts about a name?"

"A few ideas came to mind, but nothing seemed right."

"When this is all over, we'll put our heads together and select something that's just right."

We sat in silence enjoying the clams. I looked over and saw Ruth licking her fingers. I smiled. "We're a team, you know?"

She looked at me. Tears welled up in her eyes.

"What's wrong?"

"What's going to happen when you marry Ralph?"

"Marry?" I nearly shouted.

"It's going to happen, you know."

"You're being silly."

"He'll be your crime-solving partner. This is the third murder we've worked on together. We're getting really good at this, and I'm beginning to enjoy it. It might be our last murder investigation."

"You've had too many clams. I have no intention of getting married. You will always be my partner. Understand?"

"And what about Marcella?"

"Look, consider Marcella and Dixon as added staff. We can't do everything." The mention of Marcella made me recall the conversation I'd had with her the evening we dined at Gaidos. A melancholy feeling washed over me.

"What is it?" Ruth said. "The talk of domesticity upset your tummy?"

"Ruth, do you ever think about what Marcella went through while she was growing up?"

"Oh, please. She was well taken care of. My father saw to that."

"Money can't replace what was missing in her life."

"Where did this sentimentality come from all of a sudden?"

"The other night when we went to dinner—"

"The night I was kidnapped."

"Right. I was griping about Mom, and Marcella told me I was too hard on the ol' gal. She said she'd give anything to have her mother back."

"Well, she's wormed her way into our family so she should be happy. Mom thinks Marcella's just peachy. Imagine Mom taking a liking to the illegitimate daughter of her cheating husband. Soon she'll want to adopt the woman."

"Your mother is a softy."

"Right. Being too nice has always gotten her into trouble. Who started this soppy conversation anyway?"

"You did. All that talk about getting married and having partners." I rolled up our napkins and paper and stuffed them into the bag.

She smiled. "You're right. Then when I get married, we'll have another helper."

"If you're going to be my crime-solving partner, you're going to have to get you a pair of saddle shoes."

"I have my limits. What now?"

"We wait for Dixon to return from Houston. In the meantime— and I can't believe I'm saying this—we head over to Mom's and see if we can get this damn party up and running once and for all."

"Let's take my Caddy. I have a trunk full of Chinese lanterns your mother had me pick up from a Woolworth's."

"Jeez."

"Now, now, don't be negative."

CHAPTER TWENTY-EIGHT

We pulled out of the hotel parking lot just as Cahill rushed from the hotel and hopped into his car.

"He's in a hurry."

"He said he had a meeting downtown. I saw a twinge of concern in his face when we were talking at breakfast. Think you can tail him without being noticed?"

"That's my specialty."

"Sure, like the other night when you were following me but didn't notice those guys following you."

"I don't have eyes in back of my head."

Instead of making a right on 25th Street, Cahill turned left and then right onto Seawall Boulevard and hit the gas.

"Downtown is in the opposite direction."

"He's in a hurry. Don't get too close, but don't lose him."

When Cahill drove passed 61st Street, I had Ruth pull over at a gas station.

"There's not much traffic here. He'll see us if we keep following."

"We'll lose him."

"I don't think so. Unless he's going for a plate of catfish at Washington's or he's interested in buying a pig, there's only one other place."

"Smart girl, Syd. He's on his way to Boedecker's."

"We'll wait a couple of minutes. Then pull back out, but keep your distance. He'll notice us out on this road."

A few minutes later, Cahill passed the pig farm and made a right onto 8-Mile Road toward Boedecker's.

"Keep going. I don't want to take a chance of being seen, and I want to make absolutely sure he's going to Cleve's house. Let's give him a few minutes. Drive down Stewart Road and to the back of the pig farm."

"There better not be any loose pigs around. I might not be so kind next time I see another one in the middle of the road."

Ruth continued on about a mile, maneuvered another U-turn, passed the pig farm, another U-turn, and then headed back to 8-Mile Road.

"Pull over behind the clump of trees. Cahill is our missing link. He's connected with Boedecker, the hotel, the Pelican Island Development Project, and, most importantly, PoPo. He was probably the one who searched my room."

We were well hidden from Boedecker's house, but I needed to get closer. "Stay here. I'm going to walk toward the house and see what's going on. And, please, Ruth, keep the doors locked. Remember the other night and that day Mongoose nabbed you in Palacios?"

"That was just a fluke."

"A fluke that got you kidnapped."

Ruth rolled her eyes.

"You were undressed and forced to wear Pete's oil-field clothes and then Emma Fogmore's dress and shoes."

"You're right. I blocked that from my memory. Be careful."

I walked to the end of the road, glanced back, and was relieved to see that Ruth's Caddy was not visible. Boedecker's house was about two hundred yards down. From where I stood, I could only see the front, and Cahill's car was not there. I suspected he was parked in back. I needed to be sure. I started toward the house when a car pulled out of Boedecker's drive. I stepped behind a cluster of trees. When the car passed, I saw Louis driving. In the passenger seat, a head was barely visible. Looked like Louis and Buddy were running an errand for their boss. I brushed the dirt off my slacks and continued on.

A cluster of cedar hedges shaded the front of Boedecker's house. I edged my way around to the back, and my suspicions were confirmed. There was Cahill's Ford. I should have hightailed it back to the car, but with Louis and Buddy gone, I couldn't resist snooping. The garage door was open and I crept in. The door leading into the house was unlocked. I opened it a crack. All was quiet. I tiptoed down the hall until I heard laughing and chattering. Judging by the smells, I was near the kitchen. There were several doors leading from the hall. I opened the last one and finally got my bearings. It led to the front foyer. Boedecker's library door was closed. I went back into the hall and ignored the other doors. What I was looking for didn't have a typical doorknob or hinges. Then I saw it: a break in the molding and then another one about three feet away. It was the door Buddy had popped out of, the one built into the bookcase in the study.

I put my ear to it but couldn't hear anything. The kitchen door opened and a maid walked out. Her back was to me and she was giving orders to someone. I rushed back to the garage, but left the door ajar. The maid came back carrying a tray of dirty dishes. She was in the kitchen only a few seconds when she returned with a mop. The hall was off-limits now. I'd decided to try the back of the house when I heard a car drive up. When the fender edged around the corner, I ducked behind a heating unit.

The car pulled into the garage. "It's in the kitchen on the pantry board," I heard Louis say. Someone got out and slammed the door. "Get a move on."

"Don't boss me," Buddy cried. "You're the one who forgot the damn list."

I plastered myself against the unit and held my breath. If Buddy looked back over his shoulder, he'd spot me in an instant. I thought of faraway places—Austin, New York City, Jupiter—so my aura wouldn't give away my presence. It seemed to take Buddy forever to retrieve whatever list they had forgotten. When he finally returned, Louis shouted, "That took you long enough."

"Get off my back. I had to bring a bottle of scotch to the Boss. What do I look like, a servant?"

"Is he still in that meeting?"

"Yeah, ol' Leonard was madder than a wet cat. He said that redheaded broad is sticking her nose where it don't belong. The boss just laughed. I think he kinda likes her."

"What's there to like? She's pushy, smart-mouthed, and—"

"Too tall," Buddy added.

A car door slammed and the car backed out. So Louis thinks I have faults, Cleve likes those faults, and Cahill thinks I'm a threat. But a threat to what or whom? At least I knew I was on the right track, but where that track led was a mystery. I needed to get back to Ruth before she came looking for me. Then I heard a rumble and the garage began get dark. The slam of the door echoed doom. I felt around the wall for a light switch but couldn't find one. I groped my way toward the garage door, found the handle, and jerked. It didn't budge. Things weren't all that bad. Louis and Buddy would be back soon, Ruth knew where I was, and no one was holding me at gunpoint. Gun—I felt mine resting against my ribs; I thought of Dixon and felt better. Then I heard a tapping sound coming from the outside.

I listened.

Tap, tap, tap.

I froze.

Tap, tap, tap. Then I heard, "Sydney?"

"Ruth?"

"What are you doing in there?"

"Changing the oil in Boedecker's car, for God sake. See if you can open the door. I'm pretty sure it's locked."

"Stand back and I'll shoot it off."

"No!"

"It's okay. I have my little gun, the Derringer. It doesn't make much noise. Stand back."

Ping! "Sorry."

Ping! "Shit."

Jeez. "Ruth! Stop it!"

Ping!

"Got it. Oh my, the handle's gone. Try to open it on your side."

I grabbed the handle, and it fell off in my hand.

"Great! What now?"

Bam! Bam! Bam!

"Stop it! Kicking won't help!

The door bounced up a few inches. A hand appeared from underneath and waved. "Yoo-hoo! It's me. Uh-oh. Someone's coming."

"Help me pull up on this door! Hurry!"

We both tugged, and the door bounced open a couple of more inches.

"See if you can crawl through! Hurry!" Then I heard her heels tapping in retreat.

"Ruth! Wait!" I jerked the door again, but it was stuck. I had less than a foot of wiggle room and tried to slither under. A cloud of dust rose from the dirt road. If it wasn't Louis and Buddy, it was someone else heading for Boedecker's place. I pulled my head and shoulders through and knew the rest would follow easily. I blessed my father for passing on his slim build. In seconds I'd be behind the hedges edging my way toward the front of the house. As I pulled myself from under the door, someone grabbed my foot. I kicked and my shoe slipped off. I took off around the garage before the car turned into the driveway. Whoever it was stopped in front of the house. I heard someone cursing and fiddling with the garage door. I didn't have time to stick around. I'm sure the person with my saddle shoe would not graciously slip it on my foot like Prince Charming did to Cinderella. I made a dash for the road. Ruth was nowhere in sight. I ran to where we had left the car. It was gone.

I took off toward the pig farm. Behind the first roll of pens, I saw Ruth's Caddy nose out and roll toward the road. I hopped in.

"You left me there!"

"I did not! I came to get the car."

"There was no you, no car!"

"I hid it before I came looking for you. Where's your shoe? You're always losing your shoes."

"Just drive."

She gunned the engine. The car lunged forward a couple of inches and jerked to a stop. Ruth hit the gas and the Caddy whined like an angry racehorse tethered and rarin' to go. "We're stuck!"

"Throw it in reverse and try again."

We rocked back and forth, back and forth, mud slung across the back window, over the top of the car, and onto the hood. She gunned the engine again, more mud flew. Ruth turned on her wipers.

"Stop it!" Too late. Now the windshield looked as if it had been iced with chocolate frosting. I opened the door. The back tire had sunk down to the hubcap.

"One more time should do it," Ruth said and gunned the engine.

"Noooooooo!" Mud splattered across my face.

"Whoops."

"You know, Ruth, sometimes I think your brain dried up and blew away one hot summer's day out on your dad's ranch."

"Look, who was stupid enough to open the door? Just get out and push."

"Clark Kent couldn't get this car out. Didn't you watch where you parked?"

"As if I had time! You've gotten us into another mess!"

"Who would park their car in a pig wallow? We've got to get out of here."

"Maybe they won't come looking for us."

"Are you kidding? You destroyed their garage door with your 'little' gun, and they have my shoe. They know I was snooping around. They're not shrugging their shoulders and saying, 'Oh, well, just another day in the life of the Boedeckers.'"

I pulled a hanky from my pocket and wiped the mud from my eyes.

"That didn't help much. It's in your hair, too."

"Shut up." I shoved open the door. "Let's go. If we stay here, we're sitting ducks."

"I'm not going to slop around in pig mud again."

"Then stay here."

I hopped out. Ruth reached over, locked all four doors, and stuck out her tongue. I walked to the road where I could see the house. A car pulled out, and it was obvious from the gravel spewing in its wake it wasn't out for an afternoon cruise. I ran back to the car.

"They're coming. Are you getting out or not?"

Ruth rolled down the window. "Look, they're driving down 8-Mile Road. They didn't see us. We're safe."

"Not for long. Once they figure out we didn't take 8-Mile Road back to town, they'll come looking for us. Look back there. That must be the pig farmer's house. We'll tell him we broke down and ask him if we can use his phone."

"Out here? He probably doesn't have one."

She had a point. The old house hadn't seen paint since the 1800s. There were no utility lines to the house. No phone, no electricity.

"Maybe he'll give us a ride to town." I slipped off my shoe and stuck it in my purse. Then I heard the sound of a car. "Look they're coming back. Hurry! Let me help you get out of the car. You'll have to jump over the mud wallows you created."

"Get out of my way! I can do it!"

"IT DOESN'T LOOK LIKE ANYONE IS AT HOME."

"There's smoke coming from the chimney." I stepped over the holes on the rotting front porch and knocked on the door. We waited.

"Hear anything?"

"No, maybe he's in the barn."

"I'm staying right here. You go look. My green pumps are ruined; my entire outfit is ruined."

"At least you have shoes. My feet are wet and cold."

Ruth removed her scarf, spread it over the seat of a rickety rocking chair, and sat down. I started to walk over to the barn when I saw Louis and Buddy inspecting Ruth's car.

"Quick! In the house!"

"But—"

I knocked again, pushed open the door, and tiptoed in. "Hello? Anybody home?" I grabbed Ruth by the arm and pulled her inside.

"No one's here," she whispered. "This place smells bad."

A low grunting sounded caused us to jump. Two pink-and-brown splotched mounds lounged on what was once a sofa, snorting at our intrusion, but the lazy pigs weren't upset enough to remove themselves from their comfortable perch.

"I hate pigs," Ruth said.

"Hello?" I said again, and then I heard voices from the outside. I went to the window. It was Louis and Buddy talking to an old man, the pig farmer. He was holding a rifle and shaking his head. Louis looked toward the house.

"Hurry, that back room. See if there's a closet. They're coming in!"

We ducked into a closet filled with several pair of smelly overalls. Moments later the three men were standing in the front room.

"See, I told you no one's in here. Lola and Donna are the only gals ever in my house, and they don't like no strangers. Now get out before I put a bullet in your hides."

"That's not very neighborly," Buddy said. "We're from down the road, the Boedecker place. Neighbors got to stick together."

A blast sounded and the entire house shook.

"Uh-oh," Ruth whispered.

I poked her in the shoulder. We heard scrambling and Buddy's voice trailing off, "We're going, we're going! Crazy old fart!"

"I can't breathe," Ruth said.

I cracked the door a few inches. "Let's go."

"Now?"

"I've had enough! Get out your little gun." I pulled my .22 from its holster. "I'm through hiding in closets, running around barefooted, and being harassed by nitwits."

I walked up into the front room as the pig man was inspecting the hole in his wall.

"Put down that rifle!"

Startled, he dropped the rifle, discharging it and blasting another hole through his window. Lola, or maybe it was Donna, plopped off the sofa and hid behind the stove.

"Run!" I heard Buddy shout from the front porch.

"Grab his rifle," I told Ruth.

The farmer swung around and stood there. His lips pursed, his jaw locked; he didn't look too surprised. I guess at his age, he'd seen just about everything.

"Outside," I told him, then turned to Ruth. "Go get Louis and Buddy. We need them. Hurry. You," I told the farmer. "Help her! Now! Get them back here or I'll a blow a hole in your pig."

The man rushed out with Ruth following. Lola and Donna stayed behind.

CHAPTER TWENTY-NINE

Here we are. The four of us together again," Buddy said.
We stood in front of the house; two mud-splattered women, a tall sleazy guy, an old pig farmer, and a midget.

"How's my little Filly?"

"Shut up, Buddy," Ruth and I said in unison.

"Gee, you guys are too serious," Buddy said.

"This is a serious situation, your chasing after us," I said.

"We just wanted to return this," Buddy said. He tossed over my shoe. The maid took it off your foot."

"Cut the crap, Buddy," Louis said. "We came after you because you were trespassing. Boedecker oughta call the police."

"I don't think he'll do that," I said, "with all that's going on over there." I slipped on my shoes. "Now, I want some answers."

"You're insane," Louis said. "A woman with an overactive imagination."

That's when I noticed a huge bandage covering Louis's left hand. "Overactive imagination? Did I imagine you chasing me through the newsroom trying to kill me in the stairwell? You're not doing too well. Your left hand has a hole in it."

Louis looked at his injured hand but didn't respond.

"What are you going to do with us?" Buddy whined. "I'm too young to die. I got a lot left to do before I check out." He winked at Ruth. She volleyed by firing a bullet over his head.

"Feisty," Buddy said. "I like that."

"You're going to tell Boedecker I'm ready to make a deal. If he wants the coin, it will cost him—a bundle. Tell him I'll meet with him and only him."

"When?" Louis said.

"Tell him I'll call and arrange a meeting, and he'd better be ready to hand over cash."

I saw Ruth stealing glances in my direction, but she kept quiet and held the gun steady.

"Now," I said, "you three gentlemen have a job to do."

"Anything." Buddy smiled. He was enjoying this too much, and I was about to change that.

While Louis and Buddy pushed, the farmer pulled with his tractor. It took four tries before the pig wallow gave up its hold on Ruth's Caddy. When it finally lunged out, the sudden force sent Buddy face down into the mud while a spray of brown liquid splashed Ruth from head to toe. The little guy looked like a chocolate-covered marshmallow. I took Ruth's scarf from her shoulders and wiped her face.

"Thank you," she said.

"Don't mention it. Shall we get the hell out of here, dear Cousin?"

"Oh, let's."

I looked out the rear window as Ruth drove us away from the pig farm. The farmer was gone and the Balinese Room boys were walking down the 8-Mile Road back to the house, the radiator of Louis's car having had an unfortunate meeting with a bullet from my gun.

"What now?" Ruth said. "Boedecker's expecting a call from you. What are you planning?"

"I'm not sure. I just wanted to buy some time. We might want to consider moving out of the hotel. I want to see if Dixon's called."

Twenty minutes later, the scent of the Gulf of Mexico had replaced the smell of swine, and the red-shingled roof of the Galvez came into view.

"Pull around to the back," I said.

"We can't walk through the lobby looking like this."

"Just park the car and wait for me. I don't look as bad as you so I'll duck into the ladies' lounge, clean up as much as I can, and then go to the front desk and see if Dixon's left a message."

The front-desk clerk handed me a slip of paper with the phone number. Dixon had just called. The message said he would be at this number for an hour or two. I slipped into the lobby phone booth and had the operator put through a collect call.

"Find out anything about Roland?" I asked when Dixon got on the line.

"Where in the hell have you been?"

"What would you like to hear first? That I was locked in Boedecker's garage or stuck in a pig wallow on the infamous pig farm?"

"Stop being coy. Where are you?"

"At the hotel."

"Get out! Now! It's Cahill. He's dangerous. Stay away from him."

"Kind of late for that."

"Don't tell me. Ruth's been kidnapped again."

"No, but we tracked Cahill to Boedecker's place."

"Listen, Sydney. I can't give you the details over the phone. I want you out of that hotel before Cahill returns. Go to your parents' house. I'll be back from Houston in about an hour, and I'll meet you at the church near the hotel."

When I got back to the car, Ruth was filing her nails.

"Took you long enough."

"I was talking to Dixon. We need to get out of here now."

"But I need a bath."

"That will have to wait."

"I'm caked in mud!"

"People spend a lot of money to be caked in mud. It's a beauty treatment; haven't you heard?"

"Oh, please!"

"Drive. I have a plan."

"I'll bet you do."

I FOUND A PHONE BOOTH A COUPLE OF BLOCKS down on the seawall and made a call. A few minutes later, Blanche dropped off a fresh change of clothes for us, as well as our cosmetic kits and a message from my mother telling me to get my butt back to the house. I handed over Ruth's clothes and kit and tossed the note into the trash. The celebration was less than three hours away, and I still had two murders to solve.

Ruth was not very happy with my idea to clean up in the public showers on Stewart Beach. I let her go first while I kept watch. The afternoon had turned out gorgeous. The hot-dog stand was open, and I bought a cup of coffee. The man behind the counter raised his eyebrows at my mud-covered attire but didn't comment. I found a bench not too stained with bird droppings and prepared myself for a long wait. With the emergence of the sun came a few beachcombers and even a couple of surfers. The sound of children's laughter mixed with squawking seagulls relaxed me.

I took my notes from my purse and tried to connect the dots. Although mention of the Pelican Island Development Project had never come up in the many conversations I'd had with Boedecker, he must be involved somehow. If so, how does Roland's death affect the future of the development?

I looked up and noticed a vagrant down the beach making his way methodically to each trash can. If he didn't have any luck by the time he arrived at the concession area, I'd buy him a hot dog. I might buy him one anyway. A guy in an olive-green work shirt with City of Galveston stitched across his pocket stuffed bags of trash into the huge cans not far from where I sat. He shook his head in disgust, muttered something about wastefulness, and moved on. I looked at my watch. Half an hour had gone by; Ruth would be another several minutes. I put my notes away and decided to people-watch and let my brain do its work without my interfering.

"Hey, lady. Your clothes are dirty."

That teeny, screeching voice sent spikes down my spine. How long were these people going to be here?

"Don't you know horses aren't allowed on the beach?" I said to the six-shooters pointed at my head.

"You're weird."

"You've told me that before. Have anything new to report?"

"Franklin Pearce, get over here and stop bothering that lady!"

Big Bad "Frankie" just stood there.

"Didn't you hear your mother?"

"She's not my mother. She's an Indian squaw, and I'm going to scalp her after I fill you full of holes."

I did something I was sure I'd regret, hopefully later rather than sooner. I opened my jacket and slowly pulled out my pistol, showing the butt of the gun. Frankie's eyes widened and he tripped over his boots scurrying back to his mother.

Someone let out a shrill whistle and an expletive. I looked around to see the bum holding the bag the trash man had just stuffed into the can. In his hands was a bright green garment that looked familiar. The first thought that struck was that I wasn't surprised Ruth would throw away a new outfit, especially one splattered with mud. Why bother with dry cleaning when you can simply buy another? The second thought that crossed my sluggish brain had me up and running. If the trash man was able to go into the ladies' room and empty the can, then the ladies' room must be empty of occupants.

"Ruth!" I pushed open every stall door. All empty, except for the last one. Hanging on the door hook was a hanger with Ruth's clean clothes, and sitting on the shower bench was her cosmetic kit. I rushed out to the boulevard. Her car was where we had left it, but she was nowhere to be seen. Her keys were in the ignition. I spun around and headed west. Whoever nabbed her, probably Louis and Buddy, were on their way to Boedecker's. With time slipping away, I now had another task added to my list: find out who murdered Roland and why, locate the missing coin, and, now, locate my missing cousin.

Rather than rush back to 8-Mile Road, I decided to do two things. One was smart—wait for Dixon before I went chasing after my cousin on my own—and one was potentially stupid. My mud-caked hair was beginning to smell like more than just mud. I trusted that Cahill would not return to the hotel after the incident at Boedecker's so I rushed back to my room. I placed my gun and holster on the bedside table and stripped off my filthy clothes. I showered, donned a clean pair of slacks and a sweater, and strapped on my weapon, which, as Dixon said, now felt comfortable after wearing it all day.

While I waited for Dixon in the church parking lot, I tried to make sense of this latest development. Why would Boedecker have his henchmen kidnap Ruth again unless he didn't believe that I really had the coin and was ready to deal? Taking Ruth would give him assurance that I would deliver. So much for my brilliant ideas.

Someone tapped on my window, and I almost flew through the roof. Expecting Dixon, I was surprised to see the young priest who had been talking to my mother a few days ago. I rolled down the window.

"Are you in trouble, my dear?"

Was this a subtle hint that I needed to accompany him to the confessional? What would I say? I've lied, cheated, stolen, threatened to kill a few people, misplaced my cousin, dishonored my mother; the list could go on forever and so would my penance—a dozen rosaries every morning for the rest of my life.

"No, thank you, Father. I'm just waiting for a friend. He should be along any minute."

"You're Mary Lou Lockhart's daughter? Your mother is excited about the renewal of her wedding vows. I'll be there to perform the service this evening."

"I hope it sticks this time."

"Excuse me?"

"Oh, just an inside joke. I'll see you later, Father."

"I'd be careful if I were you. I'm sure you've heard what happened here in this parking lost just a few days ago."

If I ever managed to forget, the bloodstains in my trunk would remind me, but I didn't tell him that.

He tipped his hat and walked away.

In the rearview mirror, I saw Dixon pull up. I cut the engine and hopped into his car.

"Change of plans."

"Don't tell me."

"Okay, but I'm sure you've figured out that Ruth didn't decide to go on a last-minute shopping spree."

"Damn. That woman must hold some kind of record for being abducted."

"Let's go. I'm sure she's at Boedecker's. We'll talk on the way."

After I told him about my adventure in Boedecker's garage, our social call on the pig farmer, and my bluff about having the coin, Dixon filled me in on his discovery.

"Roland's design company is also the investment company."

"How did you find out?"

"With the murder of their partner, I knew I'd need some help getting them to answer questions. A P.I. walking into the office has a tendency to cause folks to clam up. I called in a favor from Larry Caldwell, a P.I. friend of mine with the Houston Police Department. We paid Mr. Briscoe of Briscoe, Roland, and Cooper a visit."

"He was willing to talk to you?"

"More than willing. Seems Briscoe was concerned about what Roland had planned when he went to Galveston for the conference."

"Which was?"

"To confront a certain investor about not anteing up his down payment."

"Boedecker?"

"Cahill. Each investor was to cough up twenty-five grand. Cahill was having trouble handing over his share. He'd been stalling, promising he'd come up with the money. Roland found out that Cahill couldn't keep away from the ponies. Roland hired a P.I. and learned that Cahill was in debt too deep to ever dig himself out. Seems that when his ponies didn't cooperate, Cahill decided to dip into another fund, the hotel's account. When Roland got to Galveston, he confronted Cahill, threatening to expose him."

"That was a stupid thing to do."

"Right. Briscoe warned him. Told him not to handle it himself and to go to the police, but Roland wanted to do things his own way and it got him killed. At least that's what Briscoe suspected happened. Seems he was right."

"Roland threatens to go to the cops, Cahill kills him, and stuffs his body in my car."

"How does Boedecker figure into this? Cahill was at his place today."

"I'm sure we'll find out when we get there."

CHAPTER THIRTY

On the way out to 8-Mile Road, sirens and flashing lights overtook us as three cop cars sped by. My heart sunk as I envisioned Ruth's body dumped somewhere out in the bay that glimmered in the distance. When the police cars skidded and took a hard right onto 8-Mile Road, my fears intensified.

"I should have followed immediately."

"You did the right thing. Coming out here alone could have gotten you both killed. She's okay," Dixon tried to assure me.

"I hope you're right. I shouldn't have been so cavalier about her abduction."

"Are you kidding? I'd worry more about her abductors."

I appreciated his positive attitude, but until I saw my cousin in one living piece, sassing someone around or pounding them with her stiletto, I couldn't share his optimism. We followed the cops but didn't get far. One car was blocking the road as we neared Boedecker's house; two officers stood there with guns drawn. Dixon slowed to a stop and rolled down his window.

"What's up, officer?"

"What business do you have out here?"

I saw the other two cop cars in Boedecker's drive. There was no way I was leaving until I found Ruth.

More cop cars pulled in behind us. I turned to see Detective Fidalgo get out of one car. "It's okay, Delton. I'll handle this," he called to the officer. Fidalgo walked over to my side of the car. I rolled down the window. "Why am I not surprised to find you here?" He bent down and eyed Dixon. "And you?"

"What happened?" I asked.

"Why don't you tell me?"

"Someone's kidnapped my cousin. The trail led me here. I'm not leaving here without her."

Fidalgo turned to the Officer Delton. "Make sure these two stay put." He turned to us. "I'll report back soon."

Dixon and I stood by the car, watching cops swarm Boedecker's house. I kept my eyes peeled on the front door, willing Ruth to storm out, fuming over the inconvenience the incident had caused her. Fifteen minutes later, I was still waiting.

"Ruth's not here," I said.

"That probably a good thing," Dixon responded. He put his arm around my shoulder.

"I should have never made up that story about having the coin and being ready to deal."

At that moment, Fidalgo walked up.

"Did you find my cousin?"

"She's not in there."

"What happened?"

"Boedecker's dead. Looks like a robbery that went wrong, or maybe not. Whoever killed Boedecker took something with him."

"It was Leonard Cahill, the manager of the Hotel Galvez. He was after the coin collection," I said.

"That'd be my guess," Fidalgo responded. "Since an empty coin case was found on Boedecker's desk."

"And he has Ruth," I added.

"Don't worry, we'll find her. We're on to it."

"Then you know about Leonard Cahill?" I asked.

Fidalgo shook his head. "The embezzlement of hotel funds—yeah, we know. You're not the only ones investigating the Roland murder. If you've screwed this up, I swear I'll throw the book at you."

"Cahill was here about an hour ago." Dixon said.

"Tell me about it," Fidalgo snorted.

He listened without popping that bulging vein in his temple. I told them everything except my bluff about having the coin.

"For once and for all, I want you two to butt out. There's nothing more you can do but make the situation worse. I don't want any more bloody bodies, understand?" He motioned for the cop behind us to move his car.

"It's your show," Dixon said.

Fidalgo looked like he was about to say more but instead turned and walked back to the house.

"Let's go," Dixon said. "What kind of car does Cahill drive?"

"A black Ford, probably a '48 or '49."

"Sounds like half the cars on the island."

EVERYTHING SEEMED TO BE RUSHING AT ME like a B-52 nose-diving for the tarmac. I'm glad Dixon was driving; in the state I was in, no telling what would happen with me behind the wheel. Why couldn't my life be normal? I could just get the story I was assigned, luxuriate in my bath at The Galvez, don my sexiest outfit, and show up at Pee-in-a-Hat with a smile on my face and a nicely wrapped candy dish. As it stood, if Ruth and I missed the party, my mother would cancel, and this saga would continue until my parents were too old to recognize one another.

"I'm sure she's just fine," Dixon said. The stab of guilt struck somewhere between my left shoulder blade and my heart. He took my silence as concern for Ruth, when in reality I was again thinking of myself. I decided to leave my parents to their chaos and devote myself to the situation at hand.

"I don't know what Cahill thinks he can accomplish now, having most likely killed three people. He's stolen a coin collection and taken a hostage, and the Galveston police force is on his tail. It's all over for him."

"That's what makes him so dangerous. He has nothing to lose."

"He can't believe he can get away with it."

"Yes, he can, easy. He could head for the border with his cache and disappear. A lot of guys have done it."

"It's a long way to the border from here. Surely, he wouldn't make his getaway with Ruth in tow."

"No. I suspect we'll hear from him soon, probably at the hotel."

"So we just go and wait?"

"You will. I'll nose around to see what I can find out."

"I'm sticking with you."

"Not a good idea. You'll be okay at the hotel. Cahill won't chance going there now. The place is probably already swarming with heat."

"I guess you're right."

On the way back to town, Dixon said, "Tell me everything you remember that day you found your grandfather."

"We've been over this before."

"I know, but we may have missed something. Humor me. Close your eyes. Start when you were walking to the hotel. What were you thinking? How were you feeling? Tell me what you saw."

I felt Dixon's warmth next to me and inhaled his clean masculine scent. I closed my eyes. "I couldn't wait to see him. PoPo had something special planned. He was always surprising me. That's what I was thinking about as I sped down the street on my bicycle. After a few blocks, I slowed down. I didn't want to appear out of breath when I walked up to the door. I wanted to be that special, sophisticated lady as he opened the door for me. That's when I heard what I thought was a car backfiring. I looked up just in time to see the car speed away, swiping the bush. I swerved out of the way onto the lawn. If I hadn't been looking, it would have hit me. I chided myself for having my head in the clouds. When I was a few feet from the front door, right by the fountain, I heard a woman scream. I dropped my bike and ran. The next thing I remember I was standing over PoPo. I saw his cap lying on the floor. I wanted to pick it up, thinking it was too nice to be on the floor. I knelt down beside him. I told myself he was playing a joke, but I knew he was dead. I remember seeing his face, noticing that his mouth was slightly opened, then I saw feet, shoes, people rushing over." I opened my eyes. "The next thing I remember, I was sitting in a hard chair at the police station. The place smelled musty, smelled of cigars and sweat."

"What had your grandfather told you about the surprise he had planned? He must have said something if you knew there was going to be a surprise."

"He said something about going bird-watching."

"Here on the island?"

"I assumed."

"Think. What else did he say?"

I closed my eyes again. "Something wasn't right. He said he'd located a special bird and he wanted me to see it. But I remembered thinking it was the wrong time of year for migratory birds to be on the coast. So what kind of special bird could it have been? Oh, wait, he said he'd had his eye on this bird for a long time, but now the bird had an eye on him."

"Do you think he was talking about a real bird, or a bird's-eye view of something?"

"Who knows? PoPo always talked in riddles."

"This doesn't tell us much. We'll leave it for now. The people who were milling around, those who came over, can you remember anything else about them?"

"I just remember that woman's fingers digging into my shoulders, trying to lead me away."

"No, I mean the others. You saw their shoes, men or women?"

"Both, but there was something odd about one of the guys, the way he was dressed; something hung down over around his pant legs."

"A coat?"

"It was summer."

"A towel or robe? He could have been at the beach or the pool."

"No, he wore black dress shoes, and black trousers. His shoes were smudged. This sounds odd, but it was more like a skirt over his trousers."

"An apron?"

I jerked. "You're right! It was an apron! The guy knelt down beside me! He put his hand on PoPo's chest. I guess to see if he was breathing."

"A waiter, then?"

The image exploded into view. The guy's hand, pulling at PoPo's jacket, his fountain pen slipping from the pocket and rolling across the tile floor. The guy grabbing the lapel of the jacket and pulling it back, exposing PoPo's white shirt stained red with blood. He patted PoPo's chest. I reached out to grab the guy's arm, to push him away. He told me to move back, blocking me with his shoulder. Then he... Oh, my God!"

I grabbed Dixon's arm. "He was searching PoPo's pockets."

"Who?" Dixon said.

"It was Cahill! He told me that he was working catering at the time. He wasn't checking to see if PoPo was alive! He reached inside PoPo's jacket pocket and was about to check the pockets of his pants when the police arrived. He was looking for the coin! Wait. I remember now how I got from the foyer to the lobby. Cahill took me by the arm and pulled me away from PoPo. I must have had my hands clenched because he tried prying open my fingers. He thought I had the coin, but before he could get my hand open, the woman was there asking me if I was all right."

"If that's true, then Cahill knew what was going on. Seems we may have found the link between the past and present."

WE PULLED UP TO THE BACK ENTRANCE OF THE HOTEL. As soon as Dixon cut the engine, someone pounded on the driver's window. Dixon and I jumped, but since I was facing the window, I was the one who screamed. Dixon threw open the door so quickly that Ruth went flying and landed in the arms of the valet.

"Where have you been?" She was wearing her green polka-dotted heels and a man's overcoat, which hung down to the ground.

"Sorry, Miss Lockhart," the valet said. "I caught this woman hanging around the back of the hotel. I called hotel security. When the security guard arrived, she kicked him in the you-know-what and he passed out, so I called the police, but they haven't arrived. She gave me a wild story about being your cousin and that she's staying here. I thought she'd left, but she was hiding behind the oleander bushes. The valet had Ruth by the arm with one hand; with the other hand he'd covered his privates.

"It's okay," I said. "Her story is true. My cousin has met with... an accident." Dixon and I grabbed Ruth and ushered her into the hotel. We took the service elevator to the fifth floor so that rest of the world wouldn't hear the obscenities spewing from

Ruth's lips. About the only thing we could make out was that Louis and Buddy were with Cahill and that Louis was the one who had nabbed her. When we closed the door to my room, I was at the point of slapping Ruth. Dixon had a more effective way of shutting down her hysterics. He turned on the shower and dumped her in. When Ruth's screams turning to sobs, I knew that things would be fine.

"Sorry, honey," Dixon said. He handed her a towel. "Get cleaned up and then tell us what happened." His silky, smooth voice stopped Ruth's sobbing. She nodded and drew the shower curtain closed.

"Where did you learn to do that?" I said.

"From my father. My mother was a nutcase. That's probably why I fell for you."

"God help us."

"Amen." He closed the bathroom door and pulled me close.

In record time, Ruth emerged from her bath with a towel around her head and her pink bathrobe tied tight. She threw her hands in the air. "I give up! You two are the ones who need the cold shower."

Dixon and I parted. He fluffed the pillows on the lounge chair and invited Ruth to sit. "We don't have much time."

"I'll say we don't! Cahill said if you don't hand over the coin by five o'clock today, he was going to have Louis and Buddy drive by your parents' house and unload. That man is crazy. Louis grabbed me before I had a chance to put on my dress! Why are people always forcing me to run around in my bare slip? Louis tied me up and threw me in the backseat with Buddy, who for once didn't say a word. He just gawked. Then we went for a 'little drive.' Cahill said he planned to keep me until you handed over the coin. Then Louis came up with the cockamamie plan to take me back to the hotel to give you a message. When we got there, I refused to get out of the car wearing just my slip, so Louis gave me his coat. Cahill said for you to meet him at The Rubaiyat. He ordered Louis and Buddy to start shooting if you didn't show up. They are holed up at Hattie Spencer's house as we speak, waiting for word from Cahill. If we call the police, your parents, my mother, Marcella, Scott, Jeremiah, and whoever else is there will be killed—an anniversary party turned into a bloodbath."

"How did Cahill know about the party?"

"I sort of told him," Ruth said. "It just kind of slipped out when he demanded to know where you were. I was trying to throw him off, confuse him a bit."

I envisioned poor old Hattie tied up like a bale of hay and hoped like hell the old gal hadn't baked her last batch of oatmeal cookies on account of me.

"He shot Boedecker," I said. "I can't believe he still thinks he can get the coin. So Buddy and Louis must now be working for him?" I said.

"They probably jumped ship when Boedecker was murdered," Dixon said.

"What are we going to do?" I said. "It's four thirty, and I don't have the coin."

"We keep the bluff going, at least long enough to keep Cahill from making that call." He looked at Ruth. "Sydney and I are going to The Rubaiyat. Wait fifteen minutes and then call the police and tell them where we are and what Cahill plans to do."

"Got it," Ruth said.

"And don't leave the hotel until you hear from us," Dixon said.

CHAPTER THIRTY-ONE

The door to The Rubaiyat was wide open. Except for Lush's friends, I swear the clientele at The Rubaiyat of Omar Khayyam had not moved since the last time we were there. Same guys at the pool table, same woman plastered at the jukebox, same old man snoring in the chair in the corner. We walked up to the bar. The bartender nodded to the door located at the end of the bar.

"Stay here," Dixon said. He turned toward the door, but the bartender stopped him. He'd pulled a snub nose from under his apron. "The redheaded chick only."

"No way," Dixon said. "I don't know what he paid you, but it isn't worth a murder rap. That guy you're hiding just killed a man and probably two others."

The confidence that shone just a second ago in the bartender's eyes disappeared. "He said he'd shoot me if I didn't do exactly as he said." He lowered the gun.

"Cahill!" Dixon shouted, and pulled out his pistol. "If you want what we have, you talk to me, understand?"

The morose clientele came to life at the sight of guns and scurried out the door like roaches under a spotlight.

The door behind the bar slowly opened. Cahill stood there. A .38 pointed at me. "You brought in reinforcements, Miss Lockhart? You were warned to come alone." Then he turned to Dixon. "Put your gun on the bar and slide it over here. You do something stupid and she gets it. And you," he said to the bartender, "do the same with yours."

The bartender laid his gun on the bar and pushed it toward Cahill. Dixon followed the guy's action, acting like the encounter was no big deal.

"You said to meet you here, so here we are," Dixon said.

"All I want is the coin, then I'm gone."

"Sure," Dixon said. He reached in his pocket.

"Stop!" Cahill said. "You." He pointed to the bartender. "Check his pocket. If the coin is not there, you're all dead."

"Hey, Mister," the bartender stuttered. "I don't want no trouble here."

Dixon tried again. "There's no way you're getting off this island, Cahill. Not after killing Boedecker."

"Maybe not, but I'm going to give it my best shot. And if those two bozos, Louis and Buddy, don't get a call from me in"—he looked at his watch—"twenty-five minutes, the Lockhart party will start off with a bang."

"Listen, Cahill, just take those coins and get the hell out of here. You can't afford to be greedy now," Dixon said. "The cops have this island covered from one end to the other."

"I'll chance that. This collection is worth ten times more with that little coin your girlfriend has been hiding." He raised the gun and drew back the hammer. "In fact, I don't need you alive anymore." The barrel was now pointed at my forehead. His hate-filled stare told me he'd have no trouble putting a bullet in my brain.

"Yes, you do," Dixon said. "Do you think we're stupid enough to bring the coin with us?"

Cahill's eyes flashed back at Dixon. The yellow light above the bar cast a sickly glow across Cahill's face. That's when I noticed the beads of sweat on his brow and a dark stain oozing from the side of his shirt. Boedecker must have gotten one good shot in before he died. Cahill swayed and drew a deep breath. He unbuttoned his shirt collar, pulled a handkerchief from his pocket, and wiped his face and neck.

That's when I saw the scratches on his neck and remembered what Louis had told me about the condition of Roland's body. He'd put up a fight against his attacker; there was blood under his fingernails. The muffler Cahill wore around his throat and the casual shirt collar buttoned up, were meant to hide the scratches.

"You, empty your pockets!" he shouted at me.

I glanced at Dixon. His eyes were fixed on Cahill. I felt like I'd changed places with Gary Cooper in High Noon. Sirens sounded from far away and gradually grew louder.

"Now!" Cahill stepped toward the bar and glanced out the window.

"You win, Cahill," I said. "You want the coin, you can have it. It's been nothing but trouble." I had only a second or two for my harebrained idea to work. I reached into my pocket and pulled out a dime. I tossed it toward the open window. Cahill lunged, and I went for my gun. When I grabbed the butt, my heart stopped. The cool, solid texture of the handle now felt light and nubby and I knew my wickedness from this morning had come back to haunt me. Big Bad Jones a.k.a. Frankie's plastic pistol wouldn't stop a butterfly if it landed on my nose. Dixon saw the look on my face, glanced at my toy pistol, and dove for his gun when a blast from behind rang out and Cahill's .38 flew from his hand. Blood spewed and it wasn't mine. Dixon flew over the bar and had Cahill in a headlock before I realized what had happened.

"I'll handle things until the police arrive. You guys run along to the party and stop those two guys," Lattie said.

Lattie, sober and fearless, had her gun trained on Cahill.

WE RAN DOWN THE STAIRS AND AROUND the block to my car. "I'll drop you off at the hotel and head to your parents' house. I hope we're not too late."

The church chimes announced five o'clock as I ran into the hotel lobby. Ruth stood at the front desk, wringing her hands. "What happened? Did the police get there in time?"

"Just barely." I ran toward the elevator. "Stay here!" I shouted over my shoulder. Being Saturday, there was a crowd of people waiting for the elevator, so I sprinted up the stairs to room 557 and pounded on the door. No answer.

"They went to the beach, honey."

I turned to see Blanche pushing the maid cart down the hall.

"Oh, God. I have to find them before it's too late."

"I wouldn't worry about them if I were you."

"You don't understand. The little boy has my gun." I slumped against the wall. "He must have gotten in my room somehow, probably when I rushed up here to clean up. I must have left the door unlocked. He's too clever for his own good."

"Your gun is in your room, honey. When I went in to clean, I saw the gun sticking out of his toy holster. I may be just a housekeeper, but I can recognize the real thing when I see it. I put it in the bottom drawer of your dresser."

"How did you know it was mine?"

"I heard the kid carrying on to his mom about you trying to hold him up on the beach. He went on about you pointing a gun at him and threatening to blow a hole through his heart. Mom didn't believe him, thank goodness. Later, when I saw the real gun in his holster, I just put two and two together. Did you really threaten to kill the little brat?"

"Of course not."

Blanche gave me that look.

"Okay, well, I thought about it." I gave the housekeeper a hug. "How are the girls?"

"Fine. Your poodle will need a bath and new pedicure. She and my collie haven't stopped chasing one another. Your cat has claimed our bed, actually our entire bedroom. I'm sleeping on the sofa, and my husband left to stay with his mother."

"You're a jewel, Blanche."

"So I've been told."

RUTH AND I RAN UP THE STEPS TO HATTIE'S door and rushed in. Nothing was out of order. The lacy doilies lay over the arms of the sofa, the porcelain dolls stood under their spotlights in their glass cabinet, the familiar smell of oatmeal cookies hung in the air. "Hattie," I called. "Louis, Buddy, come out, sea scum! It's all over."

"Back here," Dixon called.

Ruth and I found Louis and Buddy on the back porch, sitting

on Hattie's bench swing under the watchful eye of Dixon and his gun.

"You won't believe what I found when I got here," Dixon said.

"At this point, I'd believe anything."

"These two Casanovas were in the dining room playing cards."

"Cahill didn't send you over to kill my family?"

"He did," said Louis, "but once we got here, we decided that killing a bunch of innocent people was a bad idea."

"Yeah," Buddy said. "We're not killers. We're just a couple of fun guys who ended up with the wrong crowd. Hi, Ruth. You look terrific as always. Cha-cha-cha."

"You're the strangest person I've ever met," Ruth replied.

"I've been called worse," Buddy smiled.

"Wait until you hear their story," Dixon said.

"I'm ready."

"We have ten minutes before the party begins." He turned to Louis and Buddy. "Once more with feeling, boys—and talk fast."

Louis began. "I've been working for Cleve on and off for years. Nothing really bad, just an arm-twisting here and there when collecting a few debts. Then you came to town and things got out of hand. Like that night at Washington's when he nabbed your cousin. Then when you two slipped out the bathroom window, Cleve told me to bring you back to his house or else. I didn't want to find out what the 'or else' meant. "

"You seem to forget that you tried to kill me in the newsroom."

"I was just tailing you. When you saw me, I tried to get out of that building. I had to go down the stairs. I shot just to scare you. I couldn't hit an elephant two paces away. I had to use my left hand. Why didn't you leave through the alley door?"

"It was locked!"

"Go on with your story," Dixon said.

Louis shot Dixon a hateful look. "After your boyfriend here shot me in the stairwell, I realized that maybe I needed to stick with my job at the hospital and stop moonlighting for Boedecker."

"I told you that guy was bad news," Buddy whined.

"Anyway, when this wise, short guy," he nodded toward Buddy, "and I got back from the pig farm today, Cahill was still at the house, but he and Cleve were in the middle of a heated argument. Buddy and I were in the kitchen, but we heard enough of what was being said."

"Oh, boy, they were going at it like a couple of roosters at a cockfight," Buddy added.

"Next thing we knew, the two guys are shooting at one another. We ran into the study. Cleve was dead and Cahill had been hit. Cleve's coin collection was out on his desk. Cahill grabbed it and told us to get in the car or he'd give us the same treatment. We didn't argue. We drove away with Cahill in the backseat."

"What did he plan to do?" I asked.

"At first he blabbered something about driving him off the island on the Bolivar Ferry. We headed down Seawall Boulevard when we noticed Ruth going into the public showers. Cahill had us pull over and I grabbed her."

"My little filly wasn't too happy. Were you, Ruth?" Buddy chirped. "Putting you in the car was like trying to cage a wildcat."

"You didn't help much," Louis scoffed.

"I was overcome seeing her in that slip and those pumps. It's a sight I'll never forget. I mean, it was worth dying for."

"Where's my Derringer" Ruth said, digging around in her purse.

"Go on with the story," Dixon said.

"Crazy Cahill still believed you had the coin and planned to keep Ruth until you turned it over," Louis said. "But we weren't very inconspicuous, a wild woman screaming her head off, a dwarf in the front seat, and a wounded man with a gun in the back."

"A little person," Buddy cried. "Not a dwarf!"

"Cahill was ready to put a bullet in Ruth's head, and I could see myself behind bars the rest of my life. I did some quick talking and persuaded Cahill to let Ruth go with a message for you to bring the coin or we'd open fire on your family. We dropped him off at The Rubaiyat, the only place in town that wouldn't question what we were doing. Then Buddy and I came here to await our fate."

"Did you turn over the coin?" Buddy asked.

"I don't have the damn coin!"

"Where is it?" Louis asked.

"Who the hell knows? I still don't know how I got involved in all of this."

"That's easy. Something you said to Cahill made him think you recognized him. Cleve told Cahill to keep a close eye on you at the hotel and for us to follow you whenever you left."

"But how is Cahill connected to the coin?" I asked.

"Another long story," Louis said.

"Talk fast," Dixon said.

"The day James went to Houston to get Hardy to sell the coin, Warren sent Cleve to make sure everything went smoothly. When James left the Hardy house, Cleve was waiting. James told him Hardy wouldn't sell. Cleve told James to go back to Galveston. Actually, Warren's instructions were for Cleve to accompany James, but Cleve was determined to get the coin. He walked into the house and overheard Hardy tell Brewster Fallow to follow James and steal the money. Cleve watched Fallow leave, waited a while, and then confronted Hardy. Cleve said he wasn't leaving without the coin."

"Why was it so important to Cleve?"

"It had to do with his brother Monty. My sister, Monty's wife, told me that Monty was Warren's favorite. Cleve was a screw-up. This was his way to prove himself, but like usual, he made a mess of things. When Hardy refused to give him the Indian Head, Cleve pulled a gun and killed him. He took the coin and then called the police and told them that he came to see Hardy, and as he drove up, he heard shots and saw Fallow leaving. After Fallow swiped the money from James, he returned to the Hardy house and found him dead just as the police showed up. Cleve returned to Galveston with the coin, thinking his father would be pleased. Warren was furious."

"Then Warren dies three months later, and PoPo steals the coin back with the intention of taking it to the police?" I said, more puzzled than ever. "I still don't buy that. PoPo never went to the police with the coin."

"I don't know nothing about that," Louis said. "When Warren died, Cleve was afraid James would finally go to the police and rat on Cleve, so Cleve had him killed before Warren was cold in his grave. Cleve called Cahill at the hotel and told him what was coming down. He told Cahill to search James's body as soon as he was shot just in case he had the coin on him."

"After three months?" Dixon scoffed.

"Cleve didn't give a damn about the coin, but the fact that James had it always gnawed at Cleve's gut. Things eventually blew over. Warren was dead, James was dead, Fallow was in jail, and Cleve was living fat and happy. Then you show up and start talking to Cahill. He runs to Cleve, and after eighteen years, Cleve starts thinking that he may be able to get the coin after all."

"And Brewster Fallow?"

"Tell her," Buddy squeaked.

A forlorn look came across Louis's face. "That was sort of our fault."

"You killed Fallow?"

"Not exactly. I'd point the finger at you."

"Me?"

"We followed you to Fallow's bait shop and reported back to Cleve. He thought Fallow might start trouble so he had Cahill kill him."

"Cahill?"

"Cleve told Cahill that if he killed Fallow, he'd bail him out financially. Cahill was in it so deep he'd do just about anything if Cleve would help. When Cahill came over today, he realized that Cleve had no intention of bailing him out. Cahill's back was to the wall. The police were on to him in connection with the embezzlement at the hotel and Roland's murder. And when he realized that Cleve had double-crossed him—well, you know the rest."

I looked out the kitchen window. The entire neighborhood—make that the entire island—appeared to be gathered in my parents' backyard. Father Stovic was standing under the trestle Scott had so lovingly crafted, and Marcella was ushering people to their seats. Aunt Frances stood at the back door wringing her hands while Hattie flirted with Jeremiah. And there was Dad leaning against the pecan tree puffing on a Lucky.

"It's almost party time," Dixon said. "You go on over and join the fun. I'll be along as soon as I call Fidalgo and have him come collect these two."

As Mom and Dad repeated their vows, or as far as Mom believed, said them for the first time, I prayed there would be no interruptions. Myriad possible interventions flashed through my mind: a late-season hurricane roaring in from the gulf, a meteorite crashing to Earth, the ground splitting open and swallowing the entire lot, Mom changing her mind and hopping a train to Hollywood. In the middle of my imaginary maelstrom, I heard my mother's quiet "I do." Aunt Frances and Jeremiah wailed with joy, the rest of the crowd applauded, the violin trio broke out into the "Beer Barrel Polka," and Dixon squeezed my hand. Months of planning, canceling, rescheduling, and bickering were finally over. My parents had tied the knot again and vowed to remain together in all their misery. It was all over— or maybe not.

As soon as Dad kissed his wife-bride, the celebration started. Dad made a run at the keg of Lone Star and began handing out cups of foaming beer. Scott popped champagne corks under the tent set up by the West Side Country Club. A row of tables held plates of shrimp cocktail, oysters on the half shell, and crustless sandwiches. Two chefs supervised the distribution of their fancy finger food by two professionally dressed waiters. The other side of the yard contained a freshly dug fire pit, which now was ablaze and warming the late-afternoon air. Next to the fence sat a couple of card tables covered with hot dog fixings. Jeremiah roasted the dogs over the fire; Marcella wrapped them in buns and passed them out. There was no demarcation line between the hot-dog crowd and the country-club folks. Everyone mingled without the slightest hesitation. One guy who wore a tux had a beer in one hand and a glass of bubbly in the other. It wasn't the fancy reception at the new country club my mother wanted, nor the cookout on the beach that had appealed to Dad. Was that what marriage was all about? Compromise? I shook those thoughts from my head.

Ruth walked up and handed me a glass of champagne.

"Don't you look lovely?" I said. "While Dixon and I were staring down Cahill's gun, you found time to change into your Neiman's cocktail dress."

"It helped take my mind off the situation." She sipped her drink; a frown spread across her forehead. I grew concerned. Ruth never missed a chance to talk about her looks. "What is it? Is there a run in your stocking, a snag on your skirt?"

"Do you think I'll ever get married? she asked. "I'm almost thirty."

"This isn't the Victorian era, Ruth. There's no reason for a smart woman to rush into marriage simply because of her age. I'm surprised at you."

"But you can never be sure about things. Maybe I shouldn't marry. I was thinking of Mom and Dad. He had an entirely different life we knew nothing about."

"You need to get a grip on that situation."

"Mother said the same thing."

"Aunt Frances is a wise lady."

"What if I take after Dad and turn out to be a two-timing wife?"

"Don't be silly, Ruth."

"Sydney?"

"What?"

"I've made a decision."

"You're going to run away with Buddy and take him up on his cha-cha-cha offer?"

Ruth threw her glass in the bushes. "Don't insult me! I'm being serious!"

"Sorry, I just wanted to lighten things up."

"This is not easy for me, but here goes. I'm going to ask Marcella to run the Home for me."

"Oh, Ruth." I threw my arms around my dear cousin. "Marcella would be perfect for the job. She's a lawyer, a sensible businesswoman, and she..."

"She's the daughter of an unwed mother. She made something of herself. She'd make a great role model."

"She would at that. You know something?"

"What?"

"You take after your mom. You're a very wise woman, too."

"Damn right. Now, you go ask Marcella if she'll do it."

I handed her my glass of champagne. "Drink this. There she is talking to Jeremiah." I shoved her in that direction. "Go now, before you chicken out."

"I would never chicken out of anything." She turned back. "What do you think of the name the Echland/Wheatly Home for Young Women?"

"You simply take my breath away, Ruth."

"Yeah, I surprise myself sometimes."

DIXON AND I DANCED A COUPLE OF SLOW ONES, and when the string trio struck up another polka, we took a break near the birdbath. Someone had set a half-empty cup of beer on the lip. A happy seagull was enjoying the leftovers. I shooed it away and tossed the cup. "I remember when PoPo brought home this birdbath," I said. "He was so proud of it. He'd spent a lot of time digging a deep hole for the foundation. He actually put together this mosaic, cementing each little piece. He was so precise."

"It's a whooping crane," Dixon said.

"It is. He drew out the design on paper. My grandmother said it took him forever to get the tiles just right. She said he finished it that morning I came to visit. Oh, my God!"

"Sydney?" Dixon grabbed my shoulders.

There was about an inch of water left in the bath. I sloshed it out. Dixon took his handkerchief and rubbed the algae from the eye of the whooping crane. He polished a little harder and the Indian Head twinkled like a tiny lost star.

"It took you long enough."

We turned to find Dad standing there with a beer in one hand and a hot dog in the other.

"You knew!"

"If you two plan to go on with this detecting stuff, you're going to have to learn a thing or two. Actually, I only found it this morning while I was getting things ready for the party."

"George!" Mom rushed over and grabbed Dad by the arm. "Father Stovic is leaving. Come say good-bye and insist he take some of my pound cake. He says he can't take gifts." Then she was gone to chastise someone else about something of little importance.

"It has nothing to do with not accepting gifts," Dad said to us. "Father Stovic's heard about Mary Lou's cooking."

I didn't know whether I wanted to slug my dad or hug him. So I just stood there, arms folded, eyes in a squint.

"Don't look at me like that," he said. "I only started piecing things together when Fallow contacted me. Come on. Let's walk down to the seawall. I'll tell you what I know. Your mother won't miss us."

The glow of the street lamps cast amber halos across the water. The gulf was calm, the sound of waves lapping the beach made a delicate splash on the wet, packed sand. Dad began his story.

"One afternoon a few weeks ago, this scary-looking fellow appeared at the back door. That was during the time your mother was still living in the beach hut. Anyway, I thought he was a hobo looking for a handout until he called my name."

"Fallow?" I said.

"Right. He'd just gotten out of prison. He said Pop came to see him shortly after they threw him in jail. Pop knew that Fallow was innocent of murdering Hardy. He told Fallow he would go to the police even if he were implicated in the crime. According to Fallow, Pop had had enough of the Boedecker family after the robbery and Hardy's murder. Pop wanted to make up for all the trouble Warren Boedecker caused even though none of it was Pop's fault. He cashed in some of his own personal bonds and sent the Hardy family enough money to cover the cost of losing the coin. He then told Warren Boedecker what he had done. Warren felt so bad that he sent James the coin. By this time, Pop knew what his friend was really like. He believed Warren gave him the coin to keep Pop from telling the police that Cleve was the one who'd killed Hardy. Pop sent Warren a letter saying he was going to the police regardless. Then Fallow got word that Pop had been murdered. Fallow had eighteen years to sit in prison and stew about it. When he got out, he came to me for help. I didn't know whether to believe the guy or not."

"That must have been the note Cleve showed me. He told me the note referred to PoPo stealing the coin with the intention of returning it, but that wasn't true. Cleve knew the note meant that PoPo was going to tell the police that Cleve had killed Hardy."

"In the morning, we'll chisel the coin out of the birdbath. It's yours, Sydney," Dad said.

"I have no right to that coin," I said. "It's been nothing but trouble."

"You could sell it," Dixon said. "It'd make a nice nest egg for you."

"I don't need a nest egg," I said. "But if I sold it, I could give part of the money to you. Boedecker never had a chance to pay your expenses."

"I don't need my expenses paid." He put his arms around me. "I've got everything I need right here."

"That's my exit cue," Dad said. "I'm going back to the house and eat a few more hot dogs and down the rest of the beer while your mother winds things down. You don't know how glad I am that this entire separation/wedding/anniversary debacle is finally over."

"We should probably go back and help," I said.

"Your mother has enough help," Dad said. "Enjoy the rest of this nice evening. See you in the morning. You two have a lot to think about."

"One more thing, Dad. In all the excitement of the evening, there's one little detail I've failed to mention. We had a sort of incident at The Rubaiyat of Omar Kayam right before the party."

"At The Rubaiyat? What sort of incident?"

I looked at Dixon, and he related the details as only a cop could, in a professional, matter-of-fact narrative. Had I told the story, I probably would have given my father a heart attack. Dixon stopped short of our rescue and then nodded for me to continue.

"Someone's been looking out for us. And that someone arrived on the scene and shot the gun right out of Cahill's hand. It was the same someone who sent me warning messages when I checked into the Galvez."

"I see." Dad lit another cigarette and gazed out of the water for a moment before he said, "There are a few things you should know, Sydney. One, I've always been true to your mother and she to me. No doubts about that—ever. Two, when your mother lost her mind and moved out last November, Lattie and I became friends, that's friends, period. Before that time, she was just a crazy old islander, a cross between a barfly and a washed-up socialite. Right after Fallow came to see me, I started nosing around. I needed information about what was happening in Galveston at the time Pop was killed. Lattie seemed the perfect source. When I realized she took my confidence as an invitation to get involved, I asked her to meet me and I politely told her to back off."

"She didn't listen," I said.

"For that I'm grateful. You mother doesn't know about this, and I'll tell her one day. I've just gotten used to having her around again and I don't want to send her running." Dad turned to Dixon. "Don't worry, son, Sydney takes after me."

"Wait, Dad. How did you know I was coming to Galveston?"

"I spoke to Jeremiah."

"He told you!"

"Not exactly. I called to warn you about your mother's plans to hurry the party along. Jeremiah was too evasive. I knew something was up so I called the newspaper and they told me you were at The Galvez in Galveston."

"Those threatening notes I received came immediately after I checked into the hotel. I'm sure Lattie sent them. Did you tell her I was here?"

"Damn that woman. I told her you'd be in town to get a story and that I was worried about you being here, but I didn't tell her you were at The Galvez."

"Then how did Lattie know I was coming to the hotel?"

"That I don't know. There's not much that gets by her. Wait. She has a sister who works there. A woman named Blanche."

CHAPTER THIRTY-TWO

I woke the next morning to an empty room. Ruth was up and gone. I propped up my pillows and watched the sun light up the gulf. It was all over, everything—the anniversary party, discovering who killed Maurice Roland and Brewster Fallow, and, most importantly, who killed my dear, sweet grandfather eighteen years ago. I had another story for Ernest, and Ruth and Marcella were well on their way to establishing a friendship. And I possessed a coin worth several thousands of dollars, a coin that had caused too much trouble and sadness. As soon as we could pry the Indian Head from the birdbath, I planned to find a collector, sell the coin, and use the money for something worthwhile.

With all the excitement of the last few days over, melancholy settled in. I tried to shake the feeling, but it only intensified. I thought of Dixon. I'd only met the man three months ago, and we'd never even had an official date. Since I left Hot Springs in November, he'd shown up twice, unannounced, both times to get me out of trouble. I liked having him around. He had an appealing ease about him. I trusted him, but what now? I enjoyed my independence, but maybe not so much anymore. I jumped out of bed and called room service. A cup of strong coffee would cure this craziness.

When we returned to The Galvez last night there was a message from Detective Fidalgo instructing Dixon and me to be at the police station at nine o'clock this morning or he'd send a squad car for us. We had some explaining to do. I told Dixon

I'd pick him up (we never got around to finding him a room at The Galvez). I finished the last of the coffee, threw on some clothes, and applied enough makeup to disguise the effect of all the sleep I'd missed since my arrival on the island. I saved myself a few minutes to locate Blanche. She was coming out of the service elevator with a cart of clean linen. "Morning. How are my two girls?"

"Happy as clams," she said.

"I'll take them off your hands this afternoon."

"No hurry."

"Blanche, where do the goddesses manage to find eggplants at this time of year?"

"Oh," she said. "You figured that out, did you?"

"It wasn't too hard. But somehow I can't see you chumming with Asherah's gang."

"It was just something to do. Put some excitement in my life. You know after so many years of marriage—"

I wasn't ready to hear another discourse on the negative aspects of matrimony. "Who was it exactly who slashed my tires and why?"

"It wasn't me, honest! Asherah gets a little overzealous at times. When she saw you walking around on Oya's island, she thought you were part of that development project and wanted to warn you off."

"Tell her she'll receive a bill for two tires. When I get the money, I'll forget all about her. If not, I'll see to it that her eggplant-throwing days will be over."

"Will do."

"If you're looking for something to keep you busy, maybe you should try joining a bridge club."

Blanche arched her eyebrows, shook her head and pushed her cart down the hall.

"And Blanche, tell your sister I'm impressed with her sharpshooting skills."

She giggled, but didn't turn back.

When I passed through the lobby, I saw Ruth and Marcella sitting in the restaurant, papers scattered across their table.

They were head to head in what looked like a business meeting. Marcella must have agreed to Ruth's offer. As I walked by, Ruth looked up and winked at me. I left my two cousins to their plans and went to meet my detective.

Dixon was in the lobby drinking coffee with Mrs. Swainy. He wore gray slacks and a white dress shirt, no jacket, no tie, no hat. He needed a haircut and his shoes were a bit scuffed. He looked delicious, and it was a good thing Mrs. Swainy was there; otherwise I might have sunk my teeth into him.

Once at the police station, we recounted our tale of meeting Cahill at The Rubaiyat of Omar Khayyam, which confirmed the story Fidalgo had just gotten from Louis and Buddy, who were now sitting in a cell. When we got to the part about Lattie showing up with a gun at that critical moment, we told Fidalgo that we were truly surprised by her actions. Evidently he wasn't. Seemed the Lush's eccentric behavior was well known to the Galveston Police Department.

With Boedecker and Fallow dead, there was no way to prove that Boedecker had murdered PoPo. Nevertheless, we told Fidalgo what we'd learned from Dad last night. He listened, took down notes, but pretty much declared the case closed. On the way back to my car, Dixon pulled a newspaper from a rack on the corner. Cahill and Boedecker's story covered the front page and continued on page three. Below was a story entitled "Pelican Island Project on Hold." The story reported that Mayor Quinn was certain that it was only a matter of time before the project was going full steam ahead again.

"The delay will allow Asherah and her goddesses time to plan their next strategy to save Oya's island," I said.

"Who's Asherah?" Dixon asked.

"Just another local with an agenda. Not important."

We walked along Strand Street, enjoying the cool morning. "I've made a decision," I said.

"Let's hear it."

"I'm going to sell the coin and donate the money to the Echland/Wheatly Home for Young Women."

"I'm glad those two gals buried the hatchet." Dixon rubbed his chin. "But are you sure you want to give it all to them?"

This didn't sound like the Dixon I knew. Money had never seemed to be an issue with him.

"I was going to wait, but now was as good a time as any. I have a proposition for you."

I shook my head. Did he say proposition or proposal? "You have a what?"

"Proposition."

Whew! That was close. "Let's hear it."

"You know when Cleve Boedecker called Billy in Hot Springs to check on my P.I. credentials?"

"Yeah?"

"Well, Billy didn't have to fib much. We've been talking about it ever since he moved to Hot Springs. Last week we made the decision. We're going private."

"You're quitting the force?"

"Yep, putting out our own shingle."

"Dixon, that's a great idea! Do you need me to loan you money to get it up and running?"

"I would never ask you for money, hon," he laughed. "But you might consider setting some aside for yourself until we build up a reliable clientele."

"I don't get it."

"How does Dixon, Lockhart, and Ludlow sound?"

"You want me to become part of your detective agency? I don't know beans about detective work."

He hooked a strand of loose hair behind my ear. "Who are you kidding? I've known you less than three months and you've solved a half dozen murders. Besides, I'd be close by and could keep you out of trouble. You'd have to get your license, but I can help you with that."

"You assumed I'd move to Hot Springs?" What sounded like a great idea just seconds ago now caused a flutter of fear in my heart.

"Nope, but there's an office for rent on 10th Street not far from the Capitol."

"In Austin? You'd move to Austin?"

"We'd make a great team, hon." He kissed me. "Take some time; think about it."

"I will." I kissed him back.

He threw the newspaper in the trash, and hand in hand, we strolled on down the Strand.

KATHLEEN KASKA

MURDER AT THE DRISKILL

A Sydney Lockhart Mystery

Enjoy an Excerpt from

Murder at the Driskill

Book #4 in *The Sydney Lockhart Series*

by Kathleen Kaska

Chapter 1

I heard Jelly Bluesteen laughing his fool head off as I darted out the door in pursuit of the slime ball I was assigned to watch. If the guy had only swiped the till, I would have turned around and told Jelly to catch his own thief. But the guy snatched my overcoat on his way out the door. Inside was my new PI license and fifty bucks from our agency's petty cash, making the thievery a personal issue.

The man I was after was the bartender at The Blue Mist, a popular sleaze joint on Sabine, a few blocks from The Next to Nothing Live Theatre. Jelly, the owner of The Blue Mist, came to our detective agency for help. He was certain one of his bartenders had been stuffing his pockets rather than replenishing the cash drawer.

My partner and boyfriend, Ralph Dixon, advised against taking the case since he suspected Jelly of being as crooked as his employees, but I was eager to get our new agency off the ground. Being a novice investigator, I could use the practice. Besides, the nighttime work would not interfere with my day job. Dixon reluctantly agreed.

It was my third night at the bar. My sleuthing required that I dress in male disguise and smoke and drink while trying to keep a low profile, which was easy since most folks came to The Blue Mist to do just that, except for the dressing in disguise part. But, hey, I might be wrong. After all, it was 1953, and weird things happened in downtown Austin, Texas.

I suspected this particular bartender the first night. He had a pattern to his pilfering. Once the joint became busy, he'd move to the far end of the bar where the overhead lights failed to reach. When someone paid for the drink, the guy pretended to stuff the money into the register, but instead he executed a quick flicking motion with his fingers, and the bills slid up his cuff.

Tonight had been busier than normal and I watched as a small fortune filled the bartender's sleeve. At closing time, Jelly came out from the back room and caught my eye. I nodded toward the guilty party. The bartender noticed our sly communication and he suddenly became twitchy. Jelly hurriedly ushered the last drunk out the door, flipped off the neon OPEN sign, and reached for his billy club. In one swift motion, the bartender snatched a wad of cash from the register and my coat off the rack and made a beeline for the door. Since Jelly was too fat to run, I took up the chase, alone.

I pursued the guy down Sixth Street all the way to The Driskill Hotel when suddenly he darted down the alley and became swallowed up in the steam rising off the pavement. I thought I'd lost him until I heard a pile of rags bundled near the dumpster say, "He turned right at the end of the alley, Miss Sydney."

I thanked the man whom I'd come to know as Backyard Benny, a bum who earned his moniker by sleeping in backyards and alleys in the downtown area. I took off in that direction as a tower of empty food crates tumbled in my path. Thanks to my long legs, I hurdled the debris, sending an annoyed family of raccoons scattering. In dodging the scavengers, I slipped on their food refuse, regained my footing, and within seconds I had the guy in sight again. Turning down Seventh toward Red River Street, he headed away from the downtown area and the streetlights illuminating the path to the State Capitol. My youth and athletic ability gave me the only hope of catching him before he vanished into the crevices of broken down warehouses, or worse yet, into the darkness of Waterloo Park. The guy was at least twenty years my senior and had obviously not graced the inside of a gymnasium since high school. But he did have the advantage of being prey, driven by survival and escape.

I was about forty yards behind him when I caught sight of a slow moving mass on the opposite side of the street a collection of stumbling drunks, or so I thought. When I saw the glint of a switchblade, I realized the drunks were malcontents intent on relieving late-nighters of whatever cash remained in their pockets.

The guy paid no notice to the thugs following him. He leapt over a low wooden fence and disappeared behind a vacant house. I pulled my gun from my shoulder holster and fired a couple of shots into the air. Someone shouted, "Cops!" and the hoodlums fled. I wasn't often mistaken for one of Austin's finest. It must have been my man clothes. I prayed my long red hair would stay put under my fedora as I scaled the fence after him.

I should have listened to my wise and experienced partner and not gotten involved in this case. I should have also listened to him when he told me to meet him at the office as soon as the bar closed. That was almost an hour ago. But I couldn't let this guy escape. My pride was at stake.

If I were lucky, Dixon would head down to The Blue Mist and Jelly would put him on my trail. If not, I might end up like so many other women who found themselves alone after dark on the bad side of town, looking for trouble and finding it. My gun would do me little good if a thug's switchblade found its way between my ribs.

As I rounded the corner of a three-story warehouse, the side door flew opened and caught me in the right shoulder, knocking me to the ground. From the crashing noise, I knew the bartender had dashed inside. I followed, but pulled up short when the door behind me slammed shut and I was clothed in darkness. I stopped and listened. Nothing. No running footsteps. No tumbling boxes. No heavy breathing. Okay, I knew when to quit. I backed toward the door when I heard it. Music. Suddenly, the room lit up like Times Square. I now stood between a headless man and a rabbit whose nose twitched to the beat of my pounding heart. Dracula's image reflected off the blade of the guillotine.

I jerked around to confront the Transylvania bloodsucker and came face-to-face with a girl dressed in organdy and lace; a blue sash wrapped around an empire waist and tied into a bow in back. This I could see from the reflection in the mirror behind her. On her feet were patent leather Mary Janes in the brightest shade of lavender I'd ever seen. She held a Bible to her chest. When she spoke in a clear, calm voice, I knew it was beyond hope that the smell of brewing coffee would wake me from the nightmare. I blinked twice. She was still there. So, I did the only sensible thing; I placed my gun back into its holster and asked her where she bought her shoes.

"I found them. Who are you?"

"I could ask you the same question. Did you see an old chubby guy running through here?"

"No one's been here all night except me."

"Why aren't you at home?"

"I am."

"You live here?"

She raised her eyes upward. "On top. Our apartment. I come down here when my dad snores."

"Do you always dress as if you're going to your First Communion?"

"I'm considering a new persona. Dad doesn't like me coming down here at night. But I find the time alone in the prop room, playing dress-up, generates my creative side. Do you play dress-up too?"

The tone of her question was not that of an innocent child. It dripped of sarcasm spoken by a well-seasoned cynic. I looked down at my grubby suit and red cowboy boots and sighed. "I do play dress-up, evidently. Listen, I got to go, and you'd better get back upstairs before your father wakes up."

"After he comes home from work, he hits the bed and doesn't wake up until late. He runs the theater next door."

"The Next to Nothing Theater?"

"Uh-huh."

"Where's the front door to this building?"

"This way."

I followed her through the warehouse, going in one door and out another, up a half flight of stairs, and down a long narrow hallway when she reached a door and pushed it open. Until now, I hadn't realized that in chasing the guy, we'd doubled back. I was back out on Sixth Street and Sabine. The Blue Mist was across the street two blocks away. Then I noticed the marquee for the theatre. I stepped back and scanned the structures. The warehouse and theatre, and apparently this girl's apartment, were all part of one huge building. We went back inside and returned to the prop room.

"I'm sure the guy came in that backdoor," I said.

"He could have. To the left of the door are stairs that lead to the roof. He could have gone up there and down the fire escape. Why were you after him?"

"Let's just say it's business. Show me the roof."

"Sure. What's your name?" she asked, leading me to the stairs.

"Sydney."

"No, your real name. I know you're not a man."

"Thank you. Sydney with a y and you are?"

"Florence, but you can all me Lydia, with a y too."

"Is that a phonograph you're playing?"

"My favorite record. It's a special night."

I listened. Billie Holiday singing "Blue Moon."

"Great song. Why is it so special to a young girl like you?"

"Not the song, the night," she scoffed and pushed opened the door. "Tonight is a Blue Moon. Only comes around once every twenty-two months. I was a mere child the last time it happened. I wouldn't miss it this time for anything in the world."

"I wish it would show itself. It's damn dark out there."

"It was out earlier just for a moment when the clouds parted. It was magical."

"Sorry I missed it." We stepped out onto the roof and I found the fire escape, which led down into the alley. No use looking for the guy now. He could be halfway to San Antonio.

"Sorry I bothered your fantasy world, Lydia. Do me a favor and lock up after I leave. There are some dangerous people hanging around this neighborhood at night."

"Oh, I'm not worried. If the bums around here know you, they pretty much leave you alone."

"Maybe you should walk me back to my office."

"Hey, come by tomorrow and I'll get you a ticket to the show. It's great entertainment."

"I'll do that. Gotta go."

"Unless you're known around here like me, I'd stay out of these alleys. Life is too wondrous and beautiful to squander in the cesspools of the devil."

I jerked around, but Lydia had disappeared. When I shut the door behind me, I heard the lock click. I pulled out my gun for the eight-block stroll back to the office. All of a sudden, the hair on my arms stood up. I spun around, giving him the opportunity to grab my shoulders and push my back against the wall.

"You never listen, do you?" he said.

"Get used to it, buddy," I replied.

His eyes narrowed. I replaced my gun in its holster and flung my arms around his neck as the wail of sirens drifted off in the distance.

"We'll never get any work done this way," Dixon said.

"It's the Blue Moon."

"It's not the Blue Moon, believe me."

He kissed me again, this time softer and gentler. My knees buckled.

WITH THANKS TO

Mike Starring, who puts ideas into my head.
To the Hotel Galvez staff for always giving me my favorite room.

To my sisters:
Karen Stanford
Karla Klyng
Krisann Kent
Whose support and opinions I value more than anyone.

And finally, to my parents who chose Galveston as
the venue for our family vacations.

ABOUT THE AUTHOR

Kathleen Kaska is the author of the awarding-winning mystery series: the Sydney Lockhart Mystery Series set in the 1950s and the Kate Caraway Animal-Rights Mystery Series. Her first two Lockhart mysteries, Murder at the Arlington and Murder at the Luther, were selected as bonus books for the Pulpwood Queen Book Group, the country's largest book group. She also writes mystery trivia. The Sherlock Holmes Quiz Book was published by Rowman & Littlefield. Her Holmes short story, "The Adventure at Old Basingstoke," appears in Sherlock Holmes of Baking Street, a Belanger Books anthology. She is the founder of The Dogs in the Nighttime, the Sherlock Holmes Society of Anacortes, Washington, a scion of The Baker Street Irregulars.

When she is not writing, she spends much of her time with her husband, traveling the back roads and byways around the country, looking for new venues for her mysteries, and bird watching along the Texas coast and beyond. Her passion for birds led to The Man Who Saved the Whooping Crane: The Robert Porter Allen Story (University Press of Florida). Her collection of blog posts for Cave Art Press was published under the title, Do You Have a Catharsis Handy? Five-Minute Writing Tips. Catharsis was the winner of the Chanticleer International Book Award in the nonfiction Instruction and Insights category.

Check out her popular blog series, "Growing Up Catholic in a Small Texas Town." www.kathleenkaska.com

Follow her on: Twitter, Facebook, and Instagram.
https://twitter.com/KKaskaAuthor
http://www.facebook.com/kathleenkaska
https://www.instagram.com/kathleenkaska/

OTHER BOOKS YOU MIGHT ENJOY FROM ANAMCARA PRESS LLC

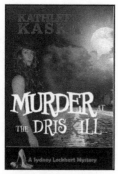

ISBN: 9781941237-85-4
$21.95

ISBN: 9781941237-85-4
$21.95

ISBN: 9781941237-38-0
$18.95

ISBN: 9781941237-33-5
$20.99

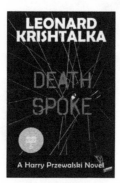

ISBN: 9781941237-30-4
$21.99

ISBN: 9781941237-32-8
$21.95

Available wherever books are sold and at:
anamcara-press.com

Thank you for being a reader! Anamcara Press publishes select works and brings writers & artists together in collaborations in order to serve community and the planet.
Your comments are always welcome!

Anamcara Press
anamcara-press.com